Praise for Janet Smith's previous mysteries

Sea of Troubles

"An intelligent heroine, a glorious setting, an ingenious murder and a romance that doesn't overwhelm the crime-solving procedures."
—*The New York Times Book Review*

"A fully charactered, cleverly plotted, active and atmospheric thriller."
—*Los Angeles Times*

"Chilling . . . A fresh, well-crafted whodunit."
—*Publishers Weekly*

Practice to Deceive

"A satisfyingly complex book."
—*Seattle Post-Intelligencer*

"The author's writing style is . . . bouncy, lively, and energetic. . . . I enjoyed this book."
—*Mystery News*

"Annie's an efficient, agreeable, no-nonsense sort—and so is this mystery."
—*Kirkus Reviews*

By Janet L. Smith
Published by Ivy Books:

SEA OF TROUBLES
PRACTICE TO DECEIVE
A VINTAGE MURDER

Books published by The Ballantine Publishing Group
are available at quantity discounts on bulk purchases
for premium, educational, fund-raising, and special
sales use. For details, please call 1-800-733-3000.

A VINTAGE MURDER

Janet L. Smith

IVY BOOKS • NEW YORK

Ivy Books
Published by Ballantine Books
Copyright © 1994 by Janet L. Smith

Library of Congress Catalog Card Number: 94-15130

ISBN 0-8041-1385-8

Manufactured in the United States of America

First Hardcover Edition: September 1994
First Mass Market Edition: November 1995

10 9 8 7 6 5 4 3 2 1

To Jim
The best is yet to come.

Acknowledgments

I would like to thank the many people who generously shared their expertise and ideas, making the research for this book an extremely pleasant task. Many thanks to the winemakers of the Yakima Valley, especially Mike Wallace, of the Hinzerling Winery, and John Rauner, of the Yakima River Winery, for answering all of my questions about the region and its wine; the Hon. Bruce Tonks, without whom Harry Braithwaite could not exist; Jean McElroy for help in thinking like a prosecutor; Dr. Darcy Johnson for medical advice; Dr. Carol Cohen for psychological input; Juanita Wagner for her chemistry expertise; to Marcia and Clyde Smith, Linda Bauer, Cathy Pappas, Karen Bargelt, Martine Andrews, and Patti Latsch for their helpful comments on the manuscript; and to Jim Gorman, of course, for everything.

... age appears to be best in four things—
old wood best to burn, old wine to drink,
old friends to trust, and old authors to read.
—FRANCIS BACON

Chapter 1

IT WAS NOT yet five o'clock on Monday morning when Galen Rockwell rose to go to work. He had grown accustomed to moving quietly and dressing in the dark so that he wouldn't disturb the woman who often lay in bed beside him. But for the last six months, he'd been sleeping alone. Even after all this time, it felt strange to dress with the light on.

He parked his truck on the hill overlooking the North Faire vineyards, leaned his shotgun against a fence post, and watched the first rose-tinted glow of dawn toward the east, coloring the hills that rimmed the Yakima Valley. From this spot, when Galen needed to feel that there was a reason to keep going, he could almost believe that the vineyards were his.

By midday, the valley would be bathed in the muted golden light of October. He looked south toward the Horse Heaven Hills and thought how different eastern Washington was from California, where he'd spent most of his forty-two years, and where he'd learned the art of making wine. The light in this valley had an old-world quality about it, not as brash or imposing as the southern sun. Although he'd never been to France, Galen imagined that this was the same kind of light as in Bordeaux, slowly ripening the grapes with long hours of daylight. He could almost picture the tower of a chateau rising in the background and imagine the sound of workers calling to each other in French.

1

Rubbing his hands together against the early morning chill, he told himself to knock off daydreaming and get to work. The gun was filled with buckshot to frighten the birds that wanted to gorge themselves on the sweet, nearly ripened grapes. Not that it was possible to scare off the birds this time of year, but at least he felt like he was doing something to protect the crop.

Even though North Faire hired a vineyard manager to be responsible for growing the grapes, it was Galen's job as winemaker to call the shots—how to prune, when and how much to irrigate, what fertilizers and sprays to use. But by far the most critical decision was when to pick the grapes. If the fruit was not at its peak of readiness, the wine would be flawed. To make this critical decision Galen liked to start early and work alone, examining the vines, tasting the fruit, collecting samples to test the sugar content and pH level. The amount of sugar was vital, because it would ultimately determine the alcohol level in the wine. But the acidity was what actually gave the wine its fresh, crisp flavor and firm character, its "personality," Galen liked to say. Taylor North might own the winery and vineyards, but when it came to making the North Faire wine, he was commander in chief. God knows, he thought with dismay, there was little else he had control over.

He started with the rows of cabernet. Tiny, dark, and tightly clustered, the fruit looked more like blueberries than grapes to the untrained eye. With a sharp knife he sliced off a bunch to take back to his lab, and he pulled off a grape to taste. The laboratory testing would probably verify his intuition, which said that the cabernet would be ready to pick in two to three days, if the warm weather lasted.

The next rows were planted with gewürztraminer, the German name describing the spicy quality of the plump pinkish-green grapes. As soon as the sun was up, busloads of migrant workers would arrive to finish picking this variety, which was at its peak of ripeness. The large wooden bins of fruit would be taken immediately back to the winery for crushing and pressing. October was always the most hectic month, but intensely satisfying as well.

Galen's musings were interrupted by the sound of a car driving up the gravel road. He recognized the sputtering cough of Steven Vick's poorly tuned Mazda. The sight of the vehicle shattered Galen's philosophical mood. The worst of it was, there was nothing the winemaker could do to keep the son of a bitch off Taylor's property.

Galen picked up his shotgun and fired at a flock of robins feasting on some clusters of chardonnay, the sharp crack echoing in the quiet morning air. The fat birds fluttered up for a moment, then realighted on the vines a few feet away. One of them seemed to cock its head insolently, reminding Galen that his efforts to control the situation were completely ineffectual. Yeah, Galen thought, the story of my life.

Taylor North rose as the autumn sunlight entered her bedroom. She went downstairs to fix coffee and toast, and she set a dish of food out on the porch for the cat. Back upstairs, she put on her usual work clothes—jeans, boots, and a cotton shirt rolled up at the sleeves—but took more care than usual, knowing that she would see *him* today. The tiny lines around her eyes or the beginnings of gray in her ash-blond hair might reveal that she was well over thirty, but he'd never know it from the cut of her jeans.

Scrutinizing her appearance in the full-length mirror, she was pleased with what she saw. There was no reason why Taylor North wouldn't still turn heads when she walked into a room. Changing her mind, she took off the chambray work shirt and substituted one of white cotton, better to show off her tanned neck and forearms, then added a gold chain and earrings to pick up the shine in her hair. As she applied just a hint of makeup, all her worries and anxieties faded farther and farther into the recesses of her memory. One way or another, she'd find a way to deal with Steven Vick.

Taylor's paperwork for the Wine Gala was spread out on

the kitchen table where she'd left it the night before. There were still dozens of details to attend to before tomorrow night—the caterers, the name tags, making sure the VIP guests were picked up at the airport and taken to their hotel. For the last several years, North Faire Winery had put on a small "library tasting," where special bottles of vintages no longer available for sale were sampled by invited guests and paying patrons. This year, a well-known wine connoisseur had invited all of the Yakima Valley wineries to participate in what they were calling a Gala—a library tasting where all of the local wineries would bring out the best from their private cellars. Even at sixty dollars a head, the two hundred and fifty tickets had sold out quickly.

When Taylor had agreed to help organize the event, she'd had no idea how much work was involved. She pulled up a chair, brought the telephone within reach, and picked up the nearest pile of paper. She wanted every item to be perfectly under control by four o'clock when she was scheduled to meet with the evening's guest of honor, Charles Marchand, to give him a tour of the facility where the Gala would be held.

Taylor had just dialed the caterers when she was startled by someone pounding on the front door as if to break it down.

Galen found it hard to keep his mind on his work, knowing that Taylor's husband was down at the house. Six months ago, when Taylor finally threw Steven Vick out, he'd thought things would finally get better. Instead, things had gotten worse. Not only did Steve still come around to bully Taylor, but the weird, malicious incidents had begun. First it was the crusher-stemmer, and then it was the ruined barrels. Now it was petty thefts, something new practically every day. He'd have to tell Taylor that just this morning he'd discovered a missing box of labels.

Not that it would do any good. He'd been nagging her for weeks trying to get her to take action. At first she said she couldn't be sure that Steven Vick was behind the thefts.

Even after Galen caught the man rifling through the old desk in the winery she had refused to respond. She just said that everyone knew she never used that desk, so it didn't matter. Every day it was becoming clearer to Galen that Taylor's unhealthy attachment to her abusive husband wasn't going to be easily broken.

A few more minutes passed, but Galen couldn't concentrate. From his vantage point on the hill, he could see that Vick's car was still parked in front of Taylor's house. He decided to walk down there and confront Vick himself.

As he walked up the steps to the porch, Galen knocked the dirt off his boots and tried to compose his opening remarks. He had no right to interfere between Taylor and her husband, but as winemaker, he had every right to be upset about the things that were happening around the winery premises. His prepared speech evaporated when he heard the shouting from inside, and the sound of a chair crashing across the living room's hardwood floor.

Using his key, Galen let himself into the house and rushed to the living room. Taylor stood frozen near the mantelpiece. Steven Vick, his face red and puffy, breathing hard, stood looking at the broken pieces of wood from the chair he'd thrown across the room.

"All right, that's it." Galen still had his shotgun in his hand. He pointed it at Vick. "You're out of here, now."

Vick shot a glance back at Taylor. "You remember what I said, babe." He winked at her insolently. "You'll come through for me, just like you always do."

Galen waited until he heard the door slam, and Steve's engine rev up. When he finally spoke, his level voice belied his anger. "Okay, Taylor. That's it. If you're not going to make a decision, I will. If you don't start whatever legal action it takes to get a court order to keep that creep off this property, then I'm out of here. Now. *This week.*"

"But the harvest—"

"Damn the harvest."

Taylor was stunned. Galen could hardly believe the words himself as they came out of his mouth. This job, the winery, meant everything to him. After all the problems he'd had in California, he'd been incredibly lucky to land this job at North Faire. All of his research into microclimates had told him that North Faire had the perfect combination of sun, rain, and elevation for the type of wine he wanted to create. And with his track record, it would be virtually impossible to find a job half as good anywhere else. But the fact was, he'd reached the end of his rope.

"We've talked about this, Galen. At least I was able to get Steve to move out. He's ... volatile. You just don't know what he's done. What he's capable of doing. I don't want to ..."

"That's precisely why you have to do something, Taylor."

"This isn't the right time. As soon as I get through the Gala ..."

"I've been hearing you complain about the timing not being right for too long. I swear, if you can't find five minutes to call a lawyer sometime today, I'll be gone by morning." He paused. "What about that friend of yours you've talked about, the lawyer in Seattle."

"Annie MacPherson? She'd never come. She's never forgiven me for what happened with Steve."

Galen glared at Taylor. "Then I'll call her." Without another word, the stocky man strode from the house, slamming the front door behind him.

Chapter 2

THE *MARTINDALE-HUBBELL* is a lawyer's directory that can be found in virtually every lawyer's office in the nation. The volumes are huge, about the size of an unabridged dictionary, and Annie MacPherson estimated that a single volume probably weighed fifteen to twenty pounds. That's why she was so startled when her client's wife heaved one of the massive books across the conference room table, aimed directly at her client's head.

He ducked and the volume hit the wall, gouging an ugly ding in the textured wallpaper. Annie stopped the husband just in time, as he was grabbing the heavy tome to hurl it back.

"All right, Mr. Biddle—Mrs. Biddle, that's enough. This is a law office, not an Olympic shot put event." She glanced across the table at opposing counsel, a law school colleague who looked genuinely mortified by his client's outburst. "So, Jeff, you think we should wrap this up for today? Somehow, I don't think the Biddles are quite ready to come to an agreement on the property settlement."

"I'd say that's a pretty fair assessment, Annie."

"It's his fault," Mrs. Biddle hissed. The ample shoulder pads in her beaded sweater made her look like a linebacker, hardly an equal match for her diminutive husband. "He's too greedy. I told him the day we moved into the Lake Sammamish house that it was *mine*, and it would always be mine, no matter what happened. I was the one who spent *weeks* traipsing around with that horrid realtor to find the house." She turned to Annie. "I designed the window treatments myself. What does *he* care about window treatments? Tell me that."

"But, honey," said her husband. "You keep forgetting that this is a community property state. Ms. MacPherson told me that without a written prenuptial agreement . . ."

"There you go again. Everything in writing, everything in writing. I'll show you something in writing, you little—"

Her attorney was prepared this time, and grabbed Mrs. Biddle's wrist before she could heft another volume. "Come on, June, let's go back to my office. We'll have a nice cup of tea and settle down." He clamped an arm around her shoulders and ushered her toward the reception area. As he passed Annie he said, "I'll call you to reschedule. And, uh, send us an invoice for the wallpaper repair."

"Thanks, Jeff. I appreciate it."

A few moments later Annie said good-bye to Mr. Biddle, who appeared not the least bit shaken. Perhaps, she thought, after twenty-five years of marriage to June, he'd seen it all.

She grabbed her stack of pink telephone slips from the receptionist's desk, and went down the hall for a refill of coffee. Even though the pot had been on for hours, she filled her cup with the dregs, drained by her afternoon sparring match. Her two law partners, Joel Feinstein and Jed Delacourt, were in Jed's office, huddled over the sports page and a scrawled list of names and numbers. "Hey, MacPherson," said Jed, "is it safe to come out yet? It sounded like World War Three in there."

She joined the two men in Jed's office and sank into a chair with exhaustion. "Somehow, when I went to law school I didn't imagine I'd need to learn how to dodge flying objects. Being a prosecutor was far less dangerous than doing dissolutions."

Jed Delacourt was dressed like the overgrown preppie that he was in gray wool slacks, navy suspenders, Harvard tie loosened at the neck. Annie thought he must spend hours every morning getting his neatly trimmed blond hair to fall forward with just the right amount of Kennedy-esque panache. "This kind of thing could hurt your stellar reputation, you know. Didn't the *National Law Journal* just name you one of the 'hottest female litigators in the state'?"

"Yes, but why do I have to be designated as a 'female' litigator, for Pete's sake? It's like calling someone a 'male nurse' or a 'lady doctor.' I swear, next thing you know, they'll be calling me 'spunky.' Have you ever heard a man being called 'spunky'?"

"Spunky. I like that," said Jed. "Spunky MacPherson— sounds like a character on a Saturday morning cartoon." He pointed at Annie's coffee cup. "And this is how you maintain all that spunk? That high-octane rocket fuel you drink is going to kill you one of these days. If they had a Breathalyzer for caffeine, you'd be *way* over the legal limit."

"You know I can't make it through the afternoon without my jolt of java. Something to make *you* work a little faster probably wouldn't hurt."

"All right, you guys," Joel interjected. "We all know that Annie's debilitating caffeine addiction is sending her to an early grave, but that's her choice. Since it's my year to be managing partner, I want to know what Annie's family feud case is worth to us. We paid through the nose to have this new office space redecorated—we can't afford to have the kind of clients who are going to tear up the wallpaper."

Annie grinned. "Since you asked, Mr. It's-My-Turn-To-Be–Managing Partner, our Mr. Biddle just happens to be one of the original Microsoft engineers. His stock in the company puts his net worth somewhere between three and four million."

Joel smiled. "That little guy?"

"And the Lake Sammamish house they're fighting over? It's conservatively valued at one point two mil, and that's not counting her antique collection, or his classic motorcycles."

"He rides motorcycles?" Jed asked, cracking up. "Does she have to give him a leg up to get on?"

"Okay," Joel interjected. "I've heard all I need to know. With that kind of property settlement at stake, his wife can wreck our wallpaper any day of the week. Now if we can just get Jed here to start bringing in major clients . . ."

"I'm working on it, I'm working on it. I guess I just don't have as much 'spunk' as Annie."

She glared at Jed, then looked at what they were working on. "I don't know how you guys can give me a hard time. Look at you—a Monday afternoon and you're spending valuable billable hours on that fantasy baseball league again. Am I the only one who does any work around here?"

"You're basing that comment on a mistaken assumption, Annie," said Joel, his long legs crowded into the space between Jed's desk and the wall. "You perceive fantasy baseball as merely a game, rather than the true mental exercise that it is. The absorption in deep, analytical, left-brain activity frees the unconscious mind to sort through other pending problems. Similar to 'sleeping on it,' as they say. When we're through with this 'game' as you call it, our minds will have automatically found solutions to other seemingly insoluble dilemmas."

"Oh, please. Excuse me while I run to my office to get my hip boots."

As Annie started flipping through her telephone messages, she asked Jed about the status of the trial they were scheduled to start on Wednesday.

"Oh, I meant to tell you. The court clerk called. We've gotten bumped by a criminal case. They're going to reschedule us for early February. I had Val call the witnesses and let them know."

"Again? That's the third time we've gotten continued. I don't know when we're ever going to get that case before a jury."

"Look on the bright side. Now we both have two weeks on our calendars completely clear. I think a little vacation time is in order. They say that October is beautiful in Maui. Or a trip to the Oregon coast would be nice. . . ."

Joel Feinstein cleared his throat. "Drumming up some new business wouldn't hurt, either."

"Uh, right, boss."

Annie continued to review her telephone messages. She was relieved to see there were no emergencies in the calls she had to return—a client with questions about an upcoming deposition, a reminder of a dental appointment, her friend Ellen calling to remind her they planned to get together for dinner that evening.

But Annie's mood changed abruptly when she saw the final message.

"What is it?" Jed asked.

Annie stuck her head into the hall and called to the receptionist. "Cyndi, when you took this message from Taylor North—did she say what she wanted?"

"She called about an hour ago, but she wouldn't say what it was about? She said you could call her collect since it's long distance, someplace in eastern Washington? She also said it was really urgent?" Cyndi, the young, newly hired receptionist, had a tendency to end every statement with a rising inflection. It was a habit that normally grated on Annie's nerves like fingernails on a chalkboard, but this time, she was too distracted by the name on the telephone message even to notice.

"You have a case in eastern Washington?" Joel asked.

"No, she's an old friend from high school. But I can't imagine what she'd be calling about."

"Probably organizing the twenty-year reunion," said Joel. "You know, I went to mine last year back in Brooklyn— what a riot. Suzy Goldman astounded everybody by losing a hundred pounds and becoming a TV sportscaster."

Jed replied, "Yeah, I can't wait to go to mine. Find out how many fellow Choate graduates I can swap AA stories with."

Annie shook her head. "No chance. The Taylor North I knew would be the last woman on earth to be on an organizing committee. Besides—we haven't spoken in . . ." Annie did the mental arithmetic. ". . . my God, it's got to be about seventeen years."

"A charity fund raiser?" Joel suggested. "Maybe she just wants to find out what you've been up to."

She shook her head. "No. I meant I haven't spoken to her, as in *not speaking*." She looked down and noticed her hands were shaking. "I'm sorry. . . ."

Without another word, Annie went into her office and closed the door. This was a call she had to return in private.

Chapter 3

TAYLOR COULD HAVE walked the mile to the Grubenmacher Mansion, which was on the property adjacent to the North Faire vineyards, but she was excited about her planning session with Charles Marchand and didn't want to show up late or out of breath. Dr. Marchand had, after all, contributed ten thousand dollars to help sponsor the event. When she arrived ten minutes early for her four o'clock meeting, she was pleased to see that the guest of honor and primary sponsor hadn't yet arrived. That would give her time to compose herself.

She pulled the van into the semicircular driveway and parked in front of the mansion, knowing the mere sight of the North Faire logo would fluster Martin Grubenmacher. She had gone to grade school with the funny-looking little man, and could vaguely recall how she and the other children had teased him unmercifully about his roly-poly shape. To this day, he couldn't be around her without dithering like a fool.

Still, it would be easier putting up with Martin's agitation than the shrewish behavior of his mother. The old woman gave Martin a figurehead post in the family business, a lucrative chain of gas station mini-marts, but she was the one who'd built the family fortune. She had trouble remembering that she was simply loaning out the mansion to be used for the Gala, and wasn't the one in control. That was precisely why Taylor had intentionally planned the meeting for

13

four o'clock on Monday, after her confidential source at Edie's Beauty Salon had informed her that was when Florence Grubenmacher always had her hair done.

Taylor closed the door of the van just as a white Lincoln Town Car with a rental agency sticker pulled up and parked behind her. She took a deep breath, reminded herself how good she looked, and walked over to the door as Charles Marchand stepped out. "Doctor Marchand, how good to see you again." Her words were demure, but her tone flirtatious. "Your flight was smooth, I hope?"

"A little turbulence, but just enough to remind me how much I like flying." He smiled and took her outstretched hand, then kissed her politely on the cheek. "You look wonderful, as always, my dear."

"As do you."

Dr. Charles Marchand was the type of man one expected to see pictured in a Dewar's profile. He had retired at fifty from a lucrative medical practice in the Bay Area, and now spent his time and money devoted to his two passions— airplanes and wine. He divided his time between his homes on the Monterey Peninsula, the San Juan Islands, and Lake Coeur d'Alene, flying himself in his private Cessna between the three destinations, with trips in between to buy, sample, and collect fine wines. It was a lifestyle most men his age could only envy.

"Is this your first chance to see the mansion?" Taylor asked.

"Yes, as a matter of fact it is. I was warned, of course, but now, seeing it in person, it's . . . uh . . . something to behold."

Taylor laughed. "Few people can find the right words to describe it. Step back here, where you can get a better view."

The Grubenmacher Mansion, which had the year before been placed on the state's register of historic homes, was a cross between a delight and a monstrosity. Taylor explained to Dr. Marchand that it had been built in 1890 by Hilda

Grubenmacher, the eccentric (some said crazy) widow of the town's first banker.

"Hilda was born in Bavaria," Taylor explained, "where she must have been influenced by the style of the nineteenth-century hunting *schlossen*. But by the time the home was being built, the widow was half-blind, and her English had never been very good. The architect who designed it was a young man who'd never traveled farther than Oregon."

They both looked up at the house, which was largely Victorian in style, but with gables, gewgaws, towers, and balconies added everywhere imaginable. The structure itself would have had a certain chaotic charm, but for the intense yellow ocher paint, with burgundy trim. "I can see that something must have been lost in the translation," Dr. Marchand replied. "Why does she keep it that detestable color?"

"Florence insists it's the original color, and that Hilda was following the Bavarian tradition. Everyone else thinks the widow was simply color-blind. Do you see the tower in the corner?"

"Yes, how tall is it?"

"I'm not sure in feet, but it's the equivalent of four stories. It was probably built as a watchtower, because the only door opens to the outside, but it got to be called the Widow's Perch after Hilda started going up there on a daily basis to converse with her dead husband. They say that as a result of all that exercise, she lived to be ninety-eight!"

Taylor's knock on the front door was answered by a very small, round man in plaid pants and a red polo shirt, who couldn't have been over five foot three. Whenever she saw him, Taylor was reminded of the three little pigs. This officious little character would have been the pig with the brick house, taunting his poor, ill-prepared brothers.

"Oh, T-Taylor, it's you. I wasn't expecting you so ... Uh, hello, Dr. Marchand." Martin nervously looked at his watch. "Oh, my goodness. Is it four already? Silly me, I guess I lost track of the time. Er, come in, I guess."

Taylor and Dr. Marchand exchanged glances.

"Mother and I are really so terribly pleased that you chose the Mansion for the Gala. We sometimes feel guilty that we get to enjoy it all to ourselves." He showed them first into the ballroom, which jutted out on the west side of the house, forming an L-shaped wing. The floor was polished hardwood, the ceiling looked about twenty feet high, and there were tall leaded glass windows lining three of the four walls, with French doors leading out to the garden. "This room is r-really the sh-showpiece of the house," Martin stammered. "There's enough room for all fifteen of the participating wineries to have their own display."

"Lovely," said Dr. Marchand. "I can see why you chose it, Taylor."

She blushed. "We thought it was more elegant than a hotel ballroom. And with fifteen of the twenty-two local wineries agreeing to participate, we needed a lot of space."

"Indeed."

Martin hurried them along to the next room. "This is the dining room. We'll have the buffet set up in here." The room was approximately half the size of the ballroom, with a heavy table and sideboard that looked antique. Mahogany paneling and a somber green rug made the room seem dark and somewhat funereal. Heavy velvet drapes hanging from brass rods looked like they'd keep out the brightest sunlight. The artworks, following a hunting motif, were as dark as the walls, with oil paintings of dogs retrieving pheasants and horses chasing foxes.

"The kitchen is through there. It's not large enough for the caterers to prepare the hors d'oeuvres, but they will have plenty of work space to get organized."

"Good, good. And the guest list?"

"We're sold out, of course," said Taylor. "Counting the invited guests, the total head count comes to two hundred and fifty. Each participating winery and the Grubenmachers were allowed six invitations, and thirty invitations were sent to prominent individuals in the wine community—

connoisseurs, dealers, critics, and restaurateurs. The rest sold very quickly."

"Well, I must say, Taylor, it looks like you've done a tremendous job. I'm expecting a flawless evening. Uh, has a final guest list been prepared? I'd love to see who's expected to come, if I may."

"Martin has the list, I believe."

"Y-yes, I'll get it right away, Taylor. Hold on." The small man scurried into the kitchen, and returned in a moment. "Here it is. I hope you can r-read my writing."

Marchand took the list, and Taylor looked on over his shoulder. The names were written in columns and grouped according to which winery had sent the invitation. Taylor noted the total number of guests, and quickly scanned the list. Her gaze stopped abruptly on the last name on the list of guests invited by Martin and Florence Grubenmacher. It was her husband, Steven Vick.

Chapter 4

THAT EVENING after work, Annie went home and threw a few things in the wash so that she could pack for her trip. She felt both excited and apprehensive about seeing Taylor North again after all these years. Annie had called the winery back around four, but Taylor had been at a meeting, and Annie was put through to the winemaker, a man named Galen Rockwell. He had insisted that Taylor wanted to see Annie urgently, that she had to come right away. There was harassment involved, an estranged husband, he had said. He made it sound like the business could be in jeopardy if she didn't get some legal help right away. The man had sounded so desperate, and her calendar was clear for a couple of weeks, so Annie agreed to leave the next morning.

Lost in her thoughts, Annie was startled when the intercom buzzed. "Who is it?" she answered tentatively. She wasn't in the mood for surprises.

"Hey, Annie, open up. It's me." Annie recognized the voice of her friend, Ellen O'Neill. "Didn't you get my message about dinner tonight?"

"Sorry. Come on up." Annie buzzed her in.

Ellen made it up the stairs to Annie's second-floor apartment in a matter of seconds. The tiny woman, whose hobby was running marathons, made a practice of going up stairs three at a time. When she knocked on Annie's door, she wasn't even winded.

"I knew you'd forget. That's why I left you a message

reminding you," Ellen said with a smile. Annie often got so frazzled by the endless details at work that she forgot she had a personal life.

"I know, it's a long story. I got your message, but completely spaced it out. You want to grab a bite somewhere? I don't feel like cooking tonight."

"What do you mean, you don't feel like cooking *tonight*? Annie, the entire time I've known you, you've *never* felt like cooking. I'm not even sure you know how to cook."

"I know how to cook perfectly well. It's just that I choose not to."

"Right. Whatever you say. You look exhausted."

Annie told her about that afternoon's call, and her decision to spend a few days in eastern Washington. "I had to rush like crazy to get everything finished up at work, and I still have to pack."

"Well, then let's do take-out. I can go get it while you finish up here."

"Sounds great." They agreed on Chinese food from Tai Tung. Half an hour later, the two women were seated on Annie's living room floor by the coffee table, dishing up orange beef, cashew chicken, mu shu pork, and something with tomatoes and eggplant that Annie didn't recognize. "My God, Ellen," Annie said when she saw all the containers. "Are you sure you got enough? I didn't know we were inviting the neighborhood army battalion."

"So there might be leftovers." Annie knew that was unlikely. Long-distance running was Ellen's second favorite hobby; her favorite pastime was eating.

Before Annie could taste a bite, the intercom buzzed again. "Don't answer it," said Ellen as she speared a piece of orange beef with her chopstick. "It's probably just some kid selling magazines."

The buzzer rang again, more insistently. Annie got up and answered it. "Yes?"

"Annie, it's Jed. I'm glad you're home. I *desperately* need solace and comfort."

Annie buzzed him in. Coming in the door, he took a deep breath and said, "Yes, I'd love to stay for dinner, and thanks for asking. What is this, a party I wasn't invited to?"

"No, just us. You know Ellen, right?"

"Yeah, hi."

"Have a seat, I'll get you a plate. So, what are you doing on Capitol Hill?"

Grabbing a mu shu pancake and spilling pork onto the carpet, Jed replied somberly, "I had a date."

Ellen looked at her watch. "*Had* a date? But it's only seven-thirty."

"I didn't say I had a *successful* date."

Annie returned with a plate, some silverware, and a roll of paper towels. She brought out two beers for herself and Ellen, and a Diet Pepsi for Jed.

"You wouldn't happen to have the caffeine-free kind, would you?" Jed asked with a smirk.

"No," Annie responded with a glare. "So the bachelorette of the week didn't work out, huh?"

He sighed. "I wasn't going to tell you, because I knew you would never let me live it down. I've turned over a new leaf. No more Barbie dates. I've decided from now on only to go out with intelligent women."

Annie almost choked. "That is a change. And just how are you going to accomplish this amazing reformation?"

Jed mumbled into his rice.

"What was that?"

"I said, I placed a personal ad in the *Weekly*. I've had three dates so far."

Annie tried not to snicker through a mouthful of mu shu.

"Don't laugh," said Ellen. "I placed an ad once, and met some nice guys. Three Boeing engineers, an insurance salesman, and an MBA student. Not a single serial killer in the bunch. No married serial killers either, now that I think of it. How's your luck been, Jed?"

"Absolutely disastrous. Date Number One on Friday was a radical feminist. I mean, I'm a sensitive-new-age-guy and all that, but she was something else. I should have made my escape the moment I saw her. She wanted to meet at the Gravity Bar on Broadway, and when I got there, she was reading a copy of *Backlash* by Susan Faludi, ferociously underlining her favorite passages with a yellow highlighter. She spent the next hour telling me why all men are scum, and how in the next world order, women will hold the positions of power and men will be the housekeepers and slaves."

"I like this woman," said Ellen, smiling.

"Hey, I barely got out of there with my anatomy intact."

"So what about Number Two?" Annie asked.

"It started out okay. I met her in the afternoon at Green Lake—she said she wanted to roller skate. And I have to admit, I was impressed when I saw her—tall, brunette, gorgeous beyond belief."

"I thought you were turning over a new leaf?"

"I didn't say they can't be beautiful as well as intelligent."

"Okay, go on."

"We get to the lake, and she strips down to nothing but a string bikini and knee pads, and proceeds to do this little dirty-dancing number on skates. I guess I was just there to be an audience, along with every other red-blooded male at the lake. She got asked out six times before we made it back to where we started." Jed picked up the eggplant dish and started eating out of the container. "This stuff's really great. What is it?"

"Eggplant," said Ellen. Jed set it down.

"I guess I'm kind of full, after all."

"So what happened tonight?" Ellen asked.

Jed put his head in his hands. "The worst. It was Cyndi—the new receptionist from the office!"

"Jed, she's only eighteen."

"Believe me, I know. Ever since she started work, it's been real clear that she had a crush on me. Not that I'm not flattered, but even I have my limits. I made the mistake of showing her the ad when it appeared in the paper. She answered, using a fake name so I wouldn't know it was her.

I met her up on Broadway—we were supposed to see a movie at the Harvard Exit. So I bought her a movie ticket, told her to enjoy herself, and that I was never, repeat never, going to go out with her. The last thing I need is to be charged with sexual harassment. I've almost decided it would be easier to be celibate." He saw Ellen raise one eyebrow. "I said, 'almost.' Hey, can I have the rest of this?"

Jed helped himself to the last of the cashew chicken. Seeing Annie's overnight bag in the corner, he asked, "You going somewhere? Is this anything to do with that mystery phone call you got today?"

Annie nodded. "Eastern Washington. This woman I used to be friends with in high school owns a winery over there in the Yakima Valley."

"This, after Joel gave me such a hard time about taking a vacation?"

"This is business. She needs legal help dealing with her estranged husband. He's harassing her, causing all kinds of trouble for the winery."

"Right. The wine country at harvest time. Really tough assignment, Annie. But I thought you said you weren't speaking to this woman."

Annie tried to think of the best way to explain her complex connection to Taylor North and her husband, Steven Vick. "Taylor and I were best friends in high school. We were transfer students at Queen Anne High, both with divorced parents, and we lived in the same neighborhood. To tell you the truth, I idolized Taylor. She was attractive, popular, outgoing—all the things I thought I wasn't. For three years, we were practically inseparable."

"And the guy?" Jed asked. "Did you know him, too?"

Annie moved the food around on her plate, her appetite suddenly gone. "Yeah. Taylor started going out with Steven Vick halfway through our senior year, really spending a lot of time with him. He and I didn't hit it off."

"Jealousy?" Ellen asked.

"Oh, it was a lot more than jealousy. We literally hated each other. It was like vinegar and baking soda—a combustible reaction if we were even in the same room together. I couldn't imagine what she saw in him. He was loud, obnoxious, went out of his way to insult everyone she cared about—not just me. And he had a terrible temper. You know the type—if someone cuts him off in his car, he's likely to get out and start a fight. The slightest thing could set him off. It was a horrible situation."

"So you stopped speaking to her because her boyfriend was a jerk?"

She took a deep breath. "There was . . . more to it than that." Annie stood up and began clearing away the plates. Her silence made it clear that the subject was closed.

Chapter 5

MARTIN GRUBENMACHER HAD always been ashamed of his appearance. It wasn't just that he was short—a lot of short men compensated for their lack of height and went on to lead wildly successful lives. Look at Napoleon. Look at Mickey Rooney. All of Martin's ancestors on his mother's side had been short, and that hadn't stopped them. His grandfather had even been able to joke about it with the name of the family business, "Short Stops, Incorporated."

No, it wasn't his height, but the thickness around the middle, combined with his stubby, somewhat bowed legs, that had caused the children at school to nickname him Humpty-Dumpty. "Humpty-Dumpty sat on a wall." "You look a little scrambled today, Humpty." "Fallen off any walls lately, Dumpty?" Taylor North—he could never forget that she was the one who started it. And as soon as she said it that first time, everyone started calling him that. But still, he didn't hold it against her. It meant that she noticed him, and that was enough.

Of course, it wouldn't have been so bad if his father hadn't liked the nickname so much he'd started using it at home. "Hide the scrambled eggs, Florence. We wouldn't want little Humpty to get a complex." "Looks like the king's horses forgot a piece of the puzzle, today, Humpty. Better go back and try again." Then he would laugh as if it were so funny.

Martin usually went to the Short Stop business office every morning precisely at nine. He knew the other employees whispered behind his back that his mother made him a vice president in the family business just to give him something to do, but Martin felt that he really made a difference. Designing the window displays at all of the gas station/mini-marts was an important task, critical to total sales volume. Someday, when she was gone, all of the mini-marts would be his.

Of course, he wished he could get a salary. He hated having to ask her for money all the time. But his mother said that vice presidents don't take salaries if they want to maximize profits. She said she didn't take a salary either.

Still, Martin felt he was luckier than most people, because he truly loved going to work every day. The business office was located on the top floor of the A. E. Larson Building, right in the heart of downtown Yakima. Even though the building was only eleven stories, it felt like a skyscraper because there were no other tall buildings around it. With its art deco shape, and flagpole perched on top, it reminded Martin of a cross between the Empire State Building and a rocket ship, ready to blast off. His office was his second favorite place. He loved the way he could turn his big leather armchair toward the corner window and look out and see for miles. It made him feel like he was on the bridge of the *Starship Enterprise*. Warp speed, Mr. Sulu!

But Martin didn't go to work that day. It was the morning of the Wine Gala, and there were too many other things to do. Details to solidify. Taylor would be very angry with him if he didn't make sure everything was perfect.

He climbed the stairs to the Widow's Perch. If his office was the bridge of the *Enterprise*, this room was his own personal landing shuttle. Clear nights were the best, when the sky was filled with billions of stars. Here, he could see everything.

Exactly at nine, Martin heard footsteps in the stairwell. A head appeared where the circular stairs came up through the floor. What the visitor saw was an octagonal room, about eight feet in diameter, with 360 degrees of windows. A door led to a narrow balcony, really only a walkway, enclosed by a wooden rail. Martin rarely went out on the walkway. The height scared him, and he was afraid that the flimsy rail wouldn't support his weight. The visitor stepped up into the room and looked around, smiling at the way Martin had decorated his special hideaway.

"I'm not disturbing you, am I?" the visitor asked sarcastically, seeing the pudgy man sitting in a beanbag chair near the floor, his hands folded in his lap.

"N-no, please, come in. There's a lot we have to talk about."

"Is there?"

Martin wasn't sure if he was being mocked. It was important to be deferential. "A-about the Wine Gala tonight . . . ?"

"You're not having second thoughts, are you?"

"Oh, no. No, not at all. I just . . . I need to go over it again. My part, that is. I'm not . . . I'm not entirely clear on what I'm supposed to do." Martin heard his own voice come out like a simpering whine, and hated it. He wanted to be confident, poised like his visitor, but it never seemed to work out that way. Martin could feel a thin layer of perspiration on his brow, but he didn't want to embarrass himself by wiping it away. Instead, he reached in his pocket for his tin of Altoids, slipping a peppermint surreptitiously into his mouth. He didn't offer a mint to his guest.

"It's really very simple. We've gone over this before." The visitor was contemptuous, and made little attempt to disguise the fact. Nevertheless, the plan was repeated, slowly, until Martin knew it by heart.

"You'll be there, won't you?"

"At the Wine Gala? Of course. Everyone will be there. But you realize we can't discuss the plan there. Too many people. That's very important. If you speak to me at all tonight, it must be about something neutral. Just act naturally."

Martin nodded. "Act naturally. All right." He'd rarely

been given this much responsibility, and it both frightened and excited him.

"But is it *really* necessary to ... uh ... you know. I mean, it seems like such a drastic step. I'm sure that if we asked him, Steve would ..."

"That's not your decision." The guest glared, reminding Martin with a glance who was in charge. Martin was ashamed that he'd even questioned the plan. Of course it was the right thing.

"You won't screw this up, will you?" the caller asked, gazing out one of the windows in the direction of North Faire. The Widow's Perch had a clear view of both the winery and Taylor North's house.

Feeling a drop of sweat beginning to roll down his forehead, the small man reached for a Kleenex. "No, of course not," he said, wiping his forehead. "The garden. I know exactly what to do." The visitor moved to the window that looked straight down to the garden below.

"Is that all?"

"Uh, uh, no ... there was another thing ... the bottles?"

The guest nodded. "You won't forget about the bottles, will you?"

Martin shook his head like a schoolboy. "I won't forget."

"Good."

Martin stood up and followed his guest to the stairwell, then listened until the descending footsteps could no longer be heard. He tried to breathe deeply, slowly, deeply, slowly. Things were going to be so much better after tonight, he thought, so much better. Taylor would be so pleased with him.

Martin went to the wooden box in the corner and opened the lid. He looked at the binoculars, but left them in their case. Not much to look at this time of day. Instead, he reached for the framed photograph. He'd taken it last year at a food and wine fair in Walla Walla, when Taylor still wore her blond hair long, to her waist. He liked it much better that way. It looked more like it had when they were in grade school together. He propped the photo up in the window, and arranged his beanbag chair so he could look at the picture, with Taylor's house in the background. Any apprehension he had about the Wine Gala slipped away, as he thought about the payoff.

Taylor's dress in the photo was black and tight. She was turned almost with her back to the camera. He imagined, as he always did, that he was reaching up to her neck, first stroking her hair, then moving it aside and pulling down the zipper. Past her waist, past her hips. Underneath, he pictured her in skimpy black lingerie, a little black bra and a garter belt holding up her black stockings. He pushed the black dress off her shoulders, let it fall to the floor, reached around her from behind and cupped her perfect breasts in his hands.

Martin Grubenmacher closed his eyes and swayed back and forth in his beanbag chair, making a small noise of delight. What he loved most about the Widow's Perch was that he could see miles and miles in any direction, but no one could see him. He was in control. He was the captain of the *Starship Enterprise*.

Chapter 6

ANNIE LEFT SEATTLE early Tuesday morning, driving east on Interstate 90. It was drizzly and cool, typical for October in the Northwest. Within half an hour she had reached the foothills of the Cascade Mountains, shrouded in a light fall mist. Gray clouds hung low in the sky, obscuring the tops of the mountains. By the time she reached the summit, a hard rain was falling.

On a whim, Annie tuned her radio to an oldies station. The first song, "Fire and Rain" by James Taylor, brought memories flooding back: Annie and Taylor on a rainy afternoon in high school, listening to records and talking for hours on end about nothing at all. Consoling themselves at the Frederick and Nelson lunch counter with hot fudge sundaes when neither had made the cheerleading squad. Lying on a friend's dock on Lake Washington working on their "tans," even though Annie's freckled complexion did nothing but burn. Annie smiled when the next song was Simon and Garfunkel's "Old Friends."

Annie could still remember the day she met Taylor. It was the first day of Annie's sophomore year, and the homeroom teacher announced the arrival of several new transfer students. One newcomer drew the entire room's attention— a tall girl wearing an embroidered denim work shirt, cowboy boots, and skin-hugging Levi's that were more revealing than any miniskirt. When it was her turn, the new girl stood to her full height of five foot eleven inches without a hint of slouch, flicked her long blond hair over her shoulder and announced, "I'm Taylor North, from Harmony, Washington," with the total poise of someone at home with her own social superiority.

A half hour beyond the summit, the terrain began to look different. Tall pine trees, virtually nonexistent on the western slopes of the mountains, were now taking the place of the Douglas firs and hemlock. The dominant color of the landscape was changing from green to brown, and the rain, blessedly, was starting to let up.

Minutes after the descent from the mountains into the central Washington valley, the landscape was marked by rolling green and brown hills of fertile ranch and farmland, punctuated with small groupings of trees, grazing cattle, barns, and irrigation systems. This land was working land—its value determined not by aesthetics but by what it could produce.

As she drove, Annie wanted to focus on the positive memories. But as hard as she tried, she couldn't keep the image of that horrible night out of her mind.

It was the summer after they graduated. Taylor and Annie were house-sitting for a friend of Taylor's mother in an elegant apartment on the east side. Taylor had told Annie that she and Steve had broken up, and that she was seeing a fellow named Frank whom she'd met at work. At the time, Annie had believed her.

Annie had never met Taylor's boyfriend, because they always went out on Friday nights, a night Annie had to work. Until one Friday night, a summer storm knocked out the electricity at the restaurant where Annie worked, and she was sent home early. Annie thought this was a great piece of luck, knowing Taylor had a date with Frank at six-thirty and that she would finally get a chance to meet him.

Annie was still rushing around the living room, straightening up, when she heard the knock. Anxious to meet the new man in Taylor's life, she rushed to the door, opening it without bothering to look through the peephole. The expectant smile vanished when she saw who was standing there.

"Steve."

Steven Vick's small eyes narrowed. "Where's Taylor?"

Annie glanced at her watch. It was six-fifteen. Taylor's date was supposed to be there at six-thirty. Pausing, she tried to think of something to say to make him go away.

"I said, where is she? And don't try to tell me she doesn't live here, because I know she does." He tried to look past her into the room. "Taylor? . . . Are you in there?"

Feet firmly planted, Annie said, "She doesn't want to see you, Steve. I think you should go."

A tinge of red appeared at his collar and began creeping up his puffy face. "She doesn't—what the fuck is that supposed to mean? What do you know about it?"

"I don't want to be having this conversation any more than you do, Steve. Now, this isn't a good time, so why don't you just—" Annie tried to close the door, but Steve forced it open with one shove. Inside the room, he looked around like he owned the place.

Steven Vick was six foot one and meaty, with the thick neck of a defensive tackle. He was not really overweight, but his face nevertheless had a flabbiness to it, even in high school. His hair was cut close to the skull. Annie assumed it was because of pre-season football practice. With eyes too small for his big face, Annie always thought he looked like a warthog. Or maybe it was just his personality.

"Taylor?" he shouted, peering down the hallway. Turning back to Annie, he plopped down on the white leather sofa and looked at the magazines on the coffee table. "*Architectural Digest, The New Yorker, Wine Spectator* . . . quite a ritzy lifestyle you got going here. No wonder Taylor never wanted to invite me over. She probably thought I'd break something."

"Look, Steve—"

"Look, nothing. You can't tell me what to do. I'm waiting for Taylor, whether it pleases your majesty or not." Absently flipping the pages of a *New Yorker*, an unpleasant smile on his face, he said, "You still can't stand me, can you, Annie? I bet just seeing me here makes your blood boil."

Annie glanced at the door. At any moment, there would be a knock, and some unsuspecting guy named Frank would be standing there. She could picture Steve starting a brawl right there in the living room. She could try to head him off outside, but that would mean leaving Steve alone in the apartment, and she didn't trust him that much. Annie decided she didn't have a choice. She'd tell Steve why he had to leave, and if that failed, call the police. She stood with her hand near the telephone on the hall table.

"Steve, listen to me. I don't know what Taylor said to make you think you were welcome here, but I've got to tell you what the situation is. Taylor's not interested in you. She's been seeing someone else all summer. His name—"

He was out of the chair before Annie could say another word. "You conniving little bitch, that you would come up with a lie like that!" He grabbed the arm that was reaching for the phone, and gripped her hard enough to leave a bruise. "Does Taylor know what a filthy little liar her roommate is, huh?"

"I'm not lying, Steve." She tried to fight the stinging pain of his grasp.

"Yeah, and have you met this guy? Who is he? What does he do?"

"No, I haven't met him, but she's told me everything about him. She met him at work. He's going to be here at six-thirty."

Laughing, Steve pushed Annie into the kitchen. "As if that isn't the oldest line in the book. Oh, my protector is going to be here any minute now. Look, the only one who's going to be here is Taylor." He opened the refrigerator. "You got anything to eat in here?"

Suddenly Annie wondered if she'd been the one lied to. What if Taylor had really been seeing Steve all along, and keeping it secret from her?

Annie felt sick. All she wanted was to get out of there, but Steve's large body blocked the door.

Steve pulled out half a cold pizza, threw it on the kitchen table next to Annie, and shut the refrigerator. She tried to run past him.

"Hey, where do you think you're going?" he said, grabbing her arm with his left hand. She struggled to pull away, but it was pointless. His hand was huge and his grip firm.

"Steve, please. I shouldn't have interfered. I didn't understand." Still, he didn't let go.

"Shouldn't have interfered? For Christ's sake, all you've been doing is interfering since Taylor and I got together. You hate my guts, and you think Taylor should, too. Well, I have to tell you, you little bitch, I'm sick and tired of it. I come over here, minding my own business, and you make up some story about another guy, like I'm some kind of moron, or something. . . ."

"Steve, stop it, you're hurting me."

"Hurting you? Like you don't deserve it, you little bitch?"

With his free right hand, he grabbed a lamp and threw it like a football across the room, where it smashed into pieces. "That's what I'd like to do to you." A ceramic vase holding a bouquet of roses was within reach, and he did the same thing, sending flowers and water dripping down the wall and onto the carpet where the vase had shattered. Annie struggled, but Steve pinned her shoulders to the wall. "Is that enough, bitch? Think you'll be able to keep your goddamned nose out of other people's lives from now on?"

Gripping her arm, he raised his right hand. She tensed, expecting a hard blow to her face at any second. Out of the corner of her eye she saw a blur in the doorway.

Steve paused. "What? What are you looking at?"

His eyes followed Annie's gaze. Taylor North stood frozen in the entryway. She had seen everything. When Taylor turned and ran from the doorway, Steven Vick followed, leaving Annie alone in the disheveled apartment.

Annie moved out of the apartment, back to her father's house, the next day. Confused and hurt, Annie waited to hear from Taylor, but the call never came. Annie never heard from Taylor North again. At least, not until her telephone call that week.

Annie drove past the city of Yakima and continued on into the agricultural valley. Following the directions that Galen Rockwell had faxed her on Monday, Annie bypassed the road that would have taken her to the center of Harmony. She took the exit for Wine Country Road and headed north into the hills. Six miles from town, a small blue and white sign for the winery was positioned at the entrance to a gravel road.

Annie had once toured some of the Napa and Sonoma wineries, and she carried an image in her mind of spacious and well-appointed tasting rooms, expansive display vineyards, and busloads of tourists hastily sampling wines before being rushed off to their next destination. She quickly learned that they did things a little differently in eastern Washington.

The gravel road ended at the top of a hill. A large wooden sign reading NORTH FAIRE WINERY—TASTING stood in front of what had once been a barn. A fresh coat of white paint made the enormous gambrel-roofed structure look only slightly less agricultural than the working barns Annie had passed on the highway.

She parked next to a Chevy Blazer with Oregon license plates. Peeking into the back, she could see that the Oregonians had already purchased five or six cases of wine at neighboring wineries. Annie wondered how many wine tastings one could enjoy in a day before being totally obliterated. With twenty-two wineries grouped along a thirty-mile stretch of highway, the Oregon tourists seemed to be attempting to find out.

She walked up a few steps into the converted barn, where the air was chilly. The floor, not the barn's original, was polished hardwood, and the walls and exposed beams had been painted white. Square-paned windows at eye level every three or four feet let in a soft, natural light.

Annie saw that the old structure didn't just house the tasting room, but much of the wine-making equipment itself. Along the sides of the building were huge wooden and stainless steel vats, about fifteen feet high. Against the opposite wall were dozens of smaller wooden barrels lying on their sides, their contents labeled in chalk. Stairs at the back of the barn led to a loft, which was stacked floor to ceiling with white shipping boxes, presumably filled with cases of bottled wine.

There was an old oak rolltop desk in one corner, and in front of it, a wine-tasting bar had been set up using a plank balanced on two metal filing cabinets. On top of the desk, an enormous marmalade cat lay curled on a stack of burgundy-colored sweatshirts, next to a sign that read SWEATSHIRTS—$22.00 (CAT NOT INCLUDED). A stocky man wearing one of the sweatshirts was pouring samples for a middle-aged couple, who Annie assumed were the Oregonians with the Blazer, explaining the wines in great detail. He looked up at Annie, reaching for a clean glass. "Can I start you with red or white today?"

"Actually, I'm not here to taste wine. I'm—"

"Annie MacPherson." Annie turned when she heard her name from the doorway behind her. She saw framed in the sunlight an older, more weathered version of the young woman Annie remembered. Chin-length blond hair framed a face that showed the lines and traces of days spent in the sun. Her tall body was lean from exercise and hard work, and Annie noted that her friend still wore cowboy boots and straight-legged Levi's. It suddenly felt very good to see Taylor North again.

Chapter 7

TAYLOR CROSSED to where Annie was standing and wrapped her in a warm embrace. "Thank you so much for coming," she said softly, a mixture of pain and gratitude in her voice. "I know it wasn't easy for you."

"No, but I'm glad I'm here," Annie replied, meaning it.

Annie stepped back to get a better look at her friend. The confident air of superiority that Taylor had carried all the way through high school was now tempered with—what? Wariness, trepidation? Annie wasn't sure. As good as Taylor looked, Annie also noted the physical signs of stress— fingernails chewed down to the quick, dark circles beneath the eyes, a tension in the rigid way Taylor held her shoulders.

"My God, you look great," Taylor said, tousling Annie's shoulder-length hair. "Is strawberry blonde *still* your natural color, or does only your hairdresser know for sure?"

"It's all mine. Gray strands and all."

"What gray hairs? I don't see a single one, you lucky thing. My golden highlights are one hundred percent L'Oreal, but hey, the commercial says I'm worth it, right? Gosh, I'm glad you could get away. I was shocked when Galen told me you were actually coming. From what I hear, all you lawyers do is work all the time."

Annie was a little confused. "The man I talked to on the phone . . . ?"

"That was Galen Rockwell, the winemaker."

"He seemed to imply that you needed help right away. I got the impression that you wanted me to come as soon as possible."

Taylor stiffened. "Yes. Well. That's Galen. He tends to be . . . protective."

Annie stopped. "Taylor, you do want me here, don't you?"

"Of course," she replied, a little too heartily. "Don't get me wrong. I really want to move ahead, I'm *ready* to move ahead with a divorce. . . . I'm just not in as much trouble as Galen seems to think I am."

Judging from Taylor's physical appearance, Annie had her doubts. "Well, I'm here now, and we can have a nice visit and catch up. You heard right about lawyers working all the time. I don't take enough time off to be with friends."

Taylor guided Annie to the door and the view south over the vineyards. Stretching out before them was a panorama of rolling hills, covered with row after row of grapevines. The sky filled Annie's view in every direction—such a pale blue that it looked almost white, the only clouds wispy and non-threatening. "When this is your office, it's not hard to come to work in the morning." The marmalade cat had stirred himself from the desk and was rubbing against Taylor's leg. "Isn't that right, Colonel Bob?" She hefted the large animal up to her chest and gave him a nuzzle. "The Colonel is our chief of security. He keeps the winery completely free of rodents and other unwanted pests. I'm trying to train him to keep creditors at bay, but we're not having much luck. Come on, let's go over to the house and get you settled in."

The two-story house was about five hundred yards from the barn, down a hill and hidden from view by a stand of trees. It looked like it might have been built near the turn of the century, and was well maintained with fresh paint and stained glass inserts in the windows flanking the front door. Annie recognized it from photographs Taylor had shown her years ago. "This is where you lived as a child, isn't it?"

"Uh-huh, till my parents split up and Gerald and I moved to Seattle with Mom in my sophomore year." Taylor opened the front door and carried Annie's bag into the foyer. "At the time, I was thrilled to be moving to the city."

Annie glanced around the room. It was feminine, yet classic, with white walls, hardwood floors, and overstuffed furniture in patterns of dusty rose and forest green. Instead of drapes, lengths of floral chintz were elegantly swagged over the windows in a style Annie had seen only in interior design magazines. Over the mantelpiece was a huge water-color painting of the house with the vineyards in the back-ground, shown in the rosy dawn so that the colors perfectly suited the room. "It's wonderful," she said, referring to both the room and the painting. "Did you . . . ?"

"No, I'm a total klutz when it comes to decorating. Gerald did it all, including the painting. Do I have a talented brother, or what? And he knows me so well. They say or-dinary siblings aren't as psychically connected as twins, but I think they're wrong. He's always known instinctively what will make me happy, and vice versa. Do you remem-ber Gerald from high school?"

"Vaguely. So he's a professional decorator?"

"No, actually, he's an artist. And he teaches art at Central Washington University in Ellensburg."

"Well, I think he missed his true calling. This is fabu-lous."

Taylor sank onto the sofa and ran a hand along the fabric as if seeing it for the first time. "This house . . . this is no longer just the place where I grew up, anymore. It was a hard life back then, and more often than not, this was a painful place to be a child. I never expected to come back. But that's all changed. This is *my* house now, and out there is *my* business. I . . . I don't know how I could leave here. It would be like cutting off my right arm."

"Is that why you've put off divorce proceedings?"

She nodded. "I've been afraid to talk to an attorney, find

out how bad the situation really is. But Steve has nothing, he isn't even employed. And I've got all this. . . . I've had friends whose lives were ruined by divorce. They lost everything. . . ."

Taylor looked like she didn't want to continue. "But we can talk about all those sordid details later."

Annie walked over to the mantelpiece to look at some framed photographs. "Look at the large one in the wooden frame," Taylor prompted.

"Oh, my God, I can't believe you kept this!" The photo was of Annie and Taylor on their high school graduation day in caps and gowns, a look of pure elation on their faces. "From the way we're grinning, you'd think we were getting out of prison, not high school."

"Look at those hairstyles—long and parted in the middle. I always envied you that yours was so *red*."

"Well, I always envied you that yours was so *straight*," Annie replied. "Naturally curly hair was simply not in vogue back then."

"Remember that time we tried to iron it, and singed the ends?"

"You mean *you* singed the ends. I was crouching under the ironing board at the time and had nothing to do with it."

"How was I to know what the proper heat setting was for hair?"

Annie picked up the next photograph in a silver frame—a picture of the wedding Annie had not been invited to. It showed the bride and groom with their shoes kicked off, whirling in a folk dance, surrounded by a circle of smiling guests. The faces of Taylor and Steve were blurred by the motion. "Well, at least it was a great party," Taylor said, her voice bitter. "My brother said the last guests didn't leave for two days." Taylor looked at her watch. "I know it's early, but would you like a sample of the home-grown product? Frankly, I need a drink."

Annie accepted, and Taylor went to the kitchen. She returned with two glasses and an unlabeled bottle of chilled white wine. She poured, then raised her glass in a toast. "To old friends."

"Old friends." Annie raised her glass, then tasted. It was good, far better than what Annie tended to buy at home.

Taylor sighed and gazed into her glass, as if she didn't know where to start. Finally, she said, "I know I owe you a lot, Annie. An apology, an explanation." She paused, searching for words. "The apology part I can handle. What I did, what I didn't do . . . was horrible, Annie. I can hardly think back to that day. I am sorry. If I were you, I wouldn't be able to forgive me. . . ."

Annie started to speak, but Taylor held up her hand. "No, let me finish. I've rehearsed what I would say when I saw you about a dozen times, and I have to get it out in one piece. As for an explanation, that's a lot harder. I'm not sure I understand it all myself. . . ." Taylor struggled to hold back tears. She reached for a tissue. "I'll be okay in a minute."

"Taylor, we don't have to talk about this right now."

She nodded. "Maybe . . . you're right. I'm so tense right now . . . the Wine Gala and all . . . but there's one thing I have to tell you. It explains in some small way why I stayed with him after that. . . ."

Annie waited while Taylor regained her composure.

"That day, I had just been to the doctor, and learned I was pregnant with Steven's child. My daughter's name is Celia, and she just turned seventeen."

"I had no idea."

"She means more to me than anything, Annie. All these years, I wouldn't have put up with him if it hadn't been for her sake." Taylor wiped her eyes. "I can't wait for you to meet her. She's so beautiful. I don't regret anything I did for her. Not one thing."

Taylor poured herself more wine. Annie's glass was still full. "He told terrible lies about you that summer, Annie. I know now they were lies. He said you had been coming on to him, trying to get him away from me. He said that . . . that afternoon . . . you had called him, begged him to come over. When he got there to try to talk to you..." She shook her head. "I can see now how crazy it all was. But at the time I believed it. That's why I could never call you. After a while, once I realized he'd lied to me, I was ashamed. I didn't think you'd ever speak to me again."

Annie reached over and touched Taylor on the arm. All these years, she had assumed that she was the only one who had been hurt by the end of their friendship. "It's okay," Annie whispered softly. "I always felt badly that I'd never called you."

"It was about five years ago," Taylor continued. "The first time I thought about calling. Steve and I had separated—one of many times, by the way—and I was thinking about that night. But I wasn't sure you'd even talk to me."

Annie remembered how disturbed she'd been the day before to see Taylor's name on the telephone message. "I might not have, then." After a pause, she said, "You two have separated before. Is there any possibility you'll get back together again this time?"

Taylor shook her head. "No. Not a chance. I've been seeing a therapist, a woman over in Spokane. She's experienced at dealing with these types of situations. I can't say I understand it myself, yet. I'm not sure anyone understands why we stay in abusive relationships...." Her voice trailed off. "It's taken me a long time, but I've finally decided that I need to get Steve out of my life, and out of my business. I need to acknowledge the kind of hold he's had over me. I thought ... since you'd seen it firsthand, you could help me."

"I'll do my best, Taylor. I may not be the best person to represent you—I could help you find an attorney closer to home."

"No, I know I'll have to pay your travel expenses and all, but I'd really like you to be my lawyer." She paused. "I guess it's my way of saying that I want the past put behind us. Will you do it, Annie?"

Annie felt warmed by the wine and the kind words. She

didn't really stop to think before agreeing. "I'd be glad to, Taylor."

Relief filled Taylor's face. "Thanks, Annie. Your support means so much to me right now. And you know what? I'm going to write you a retainer check right now. That's what it's called, isn't it, a retainer? Partial payment in advance?"

"Yes, but you really don't have to—"

"I insist." Taylor went to the desk and got her checkbook. "Is fifteen hundred okay for now?"

Annie would have asked for only a thousand, so she said that would be fine.

"Great." Taylor handed her the check. "Wow, I'm starting to feel like I'm making progress already." Taylor came back to the couch, but she wasn't relaxed. Annie could sense that her friend was jumpy, excited. "So," Taylor said, fiddling with the stem of her wine glass. "Fill me in on your life. Marriages . . . divorces . . . children . . . ?"

Annie didn't want to talk about herself. "None of the above, I'm afraid."

"You never married?"

"I've come close several times. But the closer I get to a real commitment, the greater my urge to run away." Annie thought back to the last time she'd said good-bye. David's only flaw had been his desire that Annie change her life enough to make room for him. At the time, it had seemed like too much to ask.

"But you've had your career," Annie heard Taylor say. "I let Steve support me for far too many years. It's only now, having my own business, that I realize how liberating that can be. For the first time in my life, I feel truly self-sufficient. Don't you *love* not being dependent on a man?"

Annie just smiled. She'd observed similar bursts of enthusiasm from other women she had represented in their dissolution actions, women picturing themselves free after five, ten, or twenty years of marriage. Yes, she wanted to say, independence is great. But be prepared for the occasional lonely night. The kind of night when all you want is someone to hold you very close.

There was a report of a shotgun outside, and Taylor jumped. "God, every time I hear something, I think it's him, even though I know that's just Galen trying to scare the birds."

"What do you mean, you 'think it's him'?"

Taylor stood up and began to pace. "It started about six months ago—right after I threw Steve out. He's been doing his damnedest to make my life miserable."

"In what way?"

"Awful, spiteful things. At first, I wrote them off as accidents, or kids fooling around. One day we found wire tangled in the crusher-stemmer. It took Galen a good four hours to untangle it. Another time someone had taken a can of red spray paint and sprayed some grapevines that were ready for picking, totally ruining the fruit. Another time someone had broken into a wine cask and put salt in the wine. Lately, it's taken a more serious turn. There have been thefts. We had just received a half dozen new oak aging barrels from France—they cost me over six hundred dollars apiece! Someone broke into the yard and stole three of them—almost two thousand dollars' worth. And other supplies have turned up missing. Cash flow is always a problem, and there's just no room for this sort of thing. But then . . . yesterday . . ."

"What happened?"

"Steve came here, to the house. He's been here before since he moved out. And . . . well, let's just say it's never a pleasant experience. But yesterday, his threats were even uglier than usual. He wanted money. He kept saying, he knew, he knew . . ."

"Knew what?"

Taylor had a panic-stricken look. "That's just it. I don't know. I have no idea what he was talking about. But he said he was going to expose me, ruin me, unless I paid him."

"What did you say?"

"I told him the truth—that I don't have any money. He

knows that. Everything I have is tied up in the business, and in any event, he isn't going to get a penny of it."

"What happened then?"

"He got angry, said I didn't understand that he knew everything. That's when he knocked over a chair, and Galen Rockwell heard it. He came in and had his shotgun with him. He told Steve to get out."

Taylor looked away. "My therapist thinks it's because he feels threatened. He's always hated the winery and resented my success with it. He's tried so many things that didn't pan out. He started business school—never finished. He wanted to go to law school, but never got accepted. He's tried sales jobs of various kinds—nothing's lived up to his delusions of grandeur about himself." Talking about Steve, Taylor's voice became sharper. "He always blamed his lack of success on the fact that he didn't have money growing up, said he never got a fair shake. Then the very first venture I try, the winery, is successful right from the start. He hated that. It's not like we're making money hand over fist—all of the profits go right back into production—but we've won a lot of awards, gotten write-ups in all the major wine publications. And we've gotten on just about every major wine critic's list of small wineries to watch." She turned toward Annie and smiled. "I feel such a sense of accomplishment, Annie. I've never had something that was mine, the way North Faire is. It's my entire existence."

Another red flag went up in Annie's mind. If Taylor went ahead with the divorce, the business would likely be affected by a division of community property. It didn't sound like she was going to be in any frame of mind to compromise.

"This was your father's farm, right? You inherited it when he died?"

Taylor's face took on a strange expression. "It's . . . kind of complicated. But yes, more or less."

If there's one thing a lawyer hates, it's a vague phrase like "it's kind of complicated" or "more or less." But Annie decided there would be plenty of time after the Wine Gala to get into specifics, and changed the subject. "So, tell me about this Wine Gala tonight. It sounds like quite a big deal."

Taylor bit her lip, and looked close to tears again. "Oh, Annie . . ."

The strange hesitation in Taylor's voice made Annie pause. "What is it?"

Taylor closed her eyes for a moment. "I really didn't know until yesterday. If I had, I never would have asked you to come."

"What's wrong?"

"When I was at the Grubenmacher Mansion yesterday afternoon for the final walk-through, I saw the guest list."

"Yes?"

"He's going to be there tonight. Steve is coming to the Wine Gala."

Chapter 8

ANNIE AND TAYLOR left for the Grubenmacher Mansion at a little past eight. Since learning that Steven Vick would be there, Annie had felt almost sick to her stomach, dreading the possible reunion. Taylor was affected in a different way. Her voice was high-pitched, and she seemed strangely animated, almost manic.

They pulled into the semicircular driveway in front of the Grubenmacher Mansion where a high school–aged boy hopped up to open the door, then moved Taylor's van to a gravel parking area behind the building, beyond the garden. Floodlights illuminated the front of the mansion. "Wow," was all Annie could think to say, seeing the building in all its gold and burgundy glory.

"It drives me nuts that this is all wasted on that dried-up old bat," Taylor whispered. "Gerald just cringes every time he sees it—the woman is either nuts or color-blind, maybe both."

The foyer was mobbed with arriving guests, all trading wine-related shop talk. Annie had found that almost all professional gatherings were interesting—as long as the professionals weren't lawyers. When she could get her mind off Steven Vick, she found herself looking forward to learning something new about wine.

A young woman spotted them and pushed her way through the mob. Even from across the room, Annie could tell that this must be Taylor's daughter, Celia. She had the same high cheekbones and grayish-blue eyes that had helped win Taylor so many admirers in high school. If Taylor hadn't told her Celia's age, Annie would have guessed she was closer to twenty-five than seventeen.

"Mom, thank God you're finally here. The display's almost set up, but the guys brought the '89 cabernet instead of the '88. Galen's furious, and wanted to talk to you as soon as you got here." Taylor quickly introduced Celia, and in a moment, they were joined by a stocky man in a western-style shirt and gray eelskin cowboy boots. Taylor introduced him as Galen Rockwell, North Faire's winemaker. He cracked the barest of smiles, shook Annie's hand, then apologized for having to discuss the wine display with Taylor. His voice was deep and resonant.

"Now?" said Taylor, not even trying to hide her irritation. Galen said something in a low voice that upset Taylor. "Oh, all right. Celia, I have to go with Galen. Will you show Annie around, introduce her to people?" With that, Taylor and the winemaker walked hurriedly toward the kitchen.

Celia turned to Annie, oblivious to her mother's strange mood. "Isn't this exciting? North Faire has held tasting events before, but nothing as huge as this. It's incredible."

Taylor had warned Annie not to overdress, that folks in the valley didn't go much for formality. But she apparently hadn't told Celia, who was wearing the kind of dress only a seventeen-year-old could get away with. It had a black velvet strapless bodice, and a short pouf of gold satin that was hardly long enough to be called a skirt. The fact that no one else in the room was wearing glitter didn't seem to faze her a bit.

Just inside the foyer, a tiny, elderly woman was greeting friends. "That's her highness, Florence Grubenmacher," Celia whispered conspiratorially. "Rumor has it that she hasn't seen the inside of a dress shop since 1962." Annie noted that Mrs. Grubenmacher's navy and white sheath, string of pearls, and bird's-nest hairdo did look like they were straight off the pages of *Life* magazine.

"Should we say hello?"

Celia shook her head. "No. There's so much bad blood between her and Mom, she'd probably just snub us."

"I'd noticed that Taylor didn't have very many kind things to say."

"The animosity is mutual, believe me."

"Do you know why?"

Celia shook her head. "It's something to do with her son. She thinks Taylor was mean to him in grade school or something. I wouldn't mind saying hello to the man she's talking to, though. That's Dr. Marchand. Isn't he just the sexiest thing here?"

Annie could see Celia's point, though he wasn't her type. The man was tan and fit, with the air of someone who spends most of his time pursuing leisure activities.

"And he's not married!"

"So what's the story on him?" Annie asked. "I know Taylor said to be particularly nice to him because he's the guest of honor."

"Uh-huh. He's a retired physician, and his passion is collecting wine. He really was the driving force behind this event. He came up with the idea, got all of the wineries excited, and put up ten thousand dollars of his own money. That part's between you and me—he wanted the gift to be anonymous. But the *real* reason she wants us to be nice to him is because he invests in small wineries. He has a whole lot of money invested in small wineries down in California. What he does is, he looks for young wineries that maybe have a lot of potential, but are having financial difficulties. Then he steps in as a limited partner until they get on their feet again, sort of like a patron of the arts."

"And Taylor thinks he might invest in a winery up here?"

"He's said as much. He's *very* interested in the future of

Washington wines, and North Faire is on his list of wineries to check out."

"I thought North Faire was doing well financially."

Celia's eyes widened. "I don't know where you got that idea. Mom's letting me work with the bookkeeper and build up my accounting skills. It's hand to mouth most of the time. We're doing pretty well this year, but there's nothing to spare. Some months, it's touch and go whether we'll make the payroll."

Annie thought about the fifteen-hundred-dollar check she had in her purse from Taylor. It was a lot of money to throw around, if cash flow was tight. She wondered if Taylor's legal problems were worse than she was letting on.

Celia babbled on as they skirted Mrs. Grubenmacher and tried to work their way toward the hors d'oeuvres table. "Not that there are many people *on* the payroll. Galen's an employee, and there's sometimes enough money for him to hire a helper at harvest time. The vineyard manager's on some kind of percentage contract, and he pays the men who pick the grapes. The rest of it Mom and I do—the bottling, gluing the labels on by hand, putting on the foils, making up the cases to be shipped. . . ." They had only advanced a few steps when Celia nudged Annie with her elbow. "Uh-oh. I should have warned you. Be prepared to meet Harry."

"Be prepared? For . . ."

Annie looked up to see a huge bear of a man lumbering across the room. In his mid-sixties, he had bristly salt-and-pepper hair that stood up in defiance of anything resembling a hairstyle. When he saw Celia, his rubbery face puckered with delight.

"There she is, the love of my life, the apple of my eye." The big man planted wet kisses on Celia's cheeks. "And where are you hiding that enchantress you call your mother?" The man had to be at least six foot four, and, Annie guessed, well over two hundred and fifty pounds. He wore tuxedo pants that looked twenty years old, a pale blue cotton shirt, and a bright red floral print tie. He looked down at his tie and wiped away a dab of cocktail sauce. "That was good planning to wear the red tie, I'd say." He turned to Annie and beamed, his eyes crinkling with hundreds of laugh lines. "And who is this? Why haven't I seen you before? Celia, who is your lovely friend? Don't be jealous, my dear, but she may have stolen my heart. I can't get over it. With that fiery red hair, you are identical in every way to my wonderful third-grade teacher, Mrs. Pennyworth—the source of my first and most intense schoolboy crush."

Celia, laughing with feigned embarrassment, introduced Annie. "Annie, this is Harrison Braithwaite. He lives in a big old house in town that he swears he's going to turn into a bed-and-breakfast one of these days. Before he retired, he was an ancient history professor. Isn't that right, Harry?"

"A professor of ancient history, if you please, my dear. Lest Annie think it was I who was 'ancient.' "

"But I'm upset, Harry," Celia pouted. "I thought I was the one who reminded you of your third-grade teacher."

"Oh, no, no, no. You remind me of Miss Schomakker, my *sixth*-grade teacher. I was madly in love with her, too, but the third-grade teacher came first. That was generally the case in elementary schools in those days."

"Harry is also the self-appointed mayor of Harmony."

"Mayor? That's very impressive."

"Not really. There are no job duties to speak of. I wanted to be 'town curmudgeon,' you see. I have the eyebrows for it." To demonstrate, he lifted his incredibly bushy black eyebrows and opened his eyes in a look of mock astonishment. "But to be a truly qualified curmudgeon, one has to be *negative* about things. And the trouble is, when I complain about things, no one takes me seriously. It's my face, I think. I don't have a negative face, and—"

Celia couldn't help laughing. "Harry's a marvelous mayor. Why, just last summer—"

"Hush, Celia, dear. Let me finish." He kissed her hand

and turned back to Annie. "So I figured as mayor, I could complain about things and they'd have to take me seriously, in hopes of one day elevating myself into the ranks of curmudgeonhood. Curmudgeonliness? What do you think, is it a good plan?"

"Sounds good to me."

"Good. Celia, dear, I'm going to steal your friend for a moment, and have her teach me how to taste wine."

"All right, Harry. But don't monopolize her. Taylor wanted her to meet a *few* other people this evening."

"Very well. I'll relinquish her at some point."

As Celia headed back toward the wine-tasting area, Harry guided Annie through the maze of people toward the dining room. "I'm going to let you in on the Braithwaite Rule for successful wine tasting. Always do it on a reasonably full stomach. Much more enjoyable that way. First, we must fortify ourselves at the groaning board, and then, as Oliver Wendell Holmes so aptly put it, 'the blood of the vineyard shall mingle with mine.' "

The dining room table was spread with an appetizing variety of cheeses, prawns, and pâtés, making Annie suddenly feel very hungry. At her side, Harry Braithwaite was creating a pyramid of appetizers on his plate so high that she was sure it was all going to topple at any moment.

Beyond the dining room, in the ballroom, each of the fifteen participating wineries had a small linen-covered table from which they were pouring samples from their "library," the winery's personal store of past vintages, no longer for sale. They were about to head in the direction of the wine tasting when Harry stopped and bellowed at someone across the room. As they got closer, Annie saw that their target was a handsome, uniformed state trooper standing with a young woman with maroon-tinted hair. The young woman looked up at Harry, screwing her face into an unflattering pout.

"Annie. You must meet my granddaughter, Mimi. When her mother, Violetta, named her after Puccini's great tragic heroine from *La Bohème*, we had no idea how apt the name would be. Mimi makes every effort to be as *Bohemian* as possible."

Mimi Braithwaite looked seventeen or eighteen, and was dressed in what Annie thought might be the grunge look, but she wasn't sure. She had on a black rib-knit T-shirt and black leggings, over which she wore a gauzy, ankle-length ballerina skirt. To complete the look, Mimi wore a pair of clunky Doc Martens and had tied a flannel shirt around her waist. Her short hair was practically shaved up the back of her neck, and fell forward in a heavy fringe that covered one eye. When spoken to, she glanced briefly at her grandfather, rolled her heavily made-up eyes (at least the one that was visible) and resumed her pout. "Grandpa, please don't *embarrass* me like you usually do."

Harry ignored her plea, and gave her a loud smacking kiss on each cheek. She squirmed under his embrace like a kitten that doesn't want to be held.

"Grandpa, I *told* you not to *do* that." Mimi tried to sound sophisticated and bored, imitating the Beverly Hills accents of her favorite TV stars. In reality, she just sounded whiny.

The state trooper extended his hand. "How d'you do, sir, ma'am. I'm Seth Longacre, Washington State Patrol. I just found out your granddaughter and I went to the same high school."

Mimi continued to look bored. "Yeah, like it's some big deal."

"We didn't actually know each other," the trooper explained. "I was a senior when she was a freshman, and I was pretty busy with football and basketball. I, uh, guess you didn't make it to too many games, huh, Mimi?"

"Like, duh."

"So you're a junior, now, right?" Seth Longacre asked, trying to keep the conversation going.

Mimi scowled. "The only reason I'm even at that stupid high school is 'cause I got dropped here against my will. But that doesn't mean I have to stay. Zeno—he's my boyfriend—he's the lead singer with the Nuclear Floss, and they just moved out to L.A., and he says I can come out and be, like, with the band as soon as I can pay my share of the expenses." She craned her neck as if looking for someone in the room. "And believe me, it's not going to be very long."

"Mimi, dearest. This is a festive occasion. Let's not bore our friends with the same tiresome argument that's been dampening our dinner conversation for the last three months. Hmm?"

Mimi rolled her eyes again, as if it were a gesture she had just mastered and wanted to practice until it became second nature. She must not have seen whoever she was looking for inside, because she suddenly wanted to go outside for a cigarette, pushing past the trooper toward the door. Harry looked embarrassed.

"Yes, that's my little Mimi. It's been difficult raising her, with her mother traveling so much. I really have no idea why she wanted to come tonight, but she was the one who insisted I get her a ticket. Are you here on duty?" he asked the trooper.

"Oh, no, sir. Celia Vick invited me." He glanced in the direction of the North Faire table with a moonstruck expression. "Isn't she wonderful? Not that your granddaughter isn't just as wonderful, sir."

Harry smiled. "That's quite all right. Somehow, I don't think you're Mimi's type. Tell me, though—"

Harry's question was interrupted by the sound of raised voices. Every head in the room turned toward the front door.

"I have every right to be here, you fucking asshole. I don't care what my wife told you. I've got a ticket right here—see, it's got my name on it. I was *personally* invited by Martin Grubenmacher." There was a buzz in the room as someone went to look for Martin Grubenmacher.

Annie's heart was pounding at the sound of Steven Vick's voice, so familiar in spite of all the years that had passed. She looked around for Taylor, but the room was too crowded. When she turned back toward Steve, she found him looking straight at her, his lip curled in unfriendly recognition.

Chapter 9

SEVENTEEN YEARS hadn't erased the anger and pain Annie felt, seeing him again. His hair was thinner, his face puffier. He no longer had the muscles of a football player, and the suit he wore looked like it last fit about thirty pounds ago. But his taunting, arrogant expression was exactly the same. Annie would have known Steven Vick anywhere.

Undaunted, she stood her ground as he ambled toward her, his meaty hand cupped around a glass of white wine.

"Well, well, well. Still sticking your nose into other people's business, huh?" His height meant Annie had to look up to see him. His eyes, always too small for his face, looked even smaller with the fleshy jowls of encroaching middle age. His glance darted distractedly around the room. With Harry Braithwaite and Seth Longacre close beside her, Annie felt like a sapling in a forest of large men.

"Annie MacPherson." He laughed, though it was more like a snort. "So here we are, together again."

"I'd say it's nice to see you again, Steve, but I'm not that good a liar."

"Like hell you aren't." He laughed again. "You always were too smart for your own good. I should have known it was you behind all this."

"Behind what?"

"You know damned well what I'm talking about. How long have you two been cooking up your little plan?"

Annie was glad Harry and Seth were close by. "I hate to

disappoint you, Steve, but yesterday was the first time I'd spoken to Taylor in—"

"You're a fucking liar, bitch." Steve spat out the words, his face reddening. "I know you've been feeding her your man-hating garbage. It wasn't enough that you tried to ruin what we had the first time around. Now you've got to be here for the kill. Is that it, huh? Is that what you're here for? The one thing I never could figure out was *why* she was doing it. Now that you're here, it's all starting to make sense. The whole thing is just a plot to keep me from getting what I'm entitled to, is that it? Well, I'll be damned if I let you get away with that, you little . . ." His face red, Steve hurled his glass at Annie's feet. The wine splashed her ankles as the glass broke into tiny fragments, the shattering sound bringing all the unpleasant memories flooding back. Annie could feel tiny slivers of broken glass clinging to her stockings, but was too shocked to move. Harry took her elbow and drew her back, as a waiter rushed in to sweep up the mess.

At the same time, Seth Longacre moved forward and grabbed Steve by the elbow. "All right, that's enough. Guest or not, you're leaving this party."

"Now, wait a second, you have no right . . . I've got an invitation right here, from Martin Grubenmacher. . . ." As he reached for his inside pocket, Seth Longacre pinned Steve's arms behind him. Large as he was, Steve was out of shape, and the state trooper had no difficulty restraining him.

"You just wait, MacPherson. You've got your eggs in the wrong basket this time. You think I don't know what's really going on, but . . ."

The state trooper began propelling Steve in the direction of the front door. They had almost reached it when they were stopped by a voice from behind.

"Oh, my gosh, what's the problem, here? Stop! What are you doing to one of my guests? What's going on here, officer?"

Annie looked toward the stairs, where she saw a small, round man scurrying forward, babbling nervously.

"I'm sorry, sir," said Seth. "But your, uh, *guest* here just assaulted Ms. MacPherson." The trooper nodded at Annie and the broken glass. "I felt it was my duty as an officer of the law to escort him to the door."

"Then you were mistaken. You have no jurisdiction here. I didn't hire you, I know that. I invited this man as my personal guest. I'm entitled, just like the wineries. I had six invitations to do with as I pleased, and I invited this man. Oh, this is awful. I don't have to justify myself to you. He has every right to be here." With difficulty, Martin Grubenmacher looked the trooper up and down, having to crane his neck to do so. "More than you, most likely. I don't remember anyone issuing *you* an invitation."

Seth straightened his spine. "I am an invited guest of North Faire Winery, sir."

"Humph. Well, are you going to let him go or aren't you?"

Reluctantly, Seth released his grip. Steve glowered at Annie as he made an exaggerated show of rubbing his arm and brushing himself off.

Grubenmacher mopped a sweaty brow with his handkerchief. "I'm terribly sorry about all this, Steve. I'll make sure that Officer—what was your name, boy?"

"Longacre, sir."

"—Longacre receives a harsh reprimand from his superior officer. Now, why don't we go out to the garden where we can discuss our business without being bothered by these rude party-crashers masquerading as guests."

"The garden? Why would I want to go out there? I haven't even had any wine. . . ."

"There'll be time. There'll be time. Please, it's very important that we, uh, talk. In the garden. Please. This way."

Steven Vick, still making a show of brushing himself off, looked somewhat bothered by the little man's insistence, but nevertheless let himself be led out through the French doors. The moment they were gone, the crowd erupted in chatter, as if the angry scene had been staged solely for their entertainment.

A few minutes later Taylor appeared with Galen Rockwell. She was tightly clutching a bottle of red wine, and Galen had her firmly by the elbow. Both looked upset. Celia Vick, her face flushed with excitement, was right behind them.

"Annie, are you all right?" Taylor asked, her eyes darting around the room. "Galen saw Steve arriving, and rushed me out to the kitchen. What did Steve say to you?"

"Nothing worth repeating. I just hope we don't have another scene when he comes back in."

"Don't worry," said Galen, "I called the sheriff's office the moment I saw him. Whether he was invited or not, this is still a private function, and he can be asked to leave if he's causing a disturbance. The sheriff's department is sending a deputy right over to take care of it, if it comes to that."

"Where did they go?" Taylor's eyes were bright.

"Out to the garden, supposedly to talk 'business.' Taylor, would you like me to wait with you somewhere, until the deputy arrives?" Taylor had been nervous when they arrived at the party; now her composure seemed about to disintegrate altogether.

"This is so like him, coming here and disrupting everything. I should just . . ."

"No, Taylor," Galen snapped. "We've been over this. Now isn't the time or place to try to reason with the man. I don't know why he's here tonight, but we've called the sheriff and they'll take care of the situation."

"Has anyone seen my brother?" Taylor kept looking around. "I need to talk to Gerald. He said he was going to be a little late, but he should have been here by now."

"Taylor, come on, you have to calm down," said Galen impatiently. "There's a room upstairs where the coats are. I want you to wait up there until this all blows over. Come on, I mean it."

"But, I need to wait for Gerald. . . ."

"We'll send him up when he gets here."

"No, I . . ."

"Yes, now."

Annie watched as Galen forcefully guided Taylor up the stairs. Amid the noise of the party, she couldn't hear what Taylor was saying, but could tell by the tense set of her shoulders that she was not at all happy at being told what to do.

Chapter 10

CELIA SHOWED ANNIE to the ladies' room, where Annie tried unsuccessfully to remove the fragments of glass from her pantyhose. After a few attempts, she gave up and took them off.

On her return to the party, the crowd seemed somehow to have tripled, leaving the guests barely enough elbow room to taste wine. The noise level had risen as the wine flowed. Annie looked around, and when she couldn't locate Harry Braithwaite or Seth Longacre, pushed her way through to the North Faire table, where Celia was pouring samples of wine. Seeing Annie, Celia quickly handed her the bottle.

"Thank goodness. I don't know where Galen went, and I'm under-age. If he catches me pouring, he'll have a fit. Besides," Celia giggled and lowered her voice, "Dr. Marchand is over there all by himself, and I just have to say hello. Could you stay here till Galen gets back?" Without waiting for an answer, Celia was gone. Annie saw Dr. Marchand smile broadly as the young woman approached him. He took her to taste wine at an adjacent display, apparently oblivious of her age.

Annie stood behind the display table feeling overwhelmed by everything that was happening. A guest asked if it would be possible to try a vertical tasting of merlot. "A vertical, um . . ." She tried to stall for time, having absolutely no idea what a vertical tasting was. A horizontal tast-

60

ing sounded a bit too casual. "I guess I could let you try some of this," she said tentatively, locating a bottle of merlot. She started to remove the cork. Fortunately, before she could embarrass herself too badly, Galen Rockwell appeared at her side.

It was the first time she had seen the serious man smile. "I see Celia left you holding the bottle, so to speak. Well, as much as we'd like your help, Annie, it's against the law for the guests to pour. Let me."

"By all means. I know about as much about wine as I do about nuclear technology. Except that I like wine a lot better."

"Most people do." He set out some clean glasses. In their brief prior encounters, Annie had gotten the impression that Galen Rockwell was humorless and overbearing. Now, talking about wine, he relaxed and his whole face lit up with enthusiasm. As he poured the wine, he explained to the guests in detail how weather patterns had affected each particular vintage, and that a vertical tasting involved the same wine from different vintages, generally from younger to older. It enabled one to see how a wine made with the same grapes and methods could differ from year to year, and also how well the wine aged.

When there was a lull, he said to Annie, "I just talked to the sheriff's office again. A deputy should be here at any time. It was difficult, but I finally convinced Taylor to wait upstairs. She actually wanted to confront Steve and tell him off."

"When we spoke on the phone yesterday afternoon, and you said it was an emergency, were you referring to this kind of problem?"

Galen nodded, and kept working. "The last week or so has been the worst. Several times he's confronted her, saying the same kinds of things as tonight. The threats are vague, but there's no question he's hostile toward her. I don't know how much more she can take." He picked up a small circular device and slit the foil on another bottle, then deftly inserted a two-pronged cork puller into the bottle. "She threw him out about six months ago, and he hasn't left her alone since. Yesterday morning was the last straw. If I hadn't happened in right at that moment, who knows what might have happened? And after all that, she was still not going to take action. The woman baffles me, that's all I can say." With one quick yank the cork came out with a small pop. "Makes me nervous, knowing he's right out there. He's got to come in at some point."

"I know. I was thinking the same thing."

"Let's just hope a deputy arrives first."

There was an awkward moment. Neither Annie nor Galen wanted to talk about Steven Vick. Finally, Galen said, "In all the excitement, have you had a chance to taste any wine?"

"Actually, no."

"Well, it's about time, then, isn't it?"

"I'd like that."

Galen filled two glasses about a third full. "This merlot won a gold medal at the state fair just a week ago. It's probably one of the best wines being served in this room."

Annie started to bring the glass to her mouth, but the winemaker stopped her. "First, we look." Annie followed Galen's example and held the sample up to the light. The color was a beautiful deep garnet.

"This is a little hard in artificial light. That's why judges like to do their tasting during the day. And some judges will only taste wine in the morning, when the palate is the freshest."

Annie peered into her glass. "So what am I looking for, anyway?"

"In a blind tasting, looking at the wine can tell the judge a lot about its age and quality. What we're looking for, besides just enjoying the color, is clarity and brightness. Muddiness or cloudiness could indicate a flaw in the wine, or simply that the sediment hadn't had a chance to settle. At North Faire, like a lot of the smaller wineries, we don't filter our wine, so there will always be some sediment. We think too much filtering can take away character and leave a papery taste."

"This looks pretty clear to me."

"It is. The brilliance is influenced in part by the acidity. This wine has a low pH, meaning it's fairly high in acidity."

"Is that good?"

"Very good. A wine lacking acidity will be dull and flabby, not very aggressive." He noticed Annie's smile. "I know. The descriptions we use, sometimes you'd think we were describing our in-laws."

A middle-aged couple came to the North Faire table, and Galen poured them each a sample. The man swirled it in his glass, then watched the patterns the flowing wine formed. "Look at that, Margo. Now *that's* what I call legs. Great legs."

Margo sipped her wine. "I wish he'd say that to me once in a while."

As they moved away, Galen explained that the man was referring to the pattern left by the wine on the sides of the glass. "It's supposed to tell you something about the viscosity of the wine, but in reality, it only tells you how clean the stemware is."

Annie glanced over at the next table. Dr. Marchand seemed to be delighting in Celia's company. The smile on Celia's face said the feeling was mutual.

"Now may I taste it?" Annie asked Galen.

"Not yet. Next you have to smell it. The nose is a lot more sensitive than the taste buds. Sometimes what you think is taste is really smell. What happens is, aromas inside your mouth will rise up through the passage at the back of the throat into your nasal passages. Here, hold your glass like this, by the stem, and twirl it gently." He demonstrated, with a small movement that caused the wine to circle in the glass. "Swirling causes more air to contact the wine's surface, which intensifies what you smell."

Annie did her best to copy the motion without spilling the wine.

"What you're looking for is, first, whether there are any unpleasant odors—that would tell you if the wine is flawed, or gone bad. Then you look for the aroma—that refers to the smell of the fruit of the grape. 'Bouquet' refers to the smells that come from the aging and fermentation—everything that happens to the wine once the winemaker gets his hands on it. The key factors are intensity, complexity, and balance. Now, sniff."

Annie felt somewhat silly as she stuck her nose into the glass and breathed deeply. She'd already forgotten the difference between aroma and bouquet. All she knew was that the wine smelled very nice, but she was unable to describe to Galen what she smelled. It smelled a lot like, well, wine.

"It takes practice," he said. "It's all part of learning to appreciate wine. Some of the judges are so sensitive to odor that they'll insist that no one around them wear any kind of scent—lotion, hairspray, even deodorant—when they're tasting. They probably would have ejected you." He leaned closer and breathed in her perfume. "I'm not that familiar with scents, but you're wearing something spicy, with elements of musk and vanilla. And pretty expensive, I'd say."

"You're very good."

He smiled. "Just part of my job. Actually, perfume is much easier to identify than wine, which is so subtle. And subjective. In different reviews of this particular wine, one reviewer found elements of 'citrus, loganberry, and smoke,' while another found 'black cherry, plum, and chocolate.' That's how far off tasters can be."

"Chocolate?" Annie sniffed again, but couldn't identify anything smelling even vaguely like a Hershey bar. "Can you smell chocolate in this?"

Galen sniffed again. "Yes, actually, I can. But you have to remember I've been doing this a long time. You have to develop a very good sense of smell if you're going to be any good at making wine. Just as I'm sure you're very good at spotting the fine print in a contract."

"I guess. Is it difficult marketing Washington wine?"

He shook his head. "Right now, North Faire can sell all

it produces, so we don't even worry about marketing. If we were to get bigger that might be a concern. For now, it's one less detail to worry about. The local wholesale distributor comes on the first and the fifteenth, and we just tell them to take it away."

Annie swirled the wine in her glass. "You know, a person could get awfully thirsty doing this. When do I get to have something to *drink*?"

"Okay, I get the point. Now, what you want to know here is that the four basic tastes—sweet, salty, sour, and bitter—are all detected on different parts of the tongue. Sweet is on the tip, sour down the sides, salty in the middle and bitter in the back. You've heard the phrase 'bitter finish'? That's because you don't taste the bitter until you swallow. It's the harmony of these four kinds of taste that makes up the balance and complexity of wine. That's why you want to spread the wine to as many different parts of the palate as possible. It's called 'chewing' the wine."

"Sounds unattractive."

"Hey, it is. It looks totally foolish. But don't be embarrassed, everyone does it. Here, I'll show you." He demonstrated by taking a large sip and pushing it around his mouth, cheeks and tongue in motion. He even held the wine at the front of his mouth and inhaled a stream of air. Annie almost expected the winemaker to start gargling. After fifteen or twenty seconds, he swallowed. "Now you try. Take a large enough sip, and really move it around your mouth."

Annie did as she was instructed, but it was hard to keep a straight face. She swallowed. "I like it. It's nice."

"Aw, c'mon. If I'm going to turn you into a wine connoisseur, you've gotta learn no less than forty-seven different words for 'nice.' You know, something like 'precocious, with a woody nose,' or 'light, but not too arrogant'—stuff like that. My favorite is something James Thurber said, 'It's a naive domestic Burgundy without much breeding, but I think you'll be amused by its presumption.' "

"You took the words right out of my mouth."

Annie went through the same routine with the next sample Galen poured for her, a cabernet. "I really like this one. But how can I tell if it's a 'good' wine?"

"You just did."

"No, come on. I haven't the faintest idea what's good and what's not."

"Lots of people think like that, and it keeps them from experimenting and finding what they like. For the most part, whether a wine is 'good' or not is totally subjective—it's what *you* enjoy. If you think that you would like to drink more than one glass of this wine, and it would go well with food, then it's a good wine. But it's true that as you learn more about wine, you appreciate it more."

"So I don't need to be embarrassed if I don't know a 'good' wine when I taste one?"

"Not at all. It's all pretty arbitrary. In fact, I was at a blind tasting one time, and a very prominent winemaker tasted a sample—he didn't know what it was. He stood up and berated it as the worst dreck he'd ever tasted. He sat down rather abruptly when his wife pulled on his sleeve and told him it was his."

"No."

"True story."

By the time Galen explained all the nuances of each and every wine that North Faire produced, Annie was laughing and starting to feel a little tipsy. No wonder Taylor enjoyed her work so much. But as Galen poured, the sound of the French doors being thrown open drew his attention, and he spilled a few drops on the white tablecloth. They both turned as a cool draft flew in from the garden. Celia and Dr. Marchand moved closer to get a better look.

Suddenly sober, Annie braced herself, expecting to see Steven Vick and Martin Grubenmacher returning to the party. Instead, she saw a man in his mid-thirties with short, curly hair, wearing a stylish leather jacket and black slacks. His face was completely drained of color.

"Gerald North, Taylor's brother," Galen whispered, a fact

Annie had already guessed. The blond man rushed toward the North Faire table.

"What is it, man? You look like you've seen your mother's ghost."

Taylor's brother struggled to catch his breath enough to speak. When he did, his voice was so low it was hard to make out what he was saying. "Quick . . . call nine-one-one . . . it's Steve . . . out in the garden . . . oh my God, I don't believe it. . . ."

Galen flushed. "The bastard, what's he gone and done now?"

Gerald swallowed. "Hurt . . . Badly . . ."

"What has he done, man? Did he start a fight?"

"No, no. It's Steve—dead. I think he's dead."

"What the—where's Taylor? Is she still upstairs? Has anyone told her?"

Gerald shook his head. "No, you don't understand. She's out there with him. Galen, *she killed him.*"

Chapter 11

ANNIE FOLLOWED Taylor's brother back out into the garden while Galen went to the kitchen to call 911. The grounds were practically pitch-black in the moonless night, the only illumination coming from the windows of the house. More than once Annie stumbled on an unseen obstacle in the path.

Fifty feet or so from the house was a circular herb garden, ringed by stone benches. The heavy scent of lavender hung in the air. In the darkness, Annie could barely make out the shapes of two bodies.

Gerald North handed Annie a cigarette lighter, and she flicked it on. Steven Vick lay with his head near one of the stone benches. In the scant light, he looked like he could have been asleep, but for the thin trickle of blood coming from his mouth. Quickly, Annie felt under his jawline for a pulse. There was none, nor any hint of breath. She felt the back of his skull, and her fingers came away bloody.

Gerald was right—Steven Vick was dead.

A few feet away, Gerald had gone to help Taylor. She was sitting up, but even in the darkness, Annie could see that her dress was torn, and her face was scraped and bleeding. She was cradling an unopened wine bottle in her lap.

"Are you all right? Can you stand up?"

She didn't answer.

"Come on, sis, we need to get you into the house."

Taylor's voice was barely audible. "Gerald? Who? . . . Someone . . . I don't understand."

"Shhh, now. You don't have to say anything."

Annie pried the wine bottle from Taylor's hand and set it on the bench while Gerald helped his sister up. He put an arm around her waist, slowly guiding her back to the house.

"Take her through the kitchen," said Annie. "We can take the back stairs and avoid the party." As they approached the back porch, they met Galen Rockwell coming out of the kitchen door with a deputy sheriff. When Taylor's face entered the ring of light, Annie heard Galen's sharp intake of breath.

"My God, what has he done to you this time?" He brought Taylor closer to the porch to see her injuries better. "We need to get you to a doctor."

"No." Taylor's voice was faint. "No, really, I'll be fine. I don't want to see a doctor. Lie down, that's all."

The officer, a pimply kid of eighteen or so, looked like he didn't know what to do. "Ma'am, I'm Deputy Blaisdell, from the Yakima County Sheriff's Department. Do you think . . . can you tell me what happened?"

Taylor shook her head, making a sound that was a cross between a gasp and a cry. "Steve . . . he . . . Steve . . ." She turned to put her head on Gerald's shoulder, sobbing convulsively.

"Uh, okay, ma'am. Right. You get inside now. Your friends, here, will stay with you and somebody'll be in to talk to you in a minute." To no one in particular he said, "Is there somebody I'm supposed to notify? Her husband?"

Annie's eyes met those of Gerald North, who nodded toward the garden. "Her husband's the one out there."

Upstairs in the light of the coat room, Annie saw that Taylor's injuries were unsightly, but superficial. She looked like she had fallen, or been pushed, face first into the gravel pathway. A small area under her right eye was starting to darken, but she had no major cuts or broken bones. While Gerald held his sister's hand, Annie brought a moistened towel from the bathroom. Taylor looked at it, then took it and began methodically wiping her face as if she were removing makeup.

"Will someone *please* tell me what is happening in my house? What are the police doing here?"

At the sound, Annie turned to the doorway. Florence Grubenmacher seemed even smaller than she had when surrounded by guests in the foyer, but she had a voice that could have etched glass. Even in her gold high-heeled sandals, the woman couldn't have been more than five feet tall, and her hips and shoulders were as narrow as a child's. She stood with one carefully manicured hand on her hip, the other clutching her double string of pearls, seemingly oblivious to Taylor's injuries.

"Humph." She looked Gerald up and down, taking in the silk shirt, Italian loafers, and leather jacket in one disapproving glare. Scrutinizing Annie with an equal amount of suspicion, she announced abruptly, "I don't know you."

"My name is Annie MacPherson. I'm a friend of Taylor's."

"Yes. Well. Has she taken a fall or something? I need to know why the police are here. Is this something my insurance agent needs to know about?"

Annie immediately disliked the way Mrs. Grubenmacher referred to Taylor as if she weren't present in the room. Taylor, however, did not respond for herself, but continued to wipe her face with the cloth.

"I'm sure the deputy will explain everything. He's in the garden."

"In *my* garden?" Florence walked to the window and pushed aside the heavy drapes. Down below, Deputy Blaisdell was struggling to tie plastic yellow ribbon to a rosebush and hold a flashlight at the same time. Florence grimaced, as if having a crime scene in the backyard was the ultimate display of bad manners. "You might as well wait in a room that's not full of everyone's coats. Come this way." Mrs. Grubenmacher clicked her way down the hallway, without waiting to see if she were being followed.

Gerald took Taylor's elbow and steered her into the next room.

"This is my *private* sitting room," Mrs. Grubenmacher said stiffly. "I imagine you won't be staying long. Please pull the door shut when you leave." A chill seemed to follow Mrs. Grubenmacher as she left the room.

Under stress, Annie often noticed insignificant details. Now, looking around the room, she saw that everything about it was depressingly colorless. Like Mrs. Grubenmacher's outfit, the room looked as if it hadn't been updated in decades. The wallpaper was beige on beige. The drapes were made from a nubby fabric in taupe. The carpeting was café au lait. Oak frames holding monochrome sepia photographs hung on the wall in awkward groupings. The room even smelled beige, if that were possible.

Taylor lay down on the tan sofa and closed her eyes. Gerald went to her and stroked her hair. "Tays, are you sure you're all right? Don't you want to see a doctor, just to make sure?"

"No. Please. I just want . . . to lie down."

Gerald was a handsome man, Annie noticed, with strong Teutonic features. Annie remembered Taylor saying how close they were, and wondered if Gerald was feeling Taylor's pain.

"Do you want us to stay or go?" he whispered in his sister's ear.

She sighed deeply. "I think . . . I think I'd rather be alone . . . but could you bring me my purse? I need an aspirin."

"Sure, Tays." Gerald looked up at Annie, who went back to the coat room to find Taylor's purse. Between the two rooms was a bathroom, where Annie found a glass for some water.

Taylor was lying down when Annie returned, her eyes shut. Gerald was talking to her softly and stroking her forehead. Annie handed the purse and glass of water to Gerald and quietly backed out of the room. A moment or two later,

Gerald came out, closing the door behind him. Galen Rockwell was waiting in the hallway.

"I've never seen her like this. I can't imagine what must have happened out there."

They were interrupted by a clumping sound of heavy footsteps coming up the stairs. "So, I guess this is where the real party is, huh?"

Annie jumped at the sound, and turned to see a short man in an ill-fitting polyester suit huffing his way up the stairs, carrying with him an odor of stale cigarette smoke. "Detective Shibilsky, Yakima County Sheriff's Office." He didn't offer to shake hands. "Blaisdell told me some fruity-lookin' blond guy in leather found the body. That's gotta be you, am I right?"

Gerald tensed and put a hand up to straighten his tie. He apparently thought it would be unwise to react to the detective's jibe. "Yes, I found Steve."

Shibilsky waddled into the coat room and drew open the curtain. Additional officers had finally arrived to help Deputy Blaisdell, and the herb garden was now completely cordoned off and brightly illuminated. Where there had been pitch blackness, portable lamps now flooded the area like a night game under stadium lights. Annie noticed for the first time that Steven Vick's socks were a hideous shade of yellow. A deputy was methodically running a video camera over every inch of the scene, while another took still photographs. The rookie, Blaisdell, was standing by with his hands in his pockets, waiting for someone to tell him what to do. No one did. Shibilsky drew the curtain again, shutting off the view.

"So." The short man pulled a well-chewed Bic pen out of his pocket and removed the cap with his teeth. He held it there, sucking on it noisily. "How'd you find the body?"

"I tripped over it. Literally. I didn't see it—him, I mean, or my sister until I was facedown in the dirt myself." Gerald held up his scraped palms as proof.

"Tripped—over—it," Shibilsky repeated slowly, scratching in his notebook. "And before that?"

"I arrived at the party late. I had to drive down from Ellensburg. I was teaching an art history class that lasted till eight."

"Yeah, what on?"

"You mean the subject? Tonight we were discussing the Baroque art of trompe l'oeil."

"Tramp Louie? Sounds like 'Boxcar Willie.' "

"Just write down optical illusions."

"Yeah, right." Shibilsky scowled. "Nothin' else before you got here, you parked your car, and boom, you've just fallen over a dead guy?"

"I don't understand what you're getting at. I just told you I arrived late. Look, can we sit down? I'm not accustomed to discovering dead in-laws."

Shibilsky missed Gerald's sarcasm and shrugged his approval. Gerald leaned back on the window seat, trying visibly not to get angry. Annie didn't think he was succeeding. Shibilsky remained standing.

"What about after, then?"

"I came straight into the house, through the French doors into the ballroom. Ms. MacPherson can tell you. She's a friend of my sister, and saw me when I rushed in. She came back out with me to get Taylor, while Galen Rockwell phoned nine-one-one."

Shibilsky kept writing, but looked skeptical. "Look," he said, "you got a name and address on a card or something?" Gerald handed him a business card from the art department at Central Washington University, which the detective slipped into his breast pocket. "Tripped over the body. Maybe by the time I get back to you, you'll have thought of a better story. Or the truth, even. Hey, now there's a thought." He looked at Galen and Annie. "You two, you can give your names to Blaisdell, he'll take your statement. The poor dweeb needs something to do. Right now I gotta talk to the 'grieving widow.' The old lady with the pearls said she's in the next room?"

"No, I'm right here." Taylor, looking barely strong enough to stand, was leaning in the doorway. "But I'm afraid I'm not . . ."

Galen Rockwell was barely able to catch Taylor as she stumbled into the room.

Chapter 12

"GET HER to the window seat." Gerald helped Galen get Taylor seated and, holding her face in his hands, gently tapped her cheeks. "Taylor? Taylor, come on. Talk to us."

Her eyes were open, but she didn't appear to see anything. Her skin was pale.

"Gerald?" Her voice was slurred. "Where . . . ? Where's my purse!"

"Taylor, what have you done? Have you taken something?" To Annie, he said, "Quick. Get her purse. I think she may have had some pills in there."

Annie ran to the sitting room and grabbed the purse. She hurried back, and dumped the contents on the floor. When he saw what was inside, Gerald North's face turned white. There was a small brown prescription bottle and a container of aspirin. Annie picked them up. Both were empty.

Gerald looked up at the faces in the room. "We need to get her to the hospital, now! That prescription bottle was nearly full. Galen, find Seth Longacre. He can get her to the hospital in his patrol car. I'll get Taylor downstairs. Hurry, man. This is serious."

Detective Shibilsky helped Gerald get Taylor to her feet, then got out of the way. He turned back to find Annie putting the contents back into Taylor's purse.

"Uh, 'scuse me, but you can leave that junk right where it is." The prescription bottle was still on the floor. The

detective took a pen from his pocket and rolled it over
until he could read the label. "Tylenol threes, twenty-four
tablets," he read. "I got that for my sciatica one time.
Got codeine in it. Hey, now will ya look at that? No
wonder the brother knew what was in it. It's his prescription."

Despite feeling completely fatigued, Annie rose early on
Wednesday morning. She had hardly slept all night. Gerald
had wanted to go to the hospital with his sister, but the detective insisted that he and Annie stay behind and give their
statements about finding the body. When it was decided
that Galen Rockwell would go in the patrol car with Taylor,
the winemaker gave Annie the keys to Taylor's van and the
house, and said he'd stop by in the morning to let her know
how Taylor was doing.

Annie pulled on jeans and a white cotton shirt and went
downstairs. There was a bag of Starbucks coffee beans in
the freezer and a grinder on the counter, and Annie fumbled
through Taylor's cupboards until she located coffee filters.
Once a full pot of strong coffee was brewing, she sat down
at the table and tried to figure out what she was supposed
to do next.

Seeing that it was exactly eight o'clock, she flipped
on the small black and white television that Taylor kept in
the kitchen to see if the local news would have a report.
As the screen came into focus, she heard Charles Marchand, the Wine Gala's guest of honor, being interviewed
from his hotel, voicing his deep regrets that such a tragic
incident had to occur in the midst of such a fine cele-
bration of the region's wine industry. He expressed his sin-
cerest sympathy to the family and friends of the deceased.
Next interviewed was Celia Vick, her face grim as she
said, "I'm not surprised that something like this had to
happen. Steve was a horrible, horrible man with a violent
temper. He was my own father, but I was afraid to be
around him." A solemn-faced reporter came back on the

air, and announced that the wife of the victim had been hospitalized for shock, and that a thorough investigation was under way. "Authorities have not ruled out self-defense," the reporter said. Annie clicked off the set as the graphics changed to a story about local elections, thankful that the media hadn't gotten hold of the overdose story.

She had just opened the refrigerator to look for something to eat when there was a knock on the back door. It was Galen Rockwell, who handed her a white paper bag with grease stains showing through the bottom. She noticed that the winemaker was still wearing what he'd had on the night before—jeans, white shirt, eelskin boots, and the well-worn brown felt hat. Only the bolo tie was gone. It had probably been a long night.

"I, uh, brought some sweet rolls. Wednesday's the only day Edna down at the café bakes bear claws." He shuffled from one foot to the other. "They're pretty good."

"Thanks. Come on in."

He took off his hat and stepped into the kitchen.

"Coffee?"

"Please. Black is fine."

"How's she doing?" Annie asked, pouring Galen a cup of coffee.

"Not good. They think she swallowed practically a whole bottle of those damned painkillers, plus maybe half a bottle of aspirin, and the combination—aspirin, Tylenol, and codeine—really did a number on her. She went into convulsions or something in the squad car on the way to the hospital."

"Oh, no. Is she going to be okay?"

Galen looked somber. "She's stable and conscious for now, but they're not sure about kidney damage. The doctor told us that both aspirin and codeine are a lot more dangerous than most people make 'em out to be. She'll have to stay in the hospital for a while for tests. She was also pretty disoriented, and they don't know if that's from the overdose, or if maybe she hit her head outside when she fell on the ground."

Annie shook her head slowly, moving in a daze.

Galen found plates for the pastries and paper napkins on top of the refrigerator. He placed a hand on her shoulder. "Come on. You need to eat something."

"Can she have visitors?"

"The doctors said not yet. They want her to stay real quiet for a couple of days. But I thought, if it's not too much to ask, maybe you could take her a bag with a change of underwear, her toothbrush, and whatnot. We're so busy around here with the harvest and crushing, I really can't get away."

"Of course."

Galen helped himself to a pastry from the bag, but stared at it without eating. Annie looked at him. About forty, he looked like the kind of man who had always worked hard, and who tried to do right by other people. He had an open, honest face, but one that had seen its share of troubles. Annie sensed that, like herself, he needed someone to talk to right now.

"You know, if she had died from those pills, I don't think I ever would have forgiven myself."

"For what, Galen? You weren't responsible."

He shrugged. "I'm not so sure. She's been under so much pressure lately, and I sure wasn't helping."

"What do you mean?"

The winemaker looked down at his shoes. "Did she tell you what happened on Monday?"

"A little bit."

"I came up to the house looking for Taylor. I needed to tell her there'd been another theft from the storeroom, so I was pretty mad to start off with. The last six months, ever since she got Steve out of the house, things have been disappearing from around here. Supplies, mostly. One week it was bottles. Then labels. The numbers were so small, at first I just thought it was sloppy record-keeping. But when it kept up, week after week, I knew there was something fishy going on. So I started keeping real good track. And I was sure Steve was behind it."

"Steve? Why?"

Galen shrugged. "I won't confess that I understand the man. All I know is that he's mean, and he's mad at Taylor for throwin' him out, and he's trying to get back at her any way he can. I kept telling Taylor he was behind it, but she refused to do anything about it."

"So what happened on Monday?"

"I came up here, ready to tear into her. I had three dozen cases of cabernet ready for labeling, and we were out of glue, of all the danged things. All my years of making wine, I've never run out of glue. And I sure as hell didn't have time to make a run into town to get more. So I get up to the house, I'm already on edge, and whose car is there right in front but Vick's. And as soon as I get up on the porch I can hear 'em yelling at each other. He's going on about how he wants money for something, and she's saying she doesn't know what he's talking about. I was trying to decide if I should wait and come back later when I hear a sound like a chair being pushed over." Galen stared at the floor. "I don't know what would have happened next if I hadn't rushed in there, and told him to get the hell out. I, uh, had my shotgun with me. Usually do this time of year, 'cause of the birds. Having that thing pointed at his stomach made him clear out pretty fast."

Annie poured more coffee. "But you said *you* were putting pressure on Taylor?"

"Well, as I said, I went up there pretty mad, and seeing him there didn't help my mood any. I, uh, kind of gave Taylor an ultimatum."

"What did you say?"

"All of this stuff had been going on for six months, and she hadn't done anything as far as I could tell to start divorce proceedings, or even get a court order to keep Vick away from here. I told her that if she didn't call a lawyer and take some kind of action immediately, that I was going to walk. At the time, I meant it."

"You mean walk off the job?"

"Yeah. And if there's one thing a winery owner doesn't need to hear during the crushing season, it's that the winemaker is planning to skip town. It's just that I was so angry, you see?"

Annie could hear the pain and guilt in his voice, and wanted to reassure him. "Galen, you didn't have anything to do with Taylor taking those pills."

"I don't know. She's been so worried about keeping the damned business running, she didn't need any added worries from me. It was a harsh thing to say, and I regretted it ten minutes later. I may just be an employee here, but this winery means as much to me as it does to her. I couldn't do anything that would hurt the business. Or Taylor." He laughed bitterly. "Hell, this job's about all I've got, these days."

Galen picked up a bear claw. Filling oozed out onto the napkin as he bit into it. "All these months, Steve's been driving everybody crazy, and now . . . I do feel guilty about it, but I have to admit I've been wishing some mighty bad things'd happen to him."

"I know."

"That's right, you knew him, didn't you? Why is it, when somebody dies, we're supposed to only think good things about 'em? Seems to me a rotten person's just as rotten dead as alive. Hell, don't listen to me. I don't know what I'm saying." Galen went to the sink for a glass of water. "You're an attorney, right?"

"Mm hmm."

"You do any criminal law?"

"Not as often as I used to. I spent five years as a prosecutor, but I didn't want to do that full-time when I went into private practice."

"How come? I'd think that would be the most exciting kind of work."

"It's so easy to get burned out. As a prosecutor, you get

tired of seeing the same faces, the same crimes. It's like you're chipping away at a monumental problem that just keeps getting bigger and bigger. But as bad as that is, I found criminal defense work even worse. When it comes right down to it, nearly all of your clients are guilty as sin, and it's the lawyer's job to think of creative ways to get them back out onto the street to commit another crime. It's a large, complicated cat-and-mouse game. I know all the rationales about everyone deserving a competent defense, even if they're guilty; I just don't sleep well at night if I'm the one who has to provide it."

"I can see your point."

"So now I mostly do civil work. Sometimes it's interesting, sometimes not. The work I do won't save the world, but it may make a difference in that one person's life. I'll still take a criminal case, if I really think someone is getting shafted by the system. But I have to trust that the person I'm representing is telling *me* the truth, and that there's at least a reasonable chance that they shouldn't be convicted."

Galen looked down at his boots. "I guess you can figure out why I'm asking you this." He looked away. "That homicide detective. He showed up at the hospital, but the doctor wouldn't let him in to see her. He was like a damned vulture, waiting for something to die."

Annie paused, then shook her head. "If Taylor needs me right now, I'll stay. I owe her that."

Galen didn't ask for an explanation, but his calm silence made Annie continue. For someone she knew so slightly, Galen was amazingly easy to talk to. "You were saying how you felt like you should have done more to protect Taylor. There was a time when I might have been able to help her get away from him, out from under whatever spell he had over her." Annie shrugged. "I didn't do it. You could say I turned my back on her when she needed me."

Galen got up and poured himself some more coffee, then sat down across from her.

"Taylor told me about something that happened back then. She came back, found you in the apartment with him?"

Annie nodded. "I didn't know she was pregnant with Celia then."

"Would that have made a difference?"

"I don't know. We were both so young, and I hated Steve so much. Taylor . . . it's hard to explain, Galen. High school wasn't an easy time for me. Without Taylor, it would have been horrible. Back then, she seemed older and wiser. She kind of took me under her wing, gave me access to friends and adventures I would have been too shy to pursue on my own. I still feel like I should have been more loyal to her."

Galen's mouth curved into a thin smile. "Sounds like you were asking her to choose—Steve or your friendship." He met her eyes. "Under the circumstances, I think I would have done the same thing."

They were both silent for a moment.

"How much trouble do you think she's in—with the law, I mean?"

"It's hard to say right now."

Galen sensed that she was holding back. "I need to know the truth, Annie."

She nodded. "It looks really bad. First of all, we don't know why Taylor went out to the garden. She placed herself in danger by doing that."

"But he was a violent man. Everyone knew that. And he was strong."

"From what I saw out there last night, it looked like he was struck on the back of the head. If that's the case, it could be difficult to say it was self-defense."

After a moment, Galen said, "I think you need to talk to Harry."

"Harry Braithwaite? Why?"

"I suspect that he's the only one she might have talked to about it. Oh, we all knew what was going on. The bruises that she tried to cover with makeup and dark glasses. But Harry, he might know the truth."

"About what, Galen?"

"About how much Steven Vick was beating his wife."

Chapter 13

HARRY BRAITHWAITE lived in a large Victorian house two blocks off Main Street on the hill overlooking downtown Harmony. A bronze plaque in front said it had been built in 1906 by Nathaniel Bledsoe, a vice president of the Northern Pacific Railroad, who had resided there with his wife Tillie and their fourteen children. Built over two lots and faced in rusticated concrete brick, the massive gray structure was more impressive than it was beautiful. Hulking, angular, and too ostentatious for its surroundings, Annie thought it was a perfect match for Harry Braithwaite.

Galen had said he'd call ahead and tell Harry that Annie was coming. He must have done so, because Harry was waiting for her out front as she pulled up. His baggy wool trousers, at least two sizes too large, were held up by striped suspenders, and his size-twelve wing tips looked like they'd been worn daily for years. His white shirt bore traces of that morning's bacon and egg breakfast.

Harry walked into the street and opened Annie's car door. "I'm so glad you came by, my dear. Old Mrs. Grubenmacher shooed everyone out of the place so fast last night, none of us knew what on earth had happened. And the television news this morning wasn't much help." He ushered her up the stone steps. "Come in, come in. I hope you have time to visit. I've got the coffee pot on."

"This is an incredible house, Harry."

"It is, isn't it? My wife and I bought it about ten years

84

ago. Our dream when I retired from teaching was to fix it up into a bed-and-breakfast. We moved here when I retired about four years ago—I'm not that old, mind you, I retired at sixty—but poor Eleanor died within a few months. Hodgkin's disease."

"I'm so sorry to hear that."

"Thank you, my dear. I do still miss her terribly." He sighed. "Well, someday I'll get this place cleaned out and fixed up. Mimi and I just rattle around in all this space. Problem is, I can't boil a three-minute egg, and Mimi doesn't get up before ten, so I guess it would have to be a 'bed-and-make-your-own-darned-breakfast.' " He jiggled the rusted lock. "You'll have to excuse me if the place is a mess, but that's nothing new." Annie stepped into a darkened foyer. The curving staircase seemed to go up forever. "Missing light fixture," said Harry, apologetically, and guided her to the left. "You go on into the morning room and I'll get the coffee."

The morning room, probably named for its eastern-facing bay windows, looked like the back room of a not-too-successful secondhand store. Every possible inch of space was filled with clutter. The seat of an overstuffed chair was stacked high with dusty *National Geographic*s, none of them current. There were five or six assorted end tables lined up against one wall, each with its own massive pile of books threatening to topple at any moment. An antique birdcage had become the home of a philodendron that had grown out of control, its long tendrils snaking up and over the window and around the corners of the room. Annie realized that the bed-and-breakfast would have to be a long time coming. It would take years to clear out enough stuff to make room for paying guests.

Harry returned in a moment with a stainless steel percolator, two chipped china teacups, and a plate of store-bought butter cookies. "I hope you like your coffee black, because Mimi used the last of the milk and neglected to tell me. And we rarely have visitors, except for Taylor, who doesn't care for my coffee. Here, I'll let you pour, if that's all right."

As she poured the sludge-like brew from the percolator, she immediately figured out why Taylor would have declined Harry's coffee. She sipped, and made an effort not to grimace at the bitter taste. She reminded herself that she wasn't there for the coffee.

Harry ran a hand through his wiry salt-and-pepper hair, making it stand out even more than it had when he started. "So," he said, "tell me what happened. First of all, is Taylor all right?"

Annie told Harry about the overdose and what the doctors had reported to Galen.

"Oh, my heavens, I must go see her at once."

"The doctors said no visitors for a day or two, except immediate family."

"Well, I feel like I'm practically family. Oh, my, but this is terrible, terrible. And the authorities, they think she knocked him on the head, is that it?"

She shrugged. "It seems likely, doesn't it, from the circumstances? That was my conclusion when Gerald and I found her there. She was just sitting on the ground like she was in shock, cross-legged, with the bottle in her lap. She was rocking back and forth, almost like an autistic child, moaning slightly. And there was Steve on the ground . . ." Thinking about the scene again almost made Annie ill.

Harry took a loud sip, and shook his head. "I should have known it would come to this, after everything that's happened. I should have put a stop to it. I really should have."

"A stop to what?" Annie asked. After her talk with Galen, she thought she knew the answer, but wanted to hear what Harry would volunteer.

"Why, the things he did to her, of course. Everyone knew about it. Not at the beginning, she kept it very well hidden at first. But, oh, the last six months or so, after she threw him out. It's been so obvious."

"You're sure it was Steve who beat her?"

"Why, who else could it be?" Harry munched on a cookie, ignoring the crumbs that dropped to the floor.

"Sometimes everyone suspects the husband, but it could be someone else. A co-worker. Another relative. Sometimes even another woman."

"Oh, no. It was no one but Steve." He brushed the crumbs from the front of his shirt.

"Did she tell you about it?"

"Not in so many words, no. Taylor could never have admitted that she was a battered spouse. Too ashamed, I'm sure. But there were times, she would visit me here. She had bruises on her face that she'd tried to cover with makeup, not quite succeeding."

Annie set down her cup and sat back in her chair. "This was before Steve moved out, I take it?"

"No, actually. I started to notice things *afterwards*."

"Tell me about when Taylor threw Steve out."

"Oh, it was nasty, believe me. Steve had to go to Spokane on a business trip, and as soon as he was gone, she had movers come and pack up all of his things and take them to a storage locker in town, then had all the locks changed. She asked me to come have dinner with her the evening he was due back, in case there was any trouble. I may not be that strong anymore, but I have a rather, um, intimidating physical presence. She didn't think Steve would try anything if I were there."

"And was there trouble?"

"Fortunately, nothing more than some angry yelling—a lot the way Steve was acting at the gala. All red-faced blustering. And he broke a flower pot. For effect, I think. Taylor went out on the balcony and threw down the storage locker key, and told him she never wanted to see him again, unless it was in court. He yelled back that he wasn't going to let her get away with this. That was it—vague—but no actual threats."

Annie recalled what Taylor and Galen had told her about the petty thefts around the winery. It turned out that Harry had heard the same stories. "But never any evidence directly linking Steve to the incidents?" Annie asked.

"Nothing. That's why Taylor hasn't gone to the police. She didn't feel there was anything they could do."

"Now, why was it you thought it was Steve who was beating Taylor, if she never told you directly?"

"There were clues, you see. Taylor's a very bright girl, and she never would have let anything slip accidentally. That's why I think that the clues she was dropping were an indication that she really *wanted* me to know it was Steve."

"Clues? Like what?"

"For example, one time she visited me on a Monday, and said she was going into Yakima for a meeting on Wednesday, in a building near Steve's office. She hoped she wasn't going to run into him. Then when I saw her on Thursday, and her face was covered with makeup, and I asked her about her meeting, she refused to talk about it. On another occasion that I can remember, she invited me to her house for coffee, and again, I could see that she was trying to cover a black eye. I asked her point-blank if it had been Steve, and she just turned away, wouldn't make eye contact. Didn't deny it, you see. There was a big, overstuffed chair missing from the living room. She said that he had come to take it. I presume they had a scuffle. And Celia, Taylor's daughter, told me later that she'd heard a car with a bad muffler, just like Steve's Mazda, going down the gravel road to Taylor's house the night before. But you see, Taylor wouldn't have invited me over that particular day, knowing I'd put two and two together, unless she wanted me to know."

They heard the slamming of the kitchen door, and the sound of footsteps running up the back stairs. Harry nodded in the direction of the sound. "Ah, there's my little *Bohème* now."

"If you don't mind my asking, how is it that your granddaughter lives here with you?"

"Mimi? She is a bit of a handful, isn't she? Eleanor and I had only one daughter, Violetta, who's in her forties now.

I guess we spoiled her, I don't know. Or perhaps she would have turned out the way she did without any help from us. She fancied herself a musician, but without the talent to back it up. Always flitting about here and there, singing classes in New York, running away to find herself in Fiji, four disastrous marriages squeezed in between somehow. I think she's in Italy now, or is it Cannes? I don't even try to keep up any more. Mimi's gotten the worst of it—living with Vi when the feeling suited her, getting dumped on our doorstep when it didn't. We tried our best, but I'm not terribly surprised the poor child has turned out the way she did."

More clumping was heard on the stairs. Mimi entered, an unlit cigarette hanging from her lips, and started rummaging through a pile of magazines in the corner. She wore black patterned tights and combat boots under a yellow and black minidress, making Annie think of a bumble-bee Halloween costume. One long earring brushed her shoulder. "I know, I know, no smoking in the house," Mimi whined. "Don't worry, I'm on my way out." She jangled some keys. "And I'm taking the car." She found what she was looking for—a copy of *Vogue*—and breezed out the front door, leaving it ajar behind her. Resignedly, Harry stood up to close it. He looked like he'd given up trying to discipline her long ago. "She'll be eighteen soon, and off on her own. You heard her plans—she wants to go on the road with that musician boyfriend of hers. *Zeno* his name is. The Nuclear Widgets or whatnot. My only saving grace in that regard is that she hasn't been able to save any money. There are no job opportunities for young people around here except agricultural work, and the occasional fast-food establishment, both of which she refuses to dirty her hands with."

"Maybe it's just a phase she's going through," Annie said to be polite. All she knew about teenagers was the fact that she had been one once.

"Yes, well." There was a great sense of loneliness in Harry's voice as he talked about Mimi leaving. He seemed like a man who thrived on company. Except for the clutter and inability to cook, running a bed-and-breakfast would probably suit him perfectly. After a moment, he asked softly, "Will they put Taylor in prison, do you think?"

Annie paused. The attorney side of her brain was already in the process of formulating a battered-woman's-syndrome defense, but Harry wasn't asking about legal theory. He was simply concerned about the fate of a dear friend. "I don't know, Harry," she answered. "I just don't know."

Harry reached for the percolator, and refilled his cup. "A little warm-up, my dear?"

"Sure," Annie replied, determined to make another gallant effort to drink Harry's coffee. "Taylor means a lot to you, doesn't she?"

The big man's face crinkled into a smile. "Oh, my Lord, yes. Ever since I met Taylor, I've loved her like a daughter." He chuckled. "To tell you the truth, I've loved her *more* than Violetta. Taylor's really everything I could have ever asked for in a daughter. After Eleanor died, all of the town's ladies began coming 'round with little plates of this and casseroles of that—everyone in town knows I can't cook, though why they thought it would ease my grief if they brought me a ramekin of green beans in mushroom soup with crunchy things on top, I can't for the life of me figure out. But the only one who had the decency to come to *talk* was Taylor. She knew how much I missed Eleanor. When you've had someone to talk to at the breakfast table every morning for a lifetime, and then you lose her, the silence can be deafening. Taylor was the only one who knew that stimulating conversation was more, far more, of a comfort than tamale pie. We'd talk for hours on end—philosophy, religion, politics, even theater. Can you imagine two people with such a love of theater ending up in a tiny little place like this? Years ago, right after college, I was an actor for a few years." Given Harry's expressive face, Annie didn't doubt it.

"I remember when we were in high school, Taylor was very caught up in theatrical activities."

"Oh, she was a natural, all right. Loved all aspects of the

theater—sets, costumes, lighting. We even talked about starting a little theater group here in town." He fumbled with the cookies on the plate. "Perhaps we still will . . . someday."

Annie was still thinking about Taylor as the victim of abuse. In a way, it made sense. Annie had, after all, seen a sample of Steven Vick's anger in person. But other parts of the puzzle didn't fit. Taylor had always seemed so confident and self-assured, not the type she pictured as a victim. Then she chided herself for giving in to stereotypes. Domestic violence cut across all socioeconomic lines; its victims didn't fall neatly into categories.

"Is there anyone else who Taylor might have talked to?"

"Hmmm. Possibly Edna Hinkel, the lady that owns the café in town. I may aspire to be Harmony's head curmudgeon, but she holds the undisputed title of town gossip. She was born and raised here in the valley, and I doubt if there's anything that's happened here in the last fifty, sixty years that Edna hasn't known about. And when you talk to her, tell her Harry says hello."

Annie thanked Harry for the coffee, and told him she'd let him know if she learned anything new about Taylor's condition.

"Thank you, my dear. I do appreciate that. I may be the biggest talker in town, but sometimes I'm the last to hear things." He walked her out to her car. After she got in, Harry closed the door and leaned on the window frame. "There's only one more thing I have to say, and then I'll let you go. I can't honestly say that I'm sorry Steve's dead. No woman should ever have to put up with what he did to her. Whatever happened to him last night, Steven Vick deserved it."

Chapter 14

ANNIE LEFT Harry's and drove down the hill into town. She soon realized that when the residents referred to "downtown Harmony," it was their version of local humor. The main street was about three blocks long, running parallel to and facing the railroad tracks. Only one intersection merited a four-way stop. On one side of the tracks was a row of storefronts. Opposite the tracks was a huge loading platform and a fruit canning plant.

Still, the town had all the basic necessities—one bank, one gas station, a tavern, a beauty parlor—and a few stores that appeared neither necessary nor profitable, making Annie wonder how they could compete with the shopping mall in Yakima.

Annie found Edna's café, the Apple Blossom Inn, in the middle of the third block. The building was old, with peeling red paint, but the window boxes filled with yellow mums and white petunias were well tended and inviting.

Seeing a pay phone across the street from the café, Annie decided to check in with her office before searching out the local gossip. As briefly as possible, she filled Val O'Hara in on what had happened, and explained that she would be staying over for a few days, at least until she knew Taylor was going to be all right.

"Do you think she took the pills out of guilt?" Val asked after hearing the whole story.

"I'm not sure. I haven't had a chance to speak with Taylor yet, but there are some rumors about Steve abusing her that I want to follow up on. If he had been playing mind games with her, she might have felt guilty even if it was self-defense."

"The poor dear. It sounds like a horrid experience. You think they'll bring charges against her?"

Annie paused while a loud truck from the cannery rolled by. "That's my guess. The detective seemed like the type who will want easy answers, and the easy answer would be to prosecute Taylor for murder, regardless of what Steve may have put her through."

"Well, you take your time, dear, and do what you have to for your friend. Things are under control here."

Before hanging up, Annie asked Val to prepare a retainer agreement for Taylor's signature, and some releases for medical and financial records, and fax them to a copy center in Yakima near the hospital.

Inside the café, Annie was met with the mingling aromas of freshly baked pie and simmering soup. Even though it was only about eleven, she was starting to get a little hungry for something nutritious, having had nothing but a bear claw with Galen, and a couple of cookies at Harry's.

The tiny room held four tables. Only one was occupied. Annie saw Seth Longacre, the highway patrolman she had met at the Wine Gala, at a table in the window where he was busy attacking a plate of fried chicken and mashed potatoes.

"Annie, hi. I didn't expect to see you up and about after last night."

"Thanks for getting Taylor to the hospital."

"Hey, part of my job. Have you heard how she's doing this morning?"

"Not yet. I called the hospital, but they said they wouldn't tell me anything over the phone. I'll be going there in a little while. Listen, Seth, the reason I stopped by, I'm trying to find out a little bit more about what may have been going on between Taylor and Steve. Harry Braithwaite suggested I talk to Edna Hinkel. Is she here?"

"Sure, I'll introduce you." He waved to a middle-aged woman behind the counter. She saw him and walked slowly over to the table, favoring an arthritic hip.

"Edna, have you met Annie MacPherson? She's that lawyer friend of Taylor's from Seattle. Annie, Edna Hinkel's the best baker in the Yakima Valley—if not the universe."

"I pay him plenty to say those things," said Edna, smiling. Up close, Annie could see that the woman had to be closer to seventy-five than to fifty. Soft russet hair curled around a moon-shaped face that had more lines and crevices than a dry riverbed, but her bright blue eyes belonged to a girl of twenty.

"Galen Rockwell brought over some pastries this morning. Were those yours?"

"They sure were, hon. Hope you had a bear claw. I consider them my personal best. Only bake 'em on Wednesdays."

"I did, and it was wonderful. I'll be sure to stop in and get some extras when I'm heading back to Seattle."

"You'd better. Nobody in the big city bakes like our Edna," said Seth, shoving a mouthful of mashed potatoes into his mouth.

"Can I get you something, dear, before this overgrown boy with two hollow legs eats me out of house and home?"

Annie ordered a bowl of Edna's homemade chicken soup, as Seth shoved the last bite of potatoes into his mouth, and pushed his plate away with a sigh. Edna picked it up, saying simply, "Well?"

"Oh, Edna, you know what I want."

"The apple again? Seth, I have to make two extra pies a week, just to feed you, boy. Haven't you learnt how to cook for yourself yet?"

"Nope. And I probably never will, with you around."

Edna returned in a moment with Annie's soup and Seth's pie—a wedge about four inches across heaped with two scoops of vanilla ice cream and cinnamon sauce. Annie thought her friend Ellen, the marathon runner, would adore this place.

Annie stopped Edna as she was starting to leave. "Actually, Edna, I was on my way here to talk to you, at Harry Braithwaite's suggestion. Can you sit down and join us?"

"I think that might be arranged, now that the breakfast crowd's thinned out, and the lunch boom is still an hour or so away. Let me get my coffee and I'll be right back." Seth scooped a bite of pie into his mouth, and ate as if he expected someone to take his plate away before he was done with it. Annie heard him emit a sigh of contentment.

Edna returned with a brown mug and a pitcher of cream shaped like a mooing cow. She poured a heavy measure of cream into her coffee, took a swallow, then added more. "Galen called here as soon as I opened this morning, and told me how bad-off Taylor was doing, over at the hospital. I sent some flowers, and called over there, but the nurses wouldn't tell me anything else. Have you heard any news?"

"Nothing more than what Galen knew this morning. I've got some things for Taylor in my car to drop by the hospital, but I guess her doctors have restricted her from having visitors."

Edna shook her head. "It's just a darned crying shame, that's all I can say. That poor, poor girl, with all the tragedy she's had in her life. If you get to see her, you tell her that I'm praying for her. And that she's got a meal on the house waiting for her any time. You'll tell her that, won't you?"

"I sure will. Harry told me that you might know about Steve and Taylor, whether he . . . ?" Annie paused, hoping the older woman would elaborate without much coaxing.

"Whether he beat her? Well, yes, though I don't know details. She thought she was fooling everyone, but not much gets by me. I've seen just about everything in my day. My first husband tried to slap me around once. Ran him off with my daddy's hunting rifle when I was no more than twenty. Never did hear what happened to him. Guess he thought he could do without a wife that was a better shot than he was."

"Did Taylor ever talk to you about it?"

"Oh, no, she's not like that." Edna used a corner of her

apron to wipe an imaginary spot off the table. "Fact, most of the time Taylor was always doing for somebody else. She'd stop in and see Harry two or three times a week, just to make sure that Mimi wasn't driving him crazy. And whenever she was going to Seattle, she'd stop and see if I needed anything. She even made special trips to the Pike Place Market, just to get me fancy vegetables and spices. A real caring attitude, that girl has. You don't often see it in someone of her generation."

Annie smiled. It was a side of Taylor that she had glimpsed back in high school. She remembered the dances where Taylor could have left with a gang of friends, but always made sure Annie was included. And the time they were hiking on the Mount Si trail, and Annie stumbled on a tree root and twisted her ankle. Taylor had been there, helping her down, every painful step of the way.

But there was also another side to Taylor North. There was the Taylor North who telephoned at eleven o'clock the night before a test, desperate for Annie to help her study so she wouldn't flunk. The Taylor who said cruel things about girls she didn't like. The wild Taylor who had to defy the rules, stay out too late, drive too fast. Annie was glad to hear that the caring side seemed to have prevailed as Taylor had matured.

"Do you know if she ever pressed charges against Steve?"

"No, I can't say. . . ."

Seth, his mouth full of apple pie, shook his head. "Couldn't have been," the patrolman mumbled, swallowing. " 'Scuse me. Couldn't have been more than a month ago, Taylor was here in the café on a Saturday morning, picking up pastries like everybody else, and she had those big dark glasses on, even though it was a cloudy day. I could see just a tinge of purple right there at the sides, so I knew she was hiding a shiner, and I told Edna as much. Afterwards, I called one of my buddies over at the sheriff's office and asked if they'd written anything up and they said 'no.' Never did have any domestic complaints from out at North Faire, they said."

"So this time you saw her with a black eye, that would have been *after* Steve moved out?"

"Oh, yeah. I'd say it wasn't more than a month or two ago."

"How did you know it was Steve who hit her?"

Edna stirred her coffee. Her comments were almost identical to Harry's. "It was like she wanted people to know, yet she didn't. I remember that time Seth's talking about. And somebody, might've been the Reverend, asked her how she was and if she'd had a nice week. He was kind of fishing for information, but not too pushy."

"Reverend's real good at that," said Seth. "He gets stuff out of me all the time that I have no intention of telling him."

"Anyways, he asked her in a real gentle way, and she says something ambiguous, like 'Fine, but I could've done without my husband dropping by.' And he says, 'Oh? And how's Steve doing?' and she clams up at that point and says, 'I wouldn't know. I guess you'll have to ask him,' and that was it. Never said nothing about how she got the black eye, but made it real clear to everybody in the place that Steve had been to see her. Believe me, we all got the point."

Seth had finished his pie and was trying to mop up the last smidgen of sauce. "That's pretty typical, from what my buddy at the sheriff's department says. Most of the time, the wives won't even file a complaint. Guess they're afraid the guy might retaliate and make it worse."

Annie nodded. She knew that was typical. But it still bothered her to hear the description applied to Taylor North. She never would have suspected that her friend would fit into that category.

"You said something about all the tragedy Taylor's had in her life?"

Edna nodded. "They say these things run in families. You know Taylor's mama, Lizzy, pulled up stakes and took

the kids to Seattle when they were teenagers? I don't usually like to speak ill of the dead, but Taylor's daddy, Cliff
North, used to get pretty rough with his wife. Everybody
knew it. Now, Lizzy weren't one to confide in anybody, but
I heard from a lady lived down the street that the reason
why she left all of a sudden, not a penny to her name, was
that Cliff had started beating up the kids some, once they
got older. Called it discipline. Back in those days, it was
hard for a divorced woman to get by, but from what I
heard, the judge what heard the case made her a right fair
award."

Annie tried to remember when Taylor and her family
moved to Seattle. She had known Taylor's parents were divorced, but that was about it.

Seth pushed away from the table and looked at his
watch. "Well, I guess I gotta go catch me some speeders."
He put some money on the table. Leaning over, he whispered to Annie, "Know that stretch of Highway 82 between
Granger and Grandview?"

She nodded.

"Speed trap."

"Thanks for the warning."

"Anytime," Seth said as he put on his hat and headed for
the door.

After he left, Annie asked, "So, what do you think,
Edna? Was the situation that bad?"

"I don't know, dear. I do know that there was a craziness
between Steve and Taylor. Darned near every man in town
was at least partways in love with her, but Steve . . . it was
like he had some kind of hold over Taylor. Even after she
threw him out, he was up there all the time. Sometimes to
see her, sometimes just to sneak around. The way he bad-
gered her, gosh, I wouldn't have been surprised if any of
them had wanted to kill him."

"Any of them? Who do you mean?"

Edna chuckled. "Oh, Taylor's men, I tend to think of
them as. She had a way, I don't know. There was just always some man coming to her rescue, whether she needed

it or not. That's just the type of gal she was, she didn't ask for it particularly. Harry Braithwaite, Galen, her brother Gerald, even Martin Grubenmacher. I'd say any one of them would have flown to the moon if she'd wanted them to."

"Martin Grubenmacher? He was the one who invited Steve in the first place."

Edna raised an eyebrow. "The boy has always been a mite strange, if you ask me. He and Taylor went to grade school together, before her folks split up. I remember how some of the older boys teased Martin for the way he felt about Taylor. Like on Valentine's Day, they'd put a valentine in his mailbox and pretend it was from her, just to make him do something embarrassing. You know how silly kids can be, but most of 'em grow out of it. When Taylor moved back to this area, you could see from the way he looked at her that Martin still had a thing for her. Not a real healthy attachment, neither."

Annie finished her soup. "Tell me about Gerald."

Edna thought for a moment. "Gerald North. He's a moody one. Bitter might be a better word. Goes around being quietly angry, like the world has a personal vendetta against him."

"He seemed so concerned about Taylor the other night. I take it they're close?"

"Now they are. Oh, there was a time, back a few years after their daddy died. Almost a year went by when they wasn't speaking. Gerald was sorely miffed about something, some real estate deal that went bad between him and Taylor. Steve was involved, too, somehow. That's when Gerald moved over to Ellensburg, got that teaching job. Yes, I'd say it was a year or so that not a word passed between them."

"But they patched things up, obviously."

The older woman nodded. "It's been fairly recent, I'd say."

"Within the last six months?" Annie asked.

"I couldn't pin it down exactly, but that sounds about

right. In fact, I'm pretty sure that Gerald didn't set foot back in Taylor's house until Steve was out of there." Edna looked at Annie and lowered her voice. "I've no doubt that Harry told you the same thing—nobody in town had much use for Steven Vick. Gerald couldn't stand him, neither could Galen Rockwell. He was a mean-spirited man, and even though I don't have any proof, I believe in my heart that he was the type that'd use his fists on a woman. All I can say is, if our Taylor has to go to prison for defending herself against that awful man, then there's something plain wrong with our system of justice."

Chapter 15

YAKIMA WAS about a fifteen-minute drive from Harmony. Getting off the highway one exit too soon by mistake, Annie drove through a poor residential section where all of the grocery store signs were in Spanish, and the fast-food restaurants advertised menudo.

Annie found the copy center near St. Elizabeth's hospital, about a mile west of downtown, and picked up the documents that Val had faxed. The hospital was in a sprawling red brick building, larger and more modern than Annie had anticipated for a city the size of Yakima. The woman at the information desk directed her to Three-South, Neurology. Carrying the bag with Taylor's things, she followed the maze of corridors, with only a few wrong turns, to the correct ward.

At the nurse's station, a heavyset R.N. with wiry gray hair was busy typing at a computer terminal.

"I've brought some personal items for Taylor North. And I'd like to see her, please, if that's possible."

Not knowing how long Taylor would be at the hospital, Annie hadn't known what to include. She'd brought a nightgown and some changes of underwear, a toothbrush and comb. She'd also brought Taylor's address book, in case she was feeling well enough to make calls. The nurse took the paper bag from Annie and quickly glanced through it. She handed back the address book saying, "Things have a tendency to get lost around here. If it were me, I wouldn't chance my Daytimer getting lost for anything. I'll see that she gets the other items." The nurse marked the number 313 on the bag, set it under her desk, and went back to her computer screen.

"I was wondering if I could see her?" Annie said again.

The nurse spoke without looking up. "And you are . . . ?"

"My name is Annie MacPherson."

"Immediate family?"

"No, I'm a friend."

"Sor-ry." Her voice had the sing-song quality of someone at the end of a long and tiring shift. "I have strict orders that Ms. North is to receive no visitors or telephone calls except family for the next forty-eight hours."

"It will only take five minutes to get her signature on some documents. It's quite important."

The nurse just shrugged, and went on typing.

"Then may I speak to her doctor?"

"Not if you're not immediate family or don't have a signed medical release."

Annie could tell this was not going to be easy. "I'm her attorney. One of the documents I need to have her sign is a release for medical records. If you'd let me see her, then she could sign it, and I'd be able to speak to her doctor."

The nurse went on typing.

"Well, do you know if any of her family members are here?" Annie presumed that Gerald had classes to teach, but she thought that Celia might have taken time away from the winery to come to the hospital. The nurse looked up from her work and glared at Annie over the top of her reading glasses. "Do I look like the social director around here?"

"I'm sorry, I know you're busy, but could you at least tell me what Taylor's condition is? I was told that she had convulsions in the car on the way here, and I just want to know if she's okay." The tired nurse wasn't without sympathy. "Just a second." She pulled up some data on her computer, and frowned. "Her condition is listed as serious. But that's an improvement; this morning it was critical."

Before Annie could try to squeeze more information out of her, the nurse said, "Look, why don't you have a seat over there. Her doctor's on the floor. When he comes by the station, I'll ask him if he'll agree to speak to you."

"Thank you."

Annie took a seat on one of the orange vinyl-covered chairs which, along with simulated wood grain tables, seemed common to hospitals everywhere. Annie also suspected that the same magazines could be found in every waiting room in America—a three-week-old copy of *Time*, fourteen copies of *People*, a dog-eared *Reader's Digest*, and a stack of *Highlights for Children*. Annie could remember looking at those when she went to her pediatrician as a child. They looked old enough to be the same issues.

Annie wasn't pleased to see Detective Shibilsky waddling down the hall holding a cup of vending machine coffee. When he approached, she said, "I assume you're not here to try to interview Taylor, are you? You know she's in no condition to speak to anyone, least of all the authorities."

After he took a gulp, beads of coffee hung on his mustache. "It never hurts to try, Counselor. See, when I know that a 'person of interest' in a homicide case has taken a whole slew of pills, one of the first things I think is that such a person might be feeling just a wee bit guilty, know what I mean? So I kinda like to make myself available for spontaneous confessions. It happens, ya know." He plopped down into the next chair, close enough for her to smell his bad breath and the odor of cigarette smoke on his clothes.

"Well, from now on, Detective, I'm leaving standing instructions on Ms. North's behalf that *no one* from your office is to make any attempt to speak to her unless I'm present. Do you understand?"

He shrugged his shoulders, half in acknowledgment, half in smugness. "Whatever you say, Counselor." Annie turned back to her magazine, hoping Shibilsky would leave. He didn't.

"I've been told we'll get the fingerprint analysis of the wine bottle back this afternoon, in case you're interested."

Annie didn't look up. "I assume since Taylor was found holding the bottle that her prints will be on it. Is that what you're expecting to find, Detective?" She tried to sound nonchalant, but the fact was, any hard evidence would hurt Taylor's defense.

"Yeah, that's what I'm expecting. With that evidence, I could make an arrest, ya know."

"Oh, really?" She held up one hand. "Do you want my prints? I took the bottle away from her and set it on the bench that night. Are you going to arrest me, too?"

"Now that you bring it up, I think the whole thing looks fishy. We don't get many murders where the killer makes sure their attorney is on the premises when it happens. Maybe you were part of the plot."

Annie thought Shibilsky was joking, but couldn't be entirely sure. She went back to her magazine, pretending not to be interested. She didn't think sparring with Shibilsky would get her anywhere. "I'm sure once you complete your investigation, there will be no need for any arrests. This was clearly a case of self-defense. You took statements from a number of people at the party who heard Steven Vick threaten Taylor. And if you check his background, I'm sure you'll find it wasn't the first time."

Shibilsky flipped back through his notes. "Those 'threats' as you call them were pretty vague, as I recall. And you also seem to be forgetting that *she* followed *him* out to the garden, not the other way around. Nah, I haven't had a homicide this easy in years. Even if your client hadn't been found holding a smoking gun, as they say, it all points to her."

"Oh, really?" Annie said blandly. She was actually anxious to know what Shibilsky had on Taylor, but figured he'd say more if she feigned disinterest.

"My guys have been checking this Steven Vick guy out.

Seems he didn't have a whole lot else going on in his life. No major debts, except some credit cards. No history of gambling or womanizing or drugs. Drank a little, mostly at home. Six months ago, the old lady threw him out, and he got a furnished room in a boardinghouse here in town. Nothing but a bed, dresser, and TV. No personal papers. No drugs. Nothing to indicate he was in any trouble. Neighbors said he was pretty quiet. Till a few months ago, he worked selling chemicals. Guys he worked with said it was pretty boring stuff. Nobody there he ticked off. Last few months, he's been unemployed, looking for a few jobs."

Shibilsky stretched, and drained the rest of his coffee. "Now, would you look at that," he said, snickering. He showed her his vending machine cup patterned with playing cards. "I got a full house. Guess that means I'm gonna have a run of good luck on this case."

"There are lots of hands that beat a full house, Detective."

"Yeah," he grinned. "And you wish you had one of them." He pulled a business card out of his wallet. "I want you to have this number handy in case your client wants to make a confession. You tell her I hope she's feeling better. And, uh, call me later this afternoon, if you want to know what we find on that wine bottle. I should be there till six."

Annie pocketed the card, as Shibilsky ambled down the hall, depositing his paper cup on the nurses' station as he passed.

The gray-haired nurse wasn't at the desk. Annie stood, then walked down the hall toward room 313. She glanced in. The bed nearest the door was empty, and the privacy curtain shielded her view of the bed near the window. Annie quietly stepped into the room.

There was Taylor, asleep, with her mouth slightly open. Her color was bad, and the hair on her pillow looked limp and matted, as if she had perspired all night. The side of her face where she'd fallen was discolored and slightly swollen. The sight brought tears to Annie's eyes.

For seventeen years, Annie had tried not to think about

Taylor North. Now she couldn't help wondering if she should have tried harder back then to convince Taylor that Steve was trouble. She wondered if things would have turned out differently.

Annie felt a tap on her shoulder. A bearded young man in a white lab coat gestured her out into the hall. "Ms. MacPherson? I'm Dr. Butterick, Taylor North's physician. The nurse said you wanted to speak to me?"

"Yes. How is she doing?"

The doctor shook his head. "She's not out of the woods yet, by any means. Most people have no idea how toxic an aspirin overdose can be, and in this case, combined with Tylenol and codeine . . . all I can say is we're doing everything we can. I wish I could tell you more."

The doctor's tentative tone prompted Annie to ask, "Is there anything else wrong?"

"Well, we simply don't know. She's been quite delirious, and that could be due to the overdose, but there have also been significant cognitive problems for which we've been unable to identify the etiology. When her physical condition stabilizes, she'll be scheduled for a complete neuropsychiatric battery. And she'll be monitored for depression, of course."

Annie was at a loss for words. In school, she had always felt shy and inexperienced compared to Taylor, hoping some of her friend's audacity and self-confidence would rub off. That Taylor would be depressed and confused was as hard for her to grasp as the idea of Taylor as a battered spouse.

"What do you mean by cognitive problems?"

"Her memory is quite bad. She knows who she is, she knows she's in a hospital. But she has no idea how she got here. I asked her what the last thing she remembered was, and she said it was dressing to go out. That wouldn't be an atypical response if she had had a head injury." The doctor looked into Taylor's room. "I'd prefer that you not wake her. She needs rest."

Annie explained that she had some legal documents for Taylor to sign, and wondered when she might come back.

"She really isn't in any condition to sign anything, with the mental confusion and all. You'll probably want to speak to her brother, Gerald. It was my understanding that he was going to obtain a court order giving him power of attorney while she was incapacitated. If so, then I believe that he could sign those legal documents for you."

Annie nodded. She didn't have Gerald's home number, but should be able to reach him at the college. "Doctor, when will you know if Taylor's going to be all right?"

He looked at his hands. "I don't like to sugarcoat things, and I'm not doing that now. As far as the toxins in her system, I'm fairly confident that we started treatment soon enough, and that she's going to come through this without any significant kidney damage." He took a deep breath. "What has me confused is the mental state. The memory problems and confusion bother me. On that score, I have to say I simply don't know what to tell you."

Chapter 16

GERALD NORTH'S BUSINESS CARD listed him as an associate professor of fine arts at Central Washington University in Ellensburg, about thirty miles from Yakima. Annie drove north and found the college town without too much trouble.

As she drove through town, Annie wished she had more time to look around. The architecture and businesses of the small town reflected the hard-working, no-nonsense pioneer practicality of its founders, but the college had brought with it an artistic and academic influence. Antique shops and art galleries alternated with stores selling hardware, insurance, and tractors.

It was close to three o'clock—office hours, according to Gerald's card—when Annie parked on the edge of the red-brick and tree-shaded campus, and wandered around until she found the art department building. When Gerald saw Annie in his office doorway, he quickly removed the wire-framed glasses he was wearing and slipped them into a pocket. Even though he was wearing "work clothes," Annie could tell this was a man who cared about his appearance. His white painter's pants and black T-shirt were old and stained with paint, but still showed off an athletic build. A thin gold chain at his neck highlighted his tan. Annie could tell that Gerald's hair was permed; she wondered if he had it frosted as well.

Gerald recognized her, but didn't smile. "Annie. My secretary told me you'd called, but I didn't expect you so

soon. Please, have a seat, such as it is. You can move that
pile of books onto the floor."

Gerald's office couldn't have been more than eight feet
square, and most of it was taken up by a large metal draft-
ing table and adjustable stool. The walls were covered with
what Annie assumed were student artworks, judging from
the vast variety of styles and degrees of talent. Annie
moved a pile of art books, revealing a canvas director's
chair that had seen better days. She sat down tentatively, relieved when she didn't hear the frayed seat tear.

"I've been at the hospital," said Annie. "Taylor's doctor
said she was in pretty bad shape."

"Yes, I've spoken to him a number of times today. I
guess what's troubling him is that the mental confusion and
memory loss don't appear to be related to the drug overdose, but might imply a head injury. I've hardly been able
to concentrate myself, thinking about her in the hospital."
Gerald fidgeted with a paper clip on his desk. Annie noticed that his hands were large but graceful. The paint
under his fingernails and soaked into his cuticles probably
never came clean.

"When I was at the hospital, that homicide detective,
Shibilsky, was there."

"Christ, that bastard won't leave her alone. Did he try to
talk to her again?"

"He would have liked to, but the doctor wouldn't let
him, and I left firm instructions that he was not to talk to
her under any circumstances without an attorney present."

Gerald rubbed his face. "The man's an idiot. I can't
believe he would actually charge her with murder. It was
self-defense. Anybody could see that."

"That was one of the reasons I came to see you. The doctor said you were going to obtain a power of attorney—"

"Oh, that's all taken care of. Taylor's not fit to make any
kind of decision right now. After talking to her doctor, I've
got no idea what she is going to be able to manage. And
while she's in the hospital, there's still a business to run.
Harvest is the busiest time at the winery. Decisions have to

be made, supplies purchased. And I wasn't about to let that Rockwell character have free rein with the checkbook. Not with his history." He laughed bitterly. "I guess you could say I'm protecting the family jewels."

"I can understand your concern." Annie pulled out the documents Val had faxed her. "That's the reason I stopped by. I'm not going to mince words. Taylor is in serious legal trouble. What I want from you is clear authority to represent her in any criminal action that may be brought." She handed Gerald the retainer agreement.

"I thought that was all taken care of. Didn't she already write you a check?"

"Yes, and I don't need any additional funds at this time. But Taylor asked me to help her deal with Steve. At the time we talked, I assumed she meant a dissolution action, possibly getting a restraining order. We never discussed what would happen if Steve turned up dead. She can certainly change attorneys later, but I'm worried about Detective Shibilsky. He's tough, and he would like nothing better than to arrest Taylor for murder. If it's clear that I'm representing her, then we can make sure her rights are protected."

Gerald paused for a moment, then picked up his pen and signed the agreement. "And these other documents?"

"Those are releases to obtain Taylor's medical and financial records. If they charge her, the prosecutor's office will be able to subpoena anything they think is relevant. I need to have access to the same information."

Gerald looked hesitant, but signed the papers and handed them back to Annie. "I appreciate your help in this. Now, at least I feel like someone else is bearing some of the responsibility for getting us out of this horrible situation."

Annie took the papers and put them back in the manila envelope. She certainly hoped Gerald didn't think she was acting on *his* behalf as well. Frankly, she wasn't sure she trusted Taylor's brother. As distracted as he was by the "horrible situation," he had certainly acted quickly enough to gain power over Taylor's business.

They were interrupted by a student tapping timidly on the door frame. She looked about eighteen, and wore an Indian print skirt and Birkenstocks with pink anklets. She smiled shyly at Gerald. "Hi, Professor North."

"Carolyn, are you finally bringing in your mid-term project?"

The girl blushed. "No. I came by to see if I could get another extension. I just can't seem to get it right."

"That's always one of the problems with a work of art. But at some point, you have to admit that it may not be right, but it's going to have to be *done*. Come by tomorrow with whatever you have and we can talk about it."

After the student left, Annie said, "You seem very patient. Do you enjoy teaching?"

"To be blunt, no. But I try not to let my personal feelings impact the students. The truth is, most of them will never amount to anything artistically. The classes are such a royal waste of time. The talented ones—they'll do well if they never have a lesson in their life. And the others, the good ones will end up designing ads for the local paper, or selling paintings at a street fair." He shook his head in disgust. "But that's not all. I accept the fact that I'll never make a living selling my art. But the worst of it is, I can't even make a decent living *teaching*. The status of the visual arts is so dismal in this country, I'm reduced to *this*." He pointed to a black portfolio on the corner of his desk. "Go ahead, look."

Annie opened the portfolio. Inside were a dozen matted watercolors, ready for framing. She didn't recognize the signature. "They're very nice. Did one of your students do these?"

Gerald snorted. "Nice. Would you buy something like that?"

"I might. Maybe for my office."

"When I'm not wasting my time teaching mediocre students, that's my other form of prostitution. I hate to admit it, but those are mine."

"But they're good."

He scowled. "No, they're not. It's tourist art. I won't even put my real name on them. I use my pseudonym, my *nom de junque*. I turn out three or four of these a week, and they sell quickly. One has to make money to live somehow." He looked at his watch. "I really need to drop these by the framer before four. If you have a few minutes, walk with me. I'd like to show you something."

Intrigued, Annie accompanied Gerald a few blocks to the frame shop in the historic part of town, where he dropped off the portfolio. He then led her upstairs to Gallery One. At the top of two long flights of stairs, the atrium of the gallery was flooded with natural light from five skylights. The walls were white, and the hardwood floors of the individual rooms that had once been offices were painted in subtle pastels. The displays of paintings, sculpture, jewelry, and crafts were as fine as any Annie had seen in Seattle. Gerald showed her to a room near the front. There, half a dozen large oil paintings each bore the tightly legible signature, "Gerald North."

Annie walked around the room, examining each painting. Four were abstract landscapes, and two were nude portraits. They were stunning, and she told him so. Unlike the "tourist art," as he had called his commercial watercolor paintings, these were filled with tension, emotion, and drama. The landscapes perfectly captured the indescribable quality of light that Annie had noticed since she'd been east of the Cascades. Each work was priced at over two thousand dollars. When Annie looked back at Gerald, the expression on his face was one of thinly veiled anger, or maybe resentment.

"These are absolutely incredible. But I take it, the sales aren't enough for you to live on?"

He grunted. "No. Few fine artists can. Add to that the stigma in the art community against representational art, and you see sales that are even lower. And it's not like I live high on the hog. I rent an attic room from another professor in town. I eat frugally. I don't spend money on travel or luxuries. But still, I can't make enough to have the time

for the kind of work I want to do. *Need* to do. As it is, half
the time I feel like an imposter in the classroom. I'm trying
to show these children what it is to be an artist, when most
of the time all I'm doing is turning out commercialized
crap."

Hearing Gerald complain about money, Annie wondered
about something. "I can't remember, Gerald. Are you one
year older or one year younger than Taylor?"

"Older. Why?"

"Oh, nothing, really." It didn't seem like a good time to
ask, but she wondered why Taylor had inherited the winery
from their father, instead of her older brother. When Gerald
had spoken of the winery he had seemed bitter, but maybe
that was just his manner.

Gerald looked up at the clock on the wall. "Well, I have
to be getting back. My life drawing workshop at the School
for the Terminally Unskilled will be starting soon."

Annie wasn't sorry. Gerald's pessimism was starting to
grate on her nerves. Her car was parked near his office, and
she walked back with him in silence, and said good-bye at
his office. She realized that since he'd signed her documents, he had not mentioned his sister's condition once.

Annie remembered that Detective Shibilsky said he
would have the fingerprint analysis back, and she wanted to
know what she assumed would be bad news. The art department secretary gave Annie directions to the pay phone
in the next building, where Annie called Shibilsky. She was
put through immediately when she gave her name.

"Hey, MacPherson, it's about time you called me. I been
calling all over for you, couldn't find where you'd gotten
to."

"Is something wrong? Are you arresting Taylor?"

"Nah, that's why I wanted to reach you. We got a new
development here. There's a guy here named Harry Braithwaite, says he's a friend a yours. Big guy, real talkative?"

"Yes."

"Well, here's the thing. He's here at the department,
wants to make some kinda statement. Says it's vital to our

investigation of the case, but he insists on talking to you first."

"Put him on."

"Nah, he says it's gotta be in person. How soon can you be here?"

Annie explained that she was in Ellensburg, but could leave right away. "I should be there in half an hour."

"All right. But put a move on it. Frankly, I think this guy's a bit loony, and we all want to get this thing done with and get out of here."

Chapter 17

ANNIE MADE IT BACK to Yakima in record time. As she sped along, pushing the Fiat to its maximum speed of almost eighty, she hoped that this stretch of highway was part of Seth Longacre's jurisdiction. Fortunately, the need to fix a traffic ticket didn't arise.

The Yakima County Sheriff's Department was in an ugly chrome and sandstone building on North Second. If the county had any extra money in the budget, it obviously didn't go to giving its employees an attractive work environment. She gave her name to the deputy manning the switchboard, and was quickly ushered into a conference room near the back. There was a tape recorder on the table, as well as a video camera set up in the corner. Detective Shibilsky was already seated at the green metal table reading the sports section from *USA Today*, the last remnants of a powdered sugar donut clinging to his mustache, and a 24-ounce Dunkin' Donuts coffee cup by his side. Annie knew she drank a lot of coffee, but the thought of a tumbler full of tepid, weak coffee from a donut shop made her stomach churn.

"You know, I'm starting to think there aren't any other lawyers in this town, MacPherson. If you stick around, all our local shysters are gonna end up on unemployment." The detective's oily smirk made Annie want to slap him.

"You know perfectly well I'm here as Mr. Braithwaite's

friend, not his attorney. Not that there's any reason why he should need one."

"Oh, I wouldn't be too sure about that."

"What do you mean?"

"After I got off the phone with you, and knew you had to come all the way from friggin' Ellensburg, I went back to try and find out what this jackass wanted to talk to us about, 'cause very frankly, I didn't want to wait around for you to get your fanny down here if this character was just going to regale us with some charming story about how he knew Taylor North when she was a sweet little girl. If that was the case, I was going to tell him to go on home, and we'd catch up with him later. That's when he told me what was goin' down here."

Annie was extremely tired, which only made Detective Shibilsky seem more tedious. "And what is that?"

He chuckled, though it sounded more like a hiccup. "He says he's going to confess to the murder of Steven Vick."

Annie was shocked. "And you believed him?"

"Why wouldn't I? I haven't heard what the old guy has to say yet."

"I think I had better speak to Mr. Braithwaite now."

"That's what we been waitin' on you for." He turned the page of his paper. "Take all the time you want. This confession's gonna save me and the county a few weeks' work, so I guess I can sit here for another few minutes." He bellowed into the hall for a deputy. A female officer who was no more than five foot two but looked as solid as a freight train showed Annie to another small conference room where Harry was sitting, engrossed in a back issue of *National Geographic*. The large man looked a little tired, but otherwise not too bad. His bristly salt-and-pepper hair was no more unruly than when she'd spoken to him that morning. He reached across the table and wrapped Annie's hands in his. "Thank you for coming, my dear. It means an awful lot to me to have you here. I would have preferred Taylor to be here as well, but her doctors wouldn't permit it. She's still under strict observation, from what I understand. Although they said her liver and kidney function studies were looking better."

Annie rubbed her eyes. "Harry, Taylor's doing as well as can be expected, but I'm not here to talk about her. The detective just told me you wanted to *confess* to Steve's murder? Would you tell me, please, what's going on here? You didn't have anything to do with Steve's death!"

"Oh, but I did, you see. I was lying to you when we discussed it this morning. I finally realized that trying to save myself was futile. It was time to do the right thing and turn myself in."

"Now, wait a minute." Annie tried another tack. "You've got responsibilities, Harry. What about Mimi? Without you there to exert some control, anything could—"

He shook his head. "Mimi's gone. She told me this afternoon that she's quitting school and going to L.A. to be with her boyfriend and his rock band. She insisted that I drive her to the bus station."

"Correct me if I'm wrong, but wasn't it just yesterday at the Wine Gala that she was bemoaning the fact that she didn't have the money to get out there?"

Sighing, he said, "She's been harping about wanting this money for three months, and suddenly, she's gotten it from somewhere. A thousand dollars. She even showed it to me, in hundred dollar bills. I have no doubt she obtained it illegally, but I'm afraid I no longer have the energy to fight with her."

"And your daughter?"

"Violetta sent her love in a wedding announcement from Mazatlán. Silly me, and I thought she was still in Europe. This makes husband number five, if I'm counting correctly. He's a waiter in one of the hotels. Twenty-eight years old and quite dashing, by her account. She hopes he learns English soon."

Annie reached across the table and took his hand. "Is that why you're doing this, Harry? Because of your daughter and granddaughter? Are you trying to get back at them?"

He pulled his hand away, and sat up straight. "I'm doing this because I'm guilty. I killed Steven Vick. It was right after he had his argument with you at the Gala. Galen took Taylor upstairs, you and Celia went to the ladies' room, and I followed Steven Vick and Martin Grubenmacher out to the garden. They spoke for a few moments, a bit hostilely, then Grubenmacher left. Vick was pacing, seemed to be waiting for someone. That's when I did it. Popped him over the head with a bottle."

"Why, Harry?"

"Because the man was an insufferable bastard, that's why." His voice softened. "And because I didn't want him hurting Taylor anymore."

"But she was going to divorce him, Harry. She was going to get a restraining order—"

"You, of all people, should know that the courts offer an inadequate measure of protection against such violence. Steve's type always comes back. No piece of paper can prevent that. Come on, I don't want to argue about this. Let's go put it on candid camera."

Annie stopped Harry again, and insisted that he at least discuss the case with another attorney. "You know I can't represent you, Harry. I'm Taylor's attorney. It would be a conflict of interest."

"And I'm not asking you to. I fully understand my right to see an attorney, and have waived that right. I just wanted you here as a friend, and as Taylor's proxy. As I told you, I would have wanted her to be here."

Back in the main conference room, Annie stated for the record that she was not acting as Professor Braithwaite's attorney, but had strongly urged him to retain counsel. Detective Shibilsky reiterated Harry's rights, and they began, both tape recorder and video camera recording Harry's confession.

Shibilsky asked Harry about the incident, and initially obtained the same brief account that Harry had given Annie a few minutes earlier. Harry had followed Vick out to the garden, waited until Martin Grubenmacher left, then struck him on the head with a bottle. His reason: he didn't want Vick to do any further harm to Taylor.

"Was Taylor North there when you struck the blow?"

"No, she arrived after Vick was on the ground. She was quite upset, very shaken, and pulled the bottle from my hands. She then sat down on the ground, cross-legged-style, with the bottle in her lap. She was moaning slightly."

Annie cringed at the description. She, herself, had inadvertently divulged that information to Harry.

"And then what did you do?"

"I didn't know what else to do. I heard someone coming, learning later that it was Gerald North, Taylor's brother, who had arrived at the party late. But because it was quite dark, I was able to slip unobtrusively into the shadows, and make my way back to the house. It was a selfish and heartless thing to do, leaving poor Taylor there like that."

Shibilsky slurped his coffee, unmoved by Harry's story. "I need a little more detail about Vick. Tell me everything you can. How you hit him, where you were standing, where he was standing, how he fell, all that stuff."

Harry ran a hand through his hair and took a deep breath. For a long moment he paused, holding his fingers to his temples like a charlatan psychic in a sideshow.

"After Martin Grubenmacher left, Vick was standing and looking out in the direction of the parking lot. As I said, I thought he was waiting for someone. He wasn't moving, just standing, feet slightly apart. I crept up behind him, a little to the left because I'm right-handed. Now, I'm quite a bit taller than Vick, and because I wanted the blow to hit the base of the skull, not the top, I didn't raise my arm too high. I took the bottle in both hands, and swung it like a baseball bat. Wham, leading with my left hand. I describe this in detail, you see, because from the angle of the blow, you might have assumed that a much shorter person was responsible." He paused, looking pleased with his description. "And of course I was wearing gloves, so you will not find my fingerprints on the bottle."

"Gloves, huh. What kind of gloves?"

"Leather driving gloves. I had them in the pocket of my jacket, you see."

"Right. Okay. So you hit him. How did he fall? Quick, slow?"

"There was a slight pause, like the blow was registering, then he fell to his knees, and rolled backwards and onto his side. The position, viewed from the side would be almost like that of a man praying. And I could see at that point a thin trickle of blood running from the corner of his mouth."

"Which corner?"

"Er, the left."

"Yeah?" Shibilsky sat up, no longer as uninterested, and Annie knew why. Having been one of the few people to see the body that night, she knew his description of the position and the blood was accurate. The deputy who had arrived shortly thereafter had kept the rest of the party guests away from the scene. In describing what had happened, Annie knew that she had not told Harry about the appearance of the body.

"How much blood?" the detective asked.

"Just a thin line, as I said, running from the left corner of his mouth over his chin. And his head was in an awkward position, making me wonder if I'd broken his neck."

His description so far was completely accurate, making Annie sure that Harry must have, indeed, seen Steven Vick's body. He would not have been able to guess with such unerring detail. And since the scene was well controlled after Gerald, Annie, and Taylor had left it, the only time he could have seen it was before Gerald discovered the body.

"What about hands and legs?"

Harry closed his eyes in concentration. "The hands were forward of the body, together, as I said, almost in a prayer position; the hips were bent at a slight angle, but the knees were closer to ninety degrees. The right foot, which was the side closest to the ground, was just slightly behind the left, or top, foot."

"Anything else?"

"Isn't that enough?"

"I want everything you can think of. Any detail, no matter how small. What was Vick wearing?"

"What was he wearing? Let me think . . . a suit, navy blue, I believe. White shirt. Can't recall his tie."

"Anything else?"

"Yes, actually. I don't know why I noticed this, but Vick's socks were the most unpleasant shade of mustard-yellow."

Annie couldn't listen to any more. Before Shibilsky could ask another question, she interrupted the interview and requested that the tapes be stopped.

Shibilsky sputtered, his face beet-red, and turned off both tapes. "What the hell is this all about? We're almost through here, and from what I've heard, this case is wrapped up. You got a problem with that? They must do things differently on the other side of the mountains if you're *upset* that your client's name is getting cleared."

"I'm sorry, Detective. I'm obligated to act in the best interests of my client, but that does not include letting an innocent man commit perjury. Based upon what I've just heard, there is absolutely no way that Professor Braithwaite could be telling the truth."

Chapter 18

THE DUNKIN' DONUTS COFFEE spilled across the Formica table as Shibilsky gestured wildly. Annie jumped up to keep the brew from dripping onto her lap. Shibilsky got the deputy to wait in the conference room with Harry while he asked Annie to step out into the hall.

"Look, MacPherson, I agreed to let you sit in because, and only because, the old guy insisted on it before he'd make a statement. I don't remember giving you permission to butt in. I saw the crime scene with my own eyes, and this guy's description is dead on. Now, unless some damn fool gave him a *complete rundown* on what the scene looked like—and I know none of *my* people would've done that—then we got a valid confession here. So what are you doing messin' with my case, huh?"

Annie waited a beat, then asked, "Are you through?"

Shibilsky was still red in the face and bouncing from foot to foot, but his breathing had started to slow. Annie was slightly taller than Shibilsky, and she knew it aggravated him to have to look up at her. "Yeah, I'm damn well through."

"Good. Because it's important to me that you thank Professor Braithwaite for his time in coming down here, and send him home. The man is innocent. I don't know why he's doing this, but if you accept his confession, you'll be suborning perjury and destroying an innocent man's life. I'm fully aware that this does not help my client, but I can't let you arrest Harry."

Shibilsky punched a balled-up fist into his hand. "I presume you're going to tell me why?"

"Harry Braithwaite has just described the crime scene in extremely accurate detail, even down to the color of Steven Vick's socks. You remember that I saw the crime scene as well, when Taylor's brother and I went out there before your deputy arrived. Because of the amount of detail Harry was giving in answer to your questions, I think it's highly unlikely that anyone described the scene to Harry. I'd be willing to bet that he saw it with his own eyes."

"There, now you're admitting what I just—"

"But he's not describing the crime scene at the time of the murder."

Shibilsky leveled his gaze at Annie. "And I presume you're—"

"Going to tell you why. I am. Gerald North and I were the only ones that night to see the body before the sheriff's department arrived. It was so dark, we could barely see the path to walk on, much less the color of Steve's socks. Even with Gerald North's cigarette lighter, I barely saw the blood on Vick's face. The kind of detail that Harry was describing was only visible after the lights were turned on. The crime scene wasn't visible from the main floor of the house, but it could be seen clearly from the second story, as you know."

"But I had my men watching the stairs. Braithwaite never came to the second floor."

"And were your men guarding the stairs to the Widow's Perch?"

Shibilsky looked like he didn't want to ask. "The widow's what?"

"There's a circular staircase with an exterior door at the northwest corner of the house. It goes up four flights to a small observation room. Harry was the one who told me about it, when I spoke to him earlier in the evening before Steven Vick arrived. After Steve threw the glass at me, I went to the ladies' room to clean up. When I returned to the party, I looked for Harry but I couldn't find him anywhere. That surprised me, because with his height, he shouldn't be a difficult person to find in a crowd."

"So you're saying he could have seen everything from up in the tower?"

"He probably had a much better view than from the second floor. But only *after* the garden was illuminated. Before that, you might have been able to see movement and shadows, but not much more. Certainly not color."

Without another word, Shibilsky returned to the conference room. "All right, Professor Braithwaite. You're free to go."

"But you can't let me go. I killed a man in cold blood. You . . . you have to lock me up."

"No can do. Now it's late, we all need to get home."

Annie walked Harry to where his car was parked in front of the building. His shoulders were slumped in resignation. Looking down at the car, he said, "When I drove down here, I wasn't sure what to do with this old beater, because I assumed I would not be going home again. So I had the brilliant idea of parking it at a meter. The city would then have to impound it, and eventually sell it at auction. Brilliant, eh?"

"Harry, tell me what was going on in there? Does Taylor mean that much to you that you would go to prison yourself to protect her?"

"Does she mean that much to me?" He sighed, and leaned against the car. "Yes, I have to say she does. In the last few years, I've pictured myself as something of a King Lear type, with these three young women, Taylor, Mimi, and Violetta, as my surrogate daughters. And, like Lear, two of them—the ones I had the misfortune of being biologically related to—have been as unfeeling and selfish as Regan and Goneril ever dreamed of being. And then there was Taylor, as sweet and kind as Cordelia, as loving as any natural daughter. How could I refuse anything she needed?"

"But this, Harry? Confessing to a murder you didn't commit?"

"I'm not a young man, Annie. I've had a varied and interesting life, but I'm not sure how many good years I have left. My ancestors haven't been a particularly long-lived bunch. My father had a heart attack at sixty-eight, my mother succumbed to lung cancer at seventy-one." He placed his hand at the base of his rib cage. "I've been having a terrible pain here the last two to three weeks. I haven't been to a doctor, so I don't know what it means. Frankly, I don't want to know. But if it is the first sign of a debilitating illness, then I figured that I might as well spend my last years in prison as anywhere else. I've heard the health care benefits are superb. But for Taylor, it would be so different, you see."

Annie took hold of the hand he held out. "Don't give up too soon, Harry."

"Give up. Ha!" His laugh was a cross between a bellow and a bark. "I wouldn't be giving up. I think prison would be a fascinating place to spend a few years. Think of the stories I'd hear. But you were too quick for me. You caught me in my little white lie."

"A confession to murder is hardly a little white lie, Harry. You know I couldn't let you sacrifice yourself for the real killer. Even if it is Taylor."

"Ah, but that's the rub, you see. I was protecting Taylor from prosecution, because I believe the state will eventually come up with a strong case against her. But she's *not guilty*!" Harry's eyes were twinkling with excitement.

Annie remembered the tower. "Did you see something you haven't told me, Harry?" she asked skeptically.

He glanced from one side to the other. "I would have told you sooner, but I was afraid that my testimony would hurt Taylor's case more than it helped it. I did go up to the tower that night, as you suspected." He paused dramatically.

"And?"

"It was dark, to be sure, but I could see shapes and movement."

"But it was pitch-black, Harry."

"Trust me on this, Annie. I could see what was happening. And more than that. Voices carried. I could hear a little of what was being said. I saw Steven Vick and Martin Grubenmacher go out to the garden and talk for a few moments. Steve was arguing with him, couldn't understand what they were doing out there. He wanted to go back inside and talk to Taylor. Grubenmacher said he'd send her out. He insisted that Steve wait right where he was. Grubenmacher went in, and a few minutes later, Taylor came out. All I could see was the glint of her white blouse. She stumbled a bit on the path, looked like she might be slightly inebriated, but maybe she just couldn't see the path. She went up to Vick, said something like, 'I got your message that you wanted to talk to me.' He said something about 'knowing,' he knew something, and I got the impression he was asking her for money. She was crying, or angry, I couldn't tell. Said she didn't understand. It was a very fragmented conversation.

"Then before I knew it, they were struggling. It's hard to say who started it, but my guess would have been Taylor. She was beating on his chest with both hands."

"Both hands?" Annie asked.

"Yes. No wine bottle. She was barehanded. He was trying to hold her back. The next part happened so fast, it was hard to tell what was happening. She swung at him, and Steve pushed Taylor away, hard enough that she fell to the ground. That's probably where she cut and bruised her face. But before she could get up, something moved in the bushes behind Steve, it must have been a person dressed in dark clothes, but I couldn't really see anything. I saw a glint, perhaps a reflection from a bottle, and then Steve went down to his knees, and fell over, much like I described it in there."

"And Taylor?"

"She was on the ground the entire time. Only after Steve was down did she get up and go over to him. I heard her cry out when she realized he was dead. She bent down, and it was hard to see, but I suspect that's when she picked up the wine bottle."

"And the other figure?"

"I saw motion in the direction of the parking lot. And then it was as if it were a spirit disappearing into thin air. Nothing."

Annie was dumbfounded. "You're telling me you *witnessed* Steve's murder, and you haven't told anyone?"

"I'm telling you now."

"But Harry—"

He shrugged. "It sounds so preposterous, who would have believed me? They'd say I was just making up a story to save Taylor. But unless I could name the person who really swung that bottle, they'd still go after Taylor. Frankly, I thought my confession would be far more effective. I think it would have worked, too, if I'd kept it simpler, and hadn't gotten so carried away with details."

Annie closed her eyes. "Harry, are you telling the truth now?"

"See, see what I mean? Even *you* don't believe me. Do you think I could march back into that conference room and persuade that detective I was telling the truth?"

Annie sincerely doubted it. For that matter, she sincerely doubted the whole story. Harry had already demonstrated that he would do anything to protect Taylor. And if she encouraged him to tell Shibilsky what he had just told her, it would sound even more trumped-up. All of a sudden Annie felt very tired.

"Harry, I can't advise you on this. You saw what you saw, and you'll have to do what you think is right about coming forward." And please let it be the truth, she thought to herself. "But it's getting late. Why don't you go on home tonight?"

He sighed, and had to agree she was right. Annie watched as his car pulled away, then walked back to the parking lot where she had parked her car. As she was putting her key in the door, she heard footsteps behind her and turned around.

"MacPherson, you still here?"

Annie was not thrilled to see it was Detective Shibilsky. He was grinning. "Quite an interesting scene in there, wasn't it?"

"You don't seem as upset as you were a few minutes ago."

"Upset? Now why should I be upset? Those crime lab results I was telling you about? They came in while we were wasting our precious time with that Braithwaite character." He snickered. "Do you want the bad news now, or should I wait till morning?"

Annie had a hunch he wasn't about to wait. She was right.

"The fingerprint analysis showed a match to your client's right hand—three fingers and a thumb print. And guess what else?"

Annie was quiet. She was in no mood for guessing games.

Shibilsky could barely contain his glee. "I got the autopsy results, too. Microfibers—I love this shit. You want to hear it?"

"I'm waiting."

"They found microfibers of paper and ink embedded in the head wound—an exact match for the label on that North Faire bottle we took from *your client's* lap."

Annie took a deep breath. She knew what was coming. "Go on."

"Nah, you're ahead of me already, I can tell. I don't really need to tell you I'm ready to charge Taylor North with the murder of her husband, Steven Vick. I'll have the warrant issued in the morning, just as soon as I clear it with the prosecutor."

Chapter 19

ANNIE WOKE UP Thursday morning feeling hungover, but it wasn't from drinking too much wine. This case was moving too quickly. It had all started with her wish to help Taylor, to make up for what had happened in the past, but now Annie wasn't sure she was up to the task. If Shibilsky was telling the truth, Taylor was about to be charged with her husband's murder, and Annie had nothing in the way of a defense. Self-defense would be hard to prove, as Steve had no weapon, and there were no witnesses to say that he assaulted her. Harry's version of events—a mysterious stranger in black appearing from the shadows—would probably leave a jury snickering, not to mention the fact that any prosecutor worth her salt would destroy Harry's credibility on cross-examination. Annie's only other theory—a battered-woman's-syndrome defense—would only work if Taylor could come up with convincing evidence of a pattern of abuse. Corroboration from third parties and Taylor's medical records would be critical.

Annie placed herself in the prosecutor's shoes for a moment. What evidence would the State present to make its case? There was significant circumstantial evidence linking Taylor to the crime—she was found at the scene in a distressed state, cradling in her lap what could be proven to be the murder weapon. Then, shortly after the body was discovered, Taylor took an overdose of medications, in an amount easily sufficient to kill her. The State's attorney would want to supplement that evidence with motive, which would not be hard to do. Steve and Taylor were separated, and the wife had just that day retained an attorney to stop the husband from harassing her. But here was the clincher, Annie thought. With few marital assets except the winery, a divorce with its division of community property would almost certainly destroy the business Taylor had worked so hard to build.

If she had been analyzing this case as a prosecutor, Annie would have predicted that the chance of a conviction was high. But Annie wasn't prosecuting this case. She was trying to defend a friend, whom she believed in her heart should not go to prison for striking back at the husband who tormented her. Knowing Steven Vick as she did, Annie had no doubt that he had made Taylor's life a living hell. The problem was, she didn't know how to prove it.

Annie telephoned the hospital and learned that Taylor was much improved physically, although they still wouldn't know for a day or two about permanent kidney damage from the overdose. Her mental state was another question. Her memory was still gone for the night of the Gala, and she was confused and listless. There was no possibility that she would be released for at least a week, but she would be able to see visitors briefly that evening.

Annie next tried Detective Shibilsky's office, to find out the progress of the arrest warrant. She was able to learn from an assistant only that Shibilsky had been called out of town for a few days, and had not left any written instructions regarding the Steven Vick investigation, or any arrest warrants. Annie was relieved. That gave her at least a couple more days to follow leads before Taylor was officially charged.

The one person Annie hadn't talked to since the murder was Celia Vick, Taylor and Steve's daughter. She had said in a news interview that her father was a violent man, and that she, herself, was afraid of him. Celia might be an important witness if she could back up the rumors that Steve had abused Taylor.

The two cottages were located on the gravel drive between the main house and the road, and looked like they had once been outbuildings to hold farm equipment or supplies. The smaller one, where Celia lived, was about the size of a two-car garage. Seeing a light on inside, Annie knocked.

Celia Vick opened the door with a ready smile, then looked surprised, as if she had been expecting someone else. She wore a skin-hugging maroon turtleneck and pleated wool slacks, a conservative outfit that nevertheless showed off her slim figure. "Oh, Annie . . . hi." Her voice was tentative.

Annie noticed Celia's purse and keys on a chair by the door. "I'm sorry, were you on your way out?"

"Um, yeah, actually. But you can come along if you like. Galen Rockwell is going to be giving Dr. Marchand a tour of the winery. I was just going to tag along. Why don't you come?"

Annie agreed, not sure if she was doing so because the tour might provide her with relevant information, or because she would enjoy seeing Galen Rockwell again. Then it occurred to her that if Charles Marchand were seriously interested in investing in the winery, that would have lessened Taylor's financial motive for killing Steve. A substantial investment from Marchand might have given Taylor the resources to buy Steve out.

Annie walked with Celia back down the gravel drive to the barn that housed the winery. The only car parked in front was a white Lincoln rental car. Charles Marchand was waiting just inside the barn.

"Ah, Celia." His eyes lit up when he saw her. And from Celia's similar expression, Annie surmised that it had been Charles Marchand that Celia had been expecting when Annie knocked on her door. Annie wondered if Celia had revealed her true age to the doctor. He had to be in his early fifties, a bit old for a seventeen-year-old, even one who could pass for twenty-five.

From his appearance, Annie concluded that Dr. Marchand had sufficient money to invest as much as he pleased. He wore a large but tasteful gold and onyx ring on his right hand, his shoes were Italian leather loafers, and the sweater thrown casually over his shoulders looked like cashmere. The hat he wore to ward off the chilly October air was a stylish tweed. He was an attractive man, with closely cropped black hair and a neat, perfect smile. But Annie was cautious. In her experience, wealthy doctors often made up in arrogance what they lacked in social graces.

He turned to Annie, and looked like he was struggling to remember her name. "I believe we've met. . . ." His deep voice had a hint of residual East Coast accent.

"Yes, at the Wine Gala, but very briefly. I'm Annie MacPherson, a friend of Taylor's." She held out her hand, and he shook it.

"Yes," he nodded. "I believe she mentioned you. The attorney from Seattle. Are you going to join us on our little tour this morning? I'm told it will be very enlightening."

"Yes, if I'm not intruding. I'm afraid I don't know very much about winemaking."

"I know only as much as I have to. It's much more interesting studying the final product. Ah, here's our guide now."

Galen Rockwell entered the building, brushing dust off his jeans. He looked like a man who had better things to do than give potential investors a tour of his operation, but knew where his paycheck was coming from. The corners of his mouth went up slightly when he saw Annie.

"You were such a good wine-tasting instructor," she said, "I thought I'd follow up with the advanced course."

"Well, I'll see what I can do to make it interesting for you." He looked at Marchand, then at his watch. "I'm afraid that all I can spare this morning is about an hour for a really quick overview. You understand this is our busiest time of year."

"Of course."

"Well, then. Let's see if we can get this show on the road. Why don't you all step outside here to start with."

They walked back down the steps and outside of the barn. To one side was a fenced yard containing a variety of steel tanks and equipment. To the other side was an unobstructed view of the vineyards, rising in front of them on the gentle south-facing slope of a ridge.

"I wanted to start out here," Galen said, "because my job really doesn't amount to much unless I start with the best grapes I can get my hands on. Here at North Faire, we own the vineyards, and hire a vineyard manager to do the farming. But as winemaker, my job is to tell him what to do—pruning, watering, fertilizing, spraying—you name it. I make the call."

"Excuse me if I sound a little dense," Dr. Marchand said. "But this is the first winery in the Northwest I've been interested in. All my other holdings are in Napa and Sonoma. You understand that most of us Californians believe that no other growing region can rival California."

Galen laughed. "Don't I know it. I trained at UC Davis, and worked for years in the Napa Valley, before coming up here. But the fact is, Dr. Marchand, you're just plain wrong. California wines have a lot going for them, but now that I've worked up here for a while, you couldn't pay me to go back."

"Oh, really. But I wouldn't think it's hot enough this far north to grow really *superior* grapes." Dr. Marchand had a slight smirk on his face, but Galen didn't miss a beat.

"That's a common misconception. Fact is, if it's too hot, the vine shuts down, and the grapes don't mature properly. Up here, the grapes ripen slowly and develop more acidity and a more intense varietal flavor. And that," he looked Marchand in the eye, "makes for better wine."

Annie could tell that Galen was warming up to his topic. "It is my personal belief, Doctor, that the thousand-square-mile area that makes up the Yakima Valley is perhaps the most perfect place on the face of the earth to grow quality wine grapes."

Marchand laughed. "Next to France, I assume you mean."

Galen shook his head. "No, I don't. France has a few drawbacks of its own. Bordeaux, which I would consider France's prime wine-growing region, is a maritime province, which places it at the mercy of the weather. Here, we're in the rain shadow of the Cascade Mountains, which means we get about three hundred days of sunshine a year, and very little rain. You don't have to worry about offshore storms ruining the crop. Yet, there's enough water for irrigation. What we have in common with France is a long growing season and extremely long days—two hours more sunshine per day than your beloved Napa, I'd like to point out."

Galen walked over to a vine, pulled a knife out of his back pocket, and sliced off a cluster of darkly colored grapes. "Here's a grape you won't be familiar with from California, Doctor. It's called *lemburger*, and it prefers a cooler climate. Makes a delicate, well-balanced wine, a little like a pinot noir, with a lot of character. With all this geographic variety, instead of a bunch of flat farmland, we can select whichever variety of grape is suited to a particular microclimate."

"What's a microclimate?" Celia asked. She had been following every word, and seemed eager to learn.

"It just means all of the factors that combine to influence a particular location. It might be the way a certain slope catches the sun, or the way a ridge rises above the frost level. Or the drainage, or the soil type. In this region, the same vineyard can have sand, silt, loam, or gravel within a few dozen feet of each other. You really don't want soil that's too rich for grapes. Otherwise, the vines get too woody. To keep the quality of the grape up, you have to starve the vine just a little. Believe it or not, the topsoil here is only a couple of feet deep. Below that is broken basalt that provides drainage."

Marchand was starting to nod, showing a keen interest. He crouched and picked up a handful of dirt. "Now, as I understand it, you don't have a problem with phylloxera in eastern Washington?"

"What's that?" Annie asked.

"Its a bug," Galen replied, "sort of like an aphid, that infests the roots of the vine, sucks 'em dry. There isn't any way to kill it. You just have to rip up the vines and replant with a more disease-resistant root stock. Then it takes four or five years before the vines are producing a wine-quality crop. Problem is, the damned bug keeps mutating and attacking the stock that was supposed to be resistant. It's a helluva problem in California right now. They say it's affected twenty thousand acres in Napa Valley alone."

"But it hasn't affected the vineyards here?" Annie asked.

"Not so far."

"Why is that?"

"There are a number of different theories, but the soil type is a good guess. Our soil is gravelly or sandy, and phylloxera likes more of a clay-like soil. Maybe it's because the winters are colder, or the vineyards are more spread out. California's been so devastated, I can sure understand why you're looking at Northwest wineries."

"Hmmm." Dr. Marchand tossed aside the dirt, and wiped his hands together. "You mentioned water earlier, and I'm concerned about that. I understand that North Faire is part of the Roza water district? Isn't that junior in priority to the Sunnyside District?"

Galen looked at Marchand warily. "It sounds like you've been doing your research."

Marchand returned his look and said quietly, "Water rights are very important to me."

"Well, then you probably already know that North Faire supplements its irrigation supply with well water. We have the deepest wells in the county, and have never had a problem with water."

"Yes," Dr. Marchand said with a smile. "I did know that. Shall we move along?"

"As you wish."

Galen explained how the grapes were picked by hand, then led the group into a fenced yard next to the barn to explain the various pieces of equipment. He took them up some metal steps to a machine on a raised platform that had a metal conveyor belt leading up to it. "This is the crusher-stemmer. The fruit comes up the conveyor belt and into the opening in the top of the machine." They peered over the side and saw a tubular contraption that contained a center axle with numerous wicked-looking spikes. The tube was perforated with holes about a quarter inch in diameter. Galen turned on the power, and the axle started spinning. "This part doesn't really 'crush' the grapes, but just breaks the skin. Centrifugal force pushes the pulp, seeds, and juice through the holes, where a large hose leads to a tank. The stems and leaves are pushed out at the end and used for compost."

Galen led them back down the metal steps, explaining the fermentation process for both red and white wines. He then took them back inside the barn and up onto the cat-walk near the top of the steel tanks. One vat was open, and Annie could see a layer of foamy pulp. "When the red wine is beginning its fermentation process, the skins and pulp of the grapes rise to the top. This cap traps the heat, and would eventually kill the yeast, unless we punched it down, or pumped the wine over it." The winemaker demonstrated how to punch down the cap with a wooden implement that looked a little like a rake.

Dr. Marchand was smiling, gazing around the inside of the barn. "One can really see the whole operation from here. I like it. What's there, in the back?"

"Oh, that's just the loading dock. The distributor comes by twice a month to pick up the cases we have ready for shipping. Our production is so small, most of what we sell goes to restaurants and select wine merchants. You won't see a lot of North Faire wine in the supermarket, and we like it that way."

Marchand noticed the stacks of white boxes. "It looks like quite a large shipment to me."

"This is our busiest time of year."

Galen then led them into his laboratory, a small room near the back of the barn filled with glass pipettes and flasks, test tubes, a rack of wine glasses, a Bunsen burner, and other scientific-looking objects. The winemaking process itself wasn't as complicated as Annie had imagined. What made wines so different seemed to be the decisions the winemaker made—how much and what kind of yeast to use, how long to leave the juice in contact with the skins, what temperature to use for fermentation, when to stop the fermentation process, whether to filter the wine, how to blend the wines to complement their flavors. Listening to Galen Rockwell, she could tell that he knew what he was doing and loved his job.

Galen finished by explaining the racking process, where the wine would be separated from the lees, barrel-aged, and bottled. Annie's head was spinning from all the information by the end of the tour.

"Well, I must admit, Rockwell, I'm impressed by your operation. What I see here is a professionally run establishment with excellent potential for growth." Galen accepted Dr. Marchand's compliments as stoically as he had accepted his earlier barbs.

Marchand continued, "I understand you're, uh, not under contract here, is that correct?"

"That's right," Galen replied sternly. "I'm just an employee."

"And I'm sure Taylor told you that I like to, uh, renegotiate all employment relationships when I take over an interest in a winery."

"She said that, yes."

Marchand picked up a long glass tube, and seemed to be examining it.

"That's used for taking samples from a barrel," Galen said, taking the fragile item from Marchand's hands. "It's called a 'thief.' "

"How appropriate."

Galen stiffened. "And what's that supposed to mean?"

Marchand smiled like a chess player about to make his final move. "That winery you used to own in the Napa Valley made a nice little cabernet, as I recall. Too bad you couldn't keep it going."

"If you'll excuse me, Doctor, I really need to be getting back to work now. It doesn't seem like there's anything I can tell you about North Faire that you don't already know."

Chapter 20

ANNIE STAYED BEHIND as Charles Marchand and Celia Vick drove off in Marchand's Lincoln. Galen didn't make eye contact with her as he straightened up his laboratory. He opened the dishwasher, and began carrying clean glasses out to the wine-tasting area. Annie helped, until the dishwasher was empty and the wine bar was stocked and ready to open for tourists at eleven.

Taylor's orange cat, curled up on his favorite spot on the rolltop desk, raised his head sleepily and meowed. Galen reached back and gave him a handful of oyster crackers, which the animal hungrily crunched down. "I don't know why, but Colonel Bob thinks these things are cat treats. Gotta keep our mouser happy."

"Galen, what was going on just now between you and Marchand?"

Galen wiped the bar, even though it was already clean. "Well, it seems as though the good doctor has researched the winemaker, along with the winery. I suspected as much the first time I met the man. The way he looked at me like I was a piece of cow dung. Then there's always the possibility Taylor told him. She was the only one around here who knew the whole story."

"Can you tell me about it?" Annie sensed that what Galen had to say would have some bearing on Taylor's case. But she wasn't asking as Taylor's lawyer. She wanted Galen to trust her as a friend.

He leaned back against the rolltop desk and looked at her. "I grew up in central California, worked on farms all my life. I liked the rural lifestyle, but I wasn't challenged by farming. Even as a kid, I loved science, spent hours playing with my chemistry set, making various concoctions. Still, farming was what I knew, and after working on my dad's place for a few years, I decided to go back to school to study agriculture. I came up here to Washington State University in Pullman. That was back in the seventies. Even then, there were a few crazy nuts talking about winemaking in Washington. It seemed like a perfect fit for me— part farming, part science. Plus, I learned I was good at it—I had the nose, so to speak. Pullman didn't have a program back then, so I transferred to UC Davis, got a degree, and started working for various places around the Napa Valley.

"I didn't come from a moneyed background, and banks have never been happy about loaning money to start wineries. It took me a long time to save enough to buy my own place. I didn't own any vineyards, had to buy my grapes from other growers, but I set up shop and started making wine. Damned good wine, if I say so myself."

"What happened?"

Galen shrugged. "What happens to most small businesses? I was great at making wine; I didn't know so much about selling it. I found it really hard to make ends meet. There were times when there wasn't enough money to buy supplies."

"A lot of small businesses fail, Galen. It's nothing to be ashamed of." Annie remembered when her own law firm almost went under, and would have, but for a merger with a larger firm.

"Well, if that's all there was, I wouldn't be ashamed. But truth is, what I did wasn't the right way out of my problems. Other people owed me money, and I kept thinking, if I could just make it till next week, till the next check comes in." Galen stuck his hands in his pockets and looked down at his boots. "Everybody floats checks at the bank once in a while. You write a check, knowing that a deposit will be made the next day to cover it. Well, when you set out to do it deliberately, they call it check kiting. And they arrest you for it.

"I thought I could weather the storm if I could just make it through the harvest. So I set up a bunch of different accounts with different banks and started shuffling money. I'd make a deposit in one place, then write two or three checks for that amount to my other accounts. Then write checks from those accounts back to the first one. It was like juggling, trying to keep all your balls in the air. Make a deposit here before that check clears there. And on and on." He looked up. "But when all the balls come down, there are more checks than there is money in the bank. It wasn't my intention to defraud anybody. All I wanted to do was survive till more money came in. But it didn't work. Somehow the banks got wise to me and pulled the plug."

The expression on Galen's face was one of pure remorse. Annie could tell it hurt even to talk about the incident. "What did they do?"

"I guess you could say I was lucky. Fraud's hard to prove, so they let me plead guilty to a lesser offense. And because I didn't have a record, I didn't have to serve any time. But the fines and penalties to the banks wiped me out. I had to declare bankruptcy, and pretty much lost everything."

"How did Marchand know about all this?"

"It was all over the papers down there. Some holding company ended up buying the winery equipment and inventory. Hell, it could have been one of Marchand's companies, for all I know."

"And how did you end up here?"

"Taylor and I met in college and kept in touch over the years. I knew she'd gotten into the winery business. After all this happened, I called and basically begged her to give me a job. I figured only someone who knew me would take me on, with the record I had. She was a friend, and she came through for me when I needed her."

"Galen, can I ask you something?"

"Sure."

"If Marchand were to invest in the winery, do you think he'd keep you on here, knowing what he does?"

Galen looked up at the ceiling, and his lips curled in a bitter smile. "I don't think there's a chance in hell."

Annie walked back to the house and was surprised to find the door unlocked. She was certain that she'd left it secure when she left that morning. Pushing it open, she heard a voice call to her from the living room. Gerald North was sitting on the sofa, apparently waiting for her. He wore black rayon slacks and a long-sleeved silk shirt. His one-day growth of beard looked more like a fashion statement than careless grooming. He stood up as she entered the room.

"Annie." His tone was serious, and put Annie on edge. "Have a seat, there's something we need to talk about."

Annie sat down.

"Can I get you anything? Iced tea?"

"No, thank you."

Gerald cleared his throat. "After you left Ellensburg yesterday, I got to thinking, and realized that I didn't know where you were staying. I halfway expected to get here and find that you'd already moved to a hotel."

Annie wasn't sure what to make of Gerald's demeanor. He had certainly been moody the day before, but she hadn't felt that his unpleasantness was directed at her. "I'm sorry if I was presumptuous. Your sister invited me here as her guest; I assumed she wouldn't mind if I stayed on for a day or two while I looked into her case." She was aware that she sounded defensive, and Gerald picked up on that.

"No, no. Please. It's nothing you've done. Let me explain. Celia and I spoke about it, and we decided that while Taylor is in the hospital, it would be better if the house were . . . secure."

Annie started to speak, but Gerald raised his hand. "No, I'm sure you're being very careful. It's—how can I put this—I didn't want to put you in an awkward position, but we've had the locks changed."

"The locks? But why?" Annie had her doubts that Gerald had actually discussed this with Celia. She couldn't believe that Celia wouldn't have mentioned it when they saw each other that morning.

"Did Taylor tell you about all of the thefts lately?"

"Yes, but she thought Steve was responsible. It was one of the reasons she was so angry with him."

Gerald nodded. "Taylor and I had this discussion a number of times. I never believed Steve was behind it. It didn't make sense. Why would he be interested in wine-making supplies, bottles, labels, and so on? They had no market value to speak of. Not the type of thing you'd sell to your local fence."

"Then who do you think has been doing the stealing?"

Gerald paused. "I think it was Galen Rockwell."

Annie said nothing.

"That's why we wanted to change the locks. He has a key to the house, and if you were staying here ... well, I know you two have become ... friends." Annie didn't like the spin Gerald put on the word. "We thought it would be awkward for you, staying here, if you had to explain to Galen that we didn't want him to have access to the house."

"Now, wait just a second. Why do you think Galen would steal supplies? Weren't there thefts from the other wineries around here, too? It could be anyone."

"There have been thefts, but the other wineries have all had break-ins. Signs of forced entry, broken latches. There has been none of that at North Faire. All of our supplies have just disappeared. And there was one other very strange occurrence."

"What was that?"

"A month or so ago I was working on the painting of the house." He pointed to the watercolor over the mantel. "I was trying to get the light just right. The house at dawn on a summer morning. I needed to be here so early, I drove down from Ellensburg after my last seminar the night before, got here about midnight. There was activity going on in the barn, lights on in the back room where Galen has his laboratory."

"Maybe he was just working late."

"Possibly. But as soon as I pulled into the gravel drive, all the lights went out. I was curious, so I went up to the door, and it was locked. I even knocked, and no one answered. Now my curiosity was really piqued, so I turned off the lights and waited on the porch to see who came out."

"And was it Galen?"

"I'll never know. I waited over an hour, and no one came out. They were hiding, didn't want to be seen. It was very suspicious."

"I still don't see why you think it was Galen."

"I looked around the next day. Sure enough, a supply of bottles was missing. And there was no sign of forced entry. Only two people have keys to the barn, Galen and Taylor. And Taylor was inside, asleep." Gerald stood up, signaling an end to the conversation. "So I hope you understand, I simply don't trust the man. And I don't want him letting himself into our house."

"Why did Galen have a key in the first place? Are there papers, supplies here he needs to do his work?"

Gerald shook his head and laughed. "Why does any man have a key to a woman's house?"

"Galen and Taylor?" Annie felt an odd sensation in her stomach. She didn't want to admit it might be jealousy.

"Off and on. They've known each other for years. Although I got the impression that she'd broken it off with him. That's probably why he's been stealing from her. Believe me, Annie. There are things you don't know about Rockwell. You may think he's straightforward, but he's had problems like this in the past."

Annie thought about what Galen just told her. He had

mistakenly thought Taylor was the only one in Harmony who knew.

Gerald continued. "I've told Taylor a number of times not to trust Galen. Hey, I wouldn't even be surprised if he had something to do with Vick's death."

"Why do you say that?"

"I think Taylor broke it off with Galen about the same time that she threw Vick out, but everyone knew she was still seeing Steve from time to time. Think how that must have infuriated Galen. Don't you think he might have wanted to put an end to their relationship for good, so that he could get Taylor back for himself?"

Annie tried to picture the impassive Galen Rockwell driven by a jealous rage, but the image wouldn't come. She remembered during the vineyard tour Galen mentioning that he couldn't even shoot the robins that ate his ripe grapes, but only fired shots into the air to scare them.

Annie shook her head. "I don't agree with you, Gerald. I think it's obvious that Taylor struck Steve, but it was justifiable. Steven Vick was a violent man, with a short temper. I've heard reports that those times Vick was seeing Taylor, after she made him move out, he was abusing her physically. She had bruises, black eyes. That night at the Wine Gala, she was afraid of him, of what he might do to her."

Gerald looked at Annie incredulously. "You're not serious, are you? You're saying that Taylor was a battered spouse?"

"That's what the evidence seems to point to. I know it can be hard to accept, but . . ."

"Not in this case. You're way off track."

"Why do you say that?"

"Hey, I'll be the first to admit that Steve was a first-class horse's ass. He was loud, rude, offensive to just about everyone he came into contact with, myself included. And there's no question he had a short fuse—practically anything or anyone that got in his way made him mad as a wildcat. But I'll tell you something. I know my sister, probably better than anyone alive, and there's no way Taylor North would let any man hit her more than once . . . unless she wanted him to."

Chapter 21

ANNIE DROVE the ten miles into Yakima, assuming she would have no problem finding a room. But she soon discovered that Cavanaugh's, the Red Lion, and the Rio Mirada, all of the quality business-class hotels in town, were completely full thanks to—of all things—the state bar association convention. The desk clerk at Cavanaugh's was kind enough to call around in search of a room, and when one was located at a place called the Cherry Court Motel a few blocks away, Annie took it sight unseen.

She followed the desk clerk's directions, and her heart sank when she saw it. She had stayed in her share of cheap motels, but not when she was traveling on business. Located on a residential street next to a drug rehabilitation facility, the Cherry Court was a two-story motel with a tiny kidney-shaped pool in the parking lot. A few screaming children were risking their health wading in the stagnant green water, while two surly-looking men in a corner of the parking lot were conducting some kind of transaction that Annie didn't want to know about.

She picked up her key at the desk. At least her room was on the second story, at the farthest corner from the noise of the pool. She probably would have been able to describe the decor without ever setting foot inside—chocolate-brown shag carpet, a faded bedspread in shades of burnt orange and harvest gold, a "starving artist" oil painting bolted to

148

the wall. She sat on the edge of the bed, and the mattress sagged with a spongy softness.

Spreading the contents of her briefcase out on the small round table by the window, Annie began making lists of the things she needed to do. Despite Gerald's comments, she felt that the battered-woman's defense was still Taylor's best hope, mainly because there was nothing else to go on. That afternoon, Annie would call on the local hospitals and clinics with the signed medical release in search of Taylor's records. Looking through Taylor's address book—the one the nurse had not let Annie leave at the hospital—she found the names of several potential witnesses to interview. Unfortunately, two of them were in Spokane, a couple of hundred miles east near the Idaho border. Annie called Horizon Air for their schedule of commuter flights, and discovered that she could fly over, talk to her witnesses, and fly back all in the same day. She booked a nine A.M. flight for the next morning.

Before making any more calls, Annie dialed the office to let her secretary know where she could be reached. She also needed the moral support of the one person she could count on to give her a straight evaluation of her case. Val O'Hara had always had an uncanny ability to predict what a jury would do with practically any set of facts.

The phone was picked up on the fourth ring, with the sound of raucous, high-pitched shrieking in the background. At first, Annie thought she had gotten a wrong number, until she heard Val O'Hara's, "Hold on, honey," shouted into the phone. "Let me see if I can control the volume a little bit. All right, kids, that's enough of 'dinosaur game.' I can't have Tyrannosaurus rexes playing in the reception area. Take your crayons into the conference room and draw pictures, like your daddy told you to. That's right, sweeties." The shrieking didn't stop, but Annie could tell the kids had moved into the next room. When she came back on the line, Val sighed. "Criminy, as if I don't get enough of the grandma business at home. Joel and his wife are at the bank signing loan papers, and asked if I'd watch the kids for an hour. They've been gone almost an hour and a half and I'm going out of my mind. If my hair wasn't already gray, this surely would do it. Now I know why I couldn't stay 'retired' for more than two weeks—I don't have the stamina. So how is it on your end, honey?"

Annie filled her secretary in on the events of the last couple of days, including Harry Braithwaite's fabricated confession, and ending with her abrupt move to the Cherry Court Motel. For some reason she relayed everything except what Galen had told her about his past indiscretions.

"Well, if that doesn't take all. You know what I think? I wouldn't trust that artist brother as far as I could throw him. I bet he thinks his sister is going to jail for a very long time, and he's already making plans for what he'll do with her business. Hmph. You said he hated his teaching job, didn't you? Blood is thicker than water, unless there's money involved, that's what I always say. Then it's every relative for himself. I'd check out the daughter, too. She may be seventeen, but she sounds like she's old enough to know what she wants."

"But Val, the State's going to prove that Taylor was found at the crime scene, holding the weapon. How am I going to prove that someone else killed Steve?"

"I don't know, hon, but I think you'd better work on it. Right now, you don't have a leg to stand on with that battered-woman theory."

"You don't think I could convince a jury that Taylor killed Steve out of fear for her life?"

"If you're going to get Taylor off the hook, you're going to need a whole lot more than you've got right now. Unless, of course, she's just plain guilty, and you'd be better off working on a plea bargain."

Annie sighed, feeling overwhelmed. "I don't know, Val. I'll admit that part of me *wants* Taylor to be innocent, but it's more than that. I *know* her, and she's not a murderer. I just can't believe she would have killed Steve, unless it was to defend herself."

"You know what Agatha Christie said. 'Every murderer is probably somebody's old friend.' "

"I know, and thanks for the objective viewpoint. I shouldn't let myself get so close to this case that I can't see the facts."

"Is there anything I can help you with from this end?"

"I don't think so. I just wish I could clone myself to be in two places at once. I'm going to see Taylor at the hospital this evening, and if I go talk to these witnesses tomorrow in Spokane, I'll have to wait till Monday before I can get around to checking the police and court files for reports of domestic violence, and I'd really like to do some background checking on Steven Vick, and what type of business dealings he had in the works. Any ideas?"

Annie could hear Val chuckling. "One or two. What time are you catching your plane tomorrow?"

"Nine. The airport's close to town, so I'll probably be here till eight-fifteen or so."

"I'll call you in the morning. I might have an idea of how you could get some help."

"So, how is everything going at the office? Is Jed still distracted by his personal ad?"

Val laughed. "It was interesting around here, to put it mildly. Jed seemed to think that he had to meet every single lady that responded the first week—before they got taken by someone else, I guess. But things have quieted down now that he's narrowed the field to one."

"One! I've never known Jed to date only one woman at a time in his life. This must be someone special."

Val laughed knowingly. "Oh, it is."

"Can you tell me more?"

Val paused, and Annie could almost see her smiling. "I think I'll have to let him fill you in. But I can say this. I'm positive that you'll like her."

Annie went alone to see Taylor. The halls of St. Elizabeth's were quiet, and felt cold to Annie. She had never been comfortable visiting hospitals. No matter how healthy a person might be, in a hospital bed hooked up to tubes and wires, anyone would look near death. The overhead fluorescent lights were bright but artificial, giving everything a bluish cast.

Annie had talked to Taylor's doctor that afternoon and gotten his permission for a short visit. Dr. Butterick also agreed to speak with her afterwards and update her on Taylor's condition.

With some trepidation, she approached Taylor's room. The bed closest to the door was still unoccupied. She tapped on the open door, then walked toward Taylor's side of the room. Even though she'd tried to mentally prepare for anything, the sight of her friend lying listlessly and staring out the window was disconcerting. Her blond hair was limp and unwashed. The bruises on her face had turned from dark purple to reddish-brown. Taylor turned her head when Annie softly called her name.

"I feel like I should have brought flowers."

"Not necessary," Taylor said lethargically.

"Are you feeling any better?"

A slight shrug. "The doctor says so. Take my advice. If you ever try to overdose, don't use aspirin or codeine. Big mistake."

Annie pulled a chair next to the bed and tried to think of small talk. She told Taylor how much she enjoyed the tour of the winery Galen had given, and said that Gerald was doing a good job of looking after things. She wanted to be careful in her questions. She needed information from Taylor, but didn't want to add to her depression. After a few minutes of chatting, Annie said, "Taylor, can I ask you some questions about Tuesday night?"

She closed her eyes. "You can try."

"Do you remember what happened?"

She moved her head slightly. "No. The last thing I remember is getting to the party, and going to talk to Galen about the display. The next thing I remember, I was waking up in the hospital."

"Do you know what happened to Steve?"

"The doctor didn't want to tell me, but I guessed. He's dead, isn't he?"

"Yes."

Taylor looked for a moment like she was going to cry. "Did I . . . ?"

Annie debated how much she should say. "No one saw it happen. He was hit in the back of the head with a wine bottle. You were found near the body, and your fingerprints were on the bottle."

Taylor bit her lip. "No," she said softly, her eyes welling up. "No, I couldn't. I wouldn't have. . . . Do the police think . . . ?"

"I've spoken to the homicide detective from the sheriff's department. He's indicated that he wants to issue a warrant for your arrest. But the fingerprints aren't a lot to go on. I want to make it very clear that he's not to talk to you without an attorney present."

"Are you representing me?"

"If you still want me to."

She gave a small, bitter laugh. "I guess I need you, if I'm going to be branded a murderer." Under her breath, she said, "I can't believe this is happening."

Annie had to broach another difficult topic. "I've talked to some of your friends, Taylor. Harry Braithwaite, Edna down at the café, Seth Longacre. They told me some suspicions they had about you and Steve . . ." She didn't know the right way to ask. "This might be important to your defense, Taylor. I need to know if Steve ever hit you."

Eyes still tightly shut, Taylor nodded slightly.

"And did this go on after you asked him to move out of the house? Did he come back from time to time?"

She sniffed slightly, and barely inclined her head.

"Can you tell me about it?"

A shake of the head. "Not right now," Taylor said, her voice choked with tears. Annie waited, but Taylor wouldn't say any more. "When I'm not so tired."

"Sure, Taylor. That's okay." They talked a while longer, but not about the case. When Taylor looked like she wanted to sleep, Annie left.

Chapter 22

DR. BUTTERICK HAD GIVEN Annie instructions to have him paged when she was through seeing Taylor. He arrived a few minutes later carrying Taylor's chart, and they sat down in the waiting area. Annie handed the doctor a copy of her medical release. After he had the chance to review it, she asked, "Taylor's not doing very well, is she?"

"From a physical standpoint, I'd say she's out of the woods. Her system had a pretty rough blow from the aspirin and Tylenol threes, but I don't think she's going to have any permanent damage. If there was going to be kidney failure, we probably would have seen signs by now. But we still need to watch her for a few days to be certain."

"And the memory loss?"

"We don't think that either a head injury or toxic residuals from the overdose is causing the memory loss. It's most likely psychological. Recent memory loss occurs frequently after a severe trauma. It's one of the body's survival mechanisms that allows us to go on, to recover physically. In many cases, the memories return when the victim is better able to deal with them."

"I see."

"We could attempt to release those memories through hypnosis. The relaxation involved can be fairly effective in trauma cases."

Annie shook her head. "No. If she later had to testify at

trial, anything obtained through hypnosis would be inadmissible."

"Really? I didn't know that."

After an afternoon of searching, Annie had been unable to turn up any medical records for Taylor that showed evidence of trauma. With the exception of a gynecologist Taylor saw yearly, she didn't seem to have a primary care physician. Annie decided to pursue the subject with Dr. Butterick. She briefly explained what she was looking for.

"Well," said the doctor, "we performed a thorough examination when Taylor was admitted. One wrist was swollen where she had fallen, but X rays showed it was only a sprain. Let me see if there's anything else in the chart. . . ." He flipped through the pages. "No unaccounted-for scars or evidence of healed fractures. . . . no bruises other than those she received that night. . . ." He closed the chart. "There's nothing here that would make me, as a physician, suspicious that there was abuse going on. Now, I'm not going to say there aren't cases where there are no physical marks, but most marital cases aren't that subtle. If something's going on, a physician can generally tell."

Annie stood up. "Thank you, doctor. I appreciate your time."

"No problem."

Before leaving, Annie glanced down the corridor toward Taylor's room. Galen Rockwell, brown felt hat in hand, stood in the doorway. He saw Annie and walked over and sat in the chair opposite her.

"Did you get a chance to see her?" Annie asked.

He shook his head and sighed. "No, she was asleep. Looked like she needed the rest, too, so I didn't want to wake her. God, this is a horrible thing to have to watch someone go through."

Annie told Galen what the doctor had said.

"Well, it could be a lot worse, I guess. Hell, she could've died taking those pills, so it's a blessing that she's here at all." He looked around the waiting area, seemingly at a loss for words. "I, uh, I guess I should go now. Maybe I'll try to get here a little earlier tomorrow evening, when she's not so tired." Galen looked at his hat, but made no immediate move to go. When Annie stood up, he said, "Look, Annie . . . you, uh, . . . I'm feeling a little lonely right now. Would you want to get a drink or dinner or something?"

"Sure."

Galen smiled and stood up. It was the first smile she'd seen on his face since they were tasting wine at the Gala, before Steve was killed.

They took Galen's truck to Grant's Brewery Pub housed in the old train depot on North Front Street. Galen explained that he didn't drink hard liquor, so he didn't know where the real bars were in Yakima. Annie said the pub was fine, and the brightly lit interior was probably better for their somber moods, anyway.

Like its microbrewery counterparts in Seattle, Grant's Pub was a combination of Old English and new Northwest. The booths were made of oak paneling, and the requisite dartboard was in the corner. Classic Rolling Stones played over the sound system, and the waiters in shorts, Hawaiian shirts, and Nikes were glad to explain every last detail of the beermaking process to anyone who looked even vaguely interested. Both Annie and Galen realized they'd been too busy to get dinner, and agreed to look at menus. Annie ordered the fish and chips, while Galen opted for a Scotch egg, something he'd never tried before, with bread and mustard. When the meals arrived, Galen took a look at his, which turned out to be a hard-boiled egg wrapped in pork sausage, then dipped in batter and deep-fried. "Hmmm, it's a good thing I drink a lot of red wine. They say that a glass or two a day cleans the arteries and keeps down your cholesterol level. With this meal, I'm going to need it."

Through the meal, they talked about a number of things, but the conversation kept coming back around to Taylor. Galen finished his pint of ale, and ordered them each another. After a long moment, he said, "What is this hold that she has on people, do you think? Harry was willing to go to prison for her. You're here, working night and day on her behalf, when you haven't even spoken to each other in almost two decades. I threaten to walk off the job, then regret the words as soon as I say them. What is it about Taylor that makes us do these things?"

"I don't know." Annie tried to think. "For me, I guess it might be the fact that she needs me for the first time. When we were in high school, I always felt like I was tagging along on her coattails. She was always willing to include me in her marvelous adventures. I feel like I owe her something for that, yet she never wanted anything in return."

Galen stared into the amber liquid in his glass. "In some ways she reminds me of a cat. Totally independent, totally sure of herself. Aloof, when she wants to be. A wild animal allowing itself to become domesticated. When a cat like that walks into a room, it doesn't need anything from us, yet we make fools of ourselves trying to caress it, feed it, make it comfortable. And how happy we are when the animal finally agrees to let us scratch its head."

Annie looked at Galen, and thought about what Gerald had said. "How long were you lovers?" she asked quietly.

"It shows, does it? We lived together for a second or two in Pullman, during one of her separations from Steve, and picked up again when I came up here to work for her. For a second or two." He shrugged. "I never thought it would last. Hoped it would, maybe. But Taylor's not the type to settle down with one man for very long. She gets . . . bored, I guess."

"But she always went back to Steven Vick."

Galen nodded. "Don't ask me to explain it. There was something crazy about those two."

"Is that why you wanted her to get a divorce? Were you trying to get Taylor back for yourself?"

"Did Gerald put that idea in your head? I swear, the man thinks I'm the devil incarnate. No, I honestly thought Steve was a danger to Taylor. A danger that she couldn't recognize. I'd still be trying to protect her from him, if he were alive." He chuckled to himself. "But getting her back? I don't think I'd have the stamina to be with Taylor very long. It's . . . that's not what I want. I want a lasting kind of love, something I don't think Taylor is capable of. I have her friendship now. She's a wonderful friend."

Annie looked at Galen's hands, cupped around his glass. She sensed that what he was telling her was the truth. They lingered for another hour or so, but didn't talk about Taylor anymore that evening.

As they were finishing their coffee, Annie saw the staff starting to wipe down tables and put things away.

"Gee, do you think they're trying to tell us something?" Galen asked. It felt so comfortable, sitting there talking. Neither wanted to make the first move to go.

"They're either going to ask us to leave or give us sleeping bags. I guess we should take the hint."

Galen drove Annie back to the hospital parking lot, and got out to walk her to her car. Standing in the glow of the street light, he said, "Thanks for having dinner with me tonight, Annie. Seeing Taylor like that, well, it's hard. It helped not having to be alone."

"Everyone has lonely nights, now and then."

"Do they?" He brushed the hair off her shoulder, letting his hand linger there. "Are we just two people sharing a lonely night together?" He leaned down and kissed her for a long while on the lips, then hugged her tightly. "Is that all we are?" His deep voice was so soft she could barely make out the words. He brushed his lips across her neck, breathing in the scent of her hair.

"I don't know." She leaned back to see his eyes, trying to find an answer there. "I'm not sure, Galen."

"Stay with me tonight, Annie. Please. I need to hold you tonight."

She wanted to say yes, but shook her head. Being held by Galen Rockwell all night would have felt very, very good. She just wished she knew whom he really wanted to be holding. She returned his embrace before getting into her car and driving back to her motel.

Chapter 23

ANNIE WAS FIXING her hair at seven-thirty the next morning when there was a knock on the door. "Yes?" she yelled from the bathroom.

"Room service."

"What the . . . ?" Places like the Cherry Court did not have room service. She got up and looked through the peephole, then opened the door. "What on earth?"

Annie's law partner, Jed Delacourt, stood at the door with a paper tray of orange juice and lattes, and carrying a bag of baked goods. "I hope I'm not too early. Val said your plane wasn't until nine, but I wanted to leave us enough time to discuss the case. I drove over last night after work, but I guess you didn't get in until late."

"No."

He entered the room and set breakfast on the table. " 'Double tall nonfat—no foam' for you, 'decaf mocha' for me. I couldn't believe I found a place that had lattes and fresh-squeezed O.J."

Annie looked at Jed's clothes. He wore crisp khaki slacks, a madras short-sleeved sport shirt, and white Top-Siders without socks. His Vuarnet sunglasses hung on a cord around his neck. "What? What are you looking at?"

Annie suppressed a laugh. "Oh, nothing. It's just that you're looking awfully, um, 'Dan Quayle' this morning."

"Come on, the poor man's out of office. Hasn't the statute of limitations run out on Dan Quayle jokes?"

"I'm not making fun of him. I'm making fun of you."

"Oh, that's different." He bounced on the edge of the bed. "God, I can't believe it. Your mattress is even worse than the one in my room."

"Jed, what are you doing here?"

"Well, let's see how this went. I was moping around, saying I wanted to get out of town for the weekend, because this woman that I've started dating had plans. Val told me to stop whining and go to lunch. When I got back, she had just gotten through talking to you, and said you needed help working on your case. I thought, hey, a three-day weekend in the wine country, give Annie a little help . . . sounds pretty good. Val thought it was a great idea, because it would get me out of her hair. She said you needed a document search at the courthouse, background check on the victim, that sort of thing?" He brushed his hair out of his eyes. "She also said you sounded kind of depressed."

Annie shook her head and laughed. Leave it to Val to come up with a solution to every problem. She picked up her latte and started telling Jed what she had learned so far.

When she had completed her summary, Annie still had a few minutes before she had to leave for her flight, and she directed the conversation back to gossip. "So," she asked, "what's her name, this new woman in your life? Tell me everything."

Jed grinned. "I was wondering how long it would take you to get around to that. She's very special, totally different from the other women I've gone out with. Let's see, she has a master's degree. . . ."

"Really?" As long as Annie had known Jed, which included their years at the University of Washington Law School, she'd never known him to date a woman who wasn't paddling in shallow water, intellectually speaking. She hardly expected his current love interest to be a potential "Jeopardy" champion.

"She works in health care administration. Very attractive in a no-nonsense, wholesome sort of way, extremely athletic . . ."

"Athletic?" Annie asked, starting to get suspicious.

"Extremely." Jed's smirk gave it away.

"No . . . Tell me you're *not* dating Ellen O'Neill. Please, it can't be true."

Jed just smiled. "We wanted to thank you. That night after we all had dinner at your house, she and I left together, we had coffee, we talked . . . it turns out we have a lot in common."

Annie rolled her eyes in disbelief. "You don't. You have *nothing* in common. It'll never last."

"Don't be so sure. I've turned over a new leaf. No more trophy dates." He sat up straight. "And she's really quite taken with me."

"Oh, please."

"I'm serious. She had already signed up to run a marathon in Portland this weekend, but the last few days, we've spent a lot of time together. Treat us nice, and you might get invited to the wedding."

The Yakima airport consisted of little more than a runway and a tiny terminal building. The morning commuter flight to Spokane was an eight-seater propeller plane. At five feet six inches, even Annie had to duck her head to walk down the center aisle. She told herself to look on the bright side. No matter where you sat, you got both an aisle and a window seat. Annie buckled up and gritted her teeth for the short bumpy ride to Spokane.

Both of the witnesses she needed to talk to were near downtown, so Annie took a cab in from the airport. Her most critical interview would be later that afternoon, when she spoke to Taylor's therapist. Annie had found tucked in the front cover of the address book a business card for Claire Montgomery, Ph.D., family and relationship psychotherapist. On the back of the card was written in Taylor's handwriting, CAN'T CONTINUE—HAVE TO FIND ANSWER—STEVE DRIVING ME NUTS. NEED DECISION *NOW*. There was no question; Dr. Montgomery had to know about Taylor and Steve's stormy relationship.

Annie had made the appointment with Dr. Montgomery without disclosing that she was an attorney wanting to talk about a client. In past experience, she'd learned that, of all the medical professionals, psychiatrists and psychologists were the most wary of lawyers. She was likely to have better luck simply showing up at the office with a signed release and an appointment for an hour's time.

But first, Annie had arranged to meet with Steven Vick's best friend from high school. She had immediately recognized Keith Curran's name when she came across it in the address book, and was pleased that Keith had remembered her when she called. She had arranged to meet him for lunch at Auntie's Bookstore at the edge of downtown. It was one of her favorite haunts when she came to Spokane for a trial or Division III Court of Appeals argument. With lots of wood paneling, endless stacks of well-chosen books, and an overstuffed armchair in the mystery section, it was an easy place to get lost for an hour or two. But after making the appointment, she got to wondering if she should have opted for a steak-and-potatoes place. Keith had been a big eater back in high school, and like most of the football players she knew, pretty rowdy. Hardly a Friday night went by that Keith and his buddies didn't get into a drunken brawl. Perhaps a bookstore with a health food café hadn't been the perfect choice.

When she got there, she saw a man in a plaid sport shirt and chinos sitting at one of the window tables drinking a Coke, looking slightly uncomfortable on a chair too small for his bulky frame. He looked the right age, but Annie couldn't tell if it was Keith. Playing football, he had kept his dark hair short and his face clean-shaven. This man was completely bald, but compensated for it with a bushy beard. He also had considerably more paunch than anyone on the high school football team could have gotten away with. She couldn't be sure until he saw her and waved enthusiastically.

"Keith?"

"Annie. Gosh, you look terrific. Exactly like you did in

high school." When she got to his table, he stood up and wrapped her in a bear hug. Annie stood back to get a better look. "Well, I can't say you haven't changed, but you look great."

"Thanks." He rubbed his shiny pate. "My dad and his three brothers were all cue balls, but somehow, I never thought it would happen to me. That business about inheriting hair traits from your mother's side of the family? All baloney, at least in my experience."

"Can I buy you lunch? The chili's pretty good here."

"Great. But only if they have vegetarian entrées. My doctor's got me on a strict diet. No saturated fat or red meat till I get my cholesterol down below three hundred."

Annie realized yet again that she had to stop stereotyping friends based on who or what they were back in high school. They carried trays through the buffet line, where Keith opted for stir-fried vegetables over rice and Annie selected the quiche of the day. After they sat down, Keith pulled out his wallet and showed her pictures of three little boys in Pop Warner jerseys, miniature versions of their burly dad, except for the fact that they all had hair. She asked, "You dated Carla Fuentes in high school. Did you two . . ."

"Get married? Heck no. We broke up the first quarter I was at Washington State and she went to U-Dub. Huskies and Cougars just don't mix, you know. She ended up marrying a chiropractor, so maybe she's better off. She can get her back adjusted whenever she wants. This will hardly surprise you, but I spent five years at Wazzu devoted to football and married, you guessed it, the head cheerleader. Blond, blue-eyed, and backbiting. But I thought she was God's gift to football players at the time. As I later found out, so did the rest of the team. She completed more passes than Joe Montana, even after we were married. Well, to make a long story short, she didn't think too much of sticking with a guy who sold office supplies for a living, kept nagging me to get out of typewriter ribbons and into something more lucrative, like real estate. The day Mindy figured out I wasn't likely to change was the day she ran off to Vegas with a real estate broker. At least she didn't fight me over the boys. I'd be lost without my little rug rats."

"How old are they?"

"Seven, nine, and eleven. And every one of 'em can throw a football straight as an arrow. My oldest, Keith Junior, has definite quarterback potential. His brother, Bobby, was born to be a defensive tackle. Ricky, the seven-year-old, still has to find his niche."

"So you sell office supplies?"

"Oh, no. Not any more. That's the crazy thing . . . as it turned out, it was Mindy's nagging that was holding me back. Three months after she took off, I went back to school—totally changed careers."

"Really? What do you do now?"

He reached under his collar and pulled on a gold chain. At the end hung a small gold cross. "They call me Pastor Keith now. I've got a parish over on the east side—spend a lot of time coaching kids and organizing food drives. It's a heck of a lot better than peddling typewriter ribbons, I can tell you that." He put the pictures of the boys back in his wallet. "And I've been seeing a wonderful lady who just happens to be the church secretary. We're kind of thinking about making it legal."

"That's wonderful."

"Yeah, it sure is. And what about you? I heard you went to law school? Wasn't your dad a lawyer?"

Annie nodded. "It's been a pretty good career, so far."

"Married, divorced, kids?"

"None of the above. I guess I'm still waiting for the man who can put up with a perfectionist workaholic."

"Yeah, I didn't remember you going with anybody special in high school."

"Back then, I was just too shy. That's why I liked hanging around Taylor. I thought some of her brazenness would rub off."

He laughed. "Too shy? Well, doesn't that beat all." Keith smiled and reddened a bit. "Heck, all the guys on the team thought you were just stuck-up. You were always winning some award or other, getting written up in the local paper. Tell you the truth, the guys thought you were too good for any of us. You remember the placekicker, Colin?"

"I'm not sure."

"Tall, skinny kid, transfer student from Idaho? Boy, did he have a crush on you. He even carried your yearbook picture in his wallet. He was always trying to build up the nerve to ask you out."

"Me?"

"Uh-huh. I remember he mentioned it in the locker room one time, that he wanted to ask you to one of the dances. Steve Vick just about had a fit." Keith blushed again. "Steve said some pretty nasty things about you, back then. I guess he thought you were trying to come between him and Taylor."

Annie shrugged. "He may have been right."

"Yeah, Steve Vick sure could be an A-Number-One asshole, in those days."

They were silent a moment, concentrating on their food. After a pause, Annie spoke. "I called you because I wanted to find out more about Steve's relationship with Taylor after high school. When I saw your name in Taylor's book, I hoped that meant you had kept in touch."

Keith nodded. "We kept up some, although in recent years, we'd sometimes go six months between visits. I'd usually just get together with Steve when he was in Spokane on business, but I saw them together at the college reunions and stuff."

"They were both at Washington State the same time as you? I'm kind of surprised they had time for college, what with the baby, and getting married and all."

"Oh, they didn't get married right away. They told everybody they did, for little Celia's sake. But they didn't actually tie the knot until a few years ago. I performed the ceremony, and Celia was Taylor's maid of honor." Annie remembered the photograph she'd seen from the wedding. Now that she thought about it, Taylor and Steve's faces hadn't been visible. That picture could have been taken anytime. Keith continued, "I remember Taylor telling me that they waited until after her dad died to have the ceremony, because they'd told him all along they were already hitched. Clifford North was a stern sort of fellow. Had a wild temper, that man did. He wouldn't have approved of them living together, having a child, and not being married. Steve told me that Taylor was afraid he'd disinherit her if he knew. So they kind of got stuck perpetuating the lie till he'd passed on."

Annie found that extremely interesting. If Steve and Taylor didn't marry until after her father died, then Taylor would have inherited her half of the farm as separate, not community, property. It also meant that she'd built most of her business using her own money, and not community assets. All that would greatly reduce Steve's claim in a dissolution action, as well as Taylor's financial motivation to kill Steve. But what bothered Annie was the fact that Taylor hadn't been open with her when they discussed the possibility of a divorce. It made her question whether Taylor had really intended to go through with it.

"You said you all went to college together. Were Steve and Taylor living together then?"

"Well, sort of. Steve started out at WSU with me, right after we finished high school. But Taylor stayed over in Seattle during our freshman and sophomore years." Keith finished his stir fry, and wiped up the remainder of the sauce with his roll. He looked like he could have easily eaten another helping. "I know Steve was dating lots of other women, then. And I have no idea if he was keeping in touch with Taylor. I would assume he was, considering what happened at the homecoming party." Keith got up to get a refill on his Coke. When he sat down again, he said, "I would've thought you'd known about all this, you being so close to Taylor and all."

Annie said only that they hadn't kept in touch, without explaining why. She asked what happened at the party.

"Oh, boy, was that ever a sight to see. Man. This would

have been in the fall of our junior year, and we're at the party after the game. We had a big win, so everybody was getting real drunk, whooping it up. Steve was either drunk, or high, I don't know which, but he was up on the table dancing, shouting—generally making a fool of himself, but no more so than anybody else.

"It was about midnight when who walks in but Taylor North. She was kind of disheveled, like she'd been driving for hours. She walks in, scopes out the party, and sees Steve up on the table with this gal, and they're practically getting it on. I guess it was supposed to be dancing, but you couldn't have squeezed a credit card between them. Taylor walks over to the table that Steve is dancing on, and she's shouting up at him to get down. Drunk as he is, and with the music so loud, he doesn't hear her."

"What did she do?"

"She grabbed the edge of the table—it was one of those folding tables like you see in church halls—and she started shoving it back and forth, making them lose their balance and fall. The girl sprained her ankle, but it's a wonder nobody was seriously hurt."

"What happened then?"

"The girl thought Taylor was crazy or drunk, and she got someone to help her up and get her out of there. Taylor practically grabbed Steve up off the floor—I couldn't hear what she said, but the next thing you know they're rolling around on the floor."

"They were fighting?"

He shook his head and smiled. "It wasn't fighting."

Annie wasn't surprised. Keith's story had more of a ring of truth to it than Edna Hinkel or Harry Braithwaite saying that Taylor was the victim of battering. This story sounded a lot more like the Taylor that Annie had known in high school. "And after that?"

"The next thing I knew, Steve and Taylor had moved off campus into an apartment. I learned later that she'd left the baby with her mother in Seattle, and that Celia stayed with her grandma till she was old enough for school. Anyways,

Taylor enrolled as a student and was in a couple of theater productions, but I got the impression that she flunked out. I don't think she was interested in classes other than theater. For the next couple of years, sometimes they were together, sometimes they were apart. Seemed like every time they had a fight, one or the other would move out and shack up with somebody else for awhile. To tell you the truth, I made kind of a conscious decision to steer clear of Taylor during those years. Frankly, I thought she was a little bit crazy. But I tried to keep in touch with Steve."

Annie nodded. "I have to ask you this—did you ever get the impression that Steve hit Taylor?"

Keith thought for a moment, then shook his head. "I know these things are hard to tell sometimes. As a pastor, I've counseled a lot of folks about domestic violence. Some of them, I never would have guessed in a million years that they had a problem, so I know it can be well hidden. But to give you my honest impression about Steve, I'd have to say no. I mean, back in high school and college, Steve had a pretty good temper, but even then the most I ever saw him do was yell and get red in the face. I remember one other thing about Steve—he liked to break things. Man, did he enjoy smashing something. He'd get mad, and the first thing he'd want to do was pick up something—a dish, a bottle, or a lamp, and throw it against a wall. But it was, you know, like an outlet. He had to smash *something*, but not people. In all the times in high school or college that I saw Steve Vick get mad, I never saw him hit another person. Man, I got into fist fights all the time, but Steve didn't even do that." He paused, drained the last of his Coke. "If anything, I'd suspect it would be the other way around. Taylor was the one who was really out of control."

Annie thought back to that long-ago summer night, and her encounter with Steven Vick. She had been so sure that after breaking the lamp and the vase, she was next. In her nightmares, she always saw his huge beefy fist coming at her face. But maybe she had been wrong.

"You said, *back then* he had a temper. What did you mean by that?"

"As I told you, Steve's been a good friend over the years. We grew up and became men together. I'm certainly not the same crazy kid I was back then, and neither was Steve. As he got older, he realized that there were times when his anger was out of control. When he started seeing his daughter throwing temper tantrums, he knew he had to get a handle on it. And he did."

"Did he get professional help?"

Keith laughed. "I guess so. He talked to me about it a lot, and I'm a professional. All I can say is, he got it a little more in check. He'd still get red in the face, and he'd cuss somebody out. He might have still needed to break something now and again. But all I can tell you is that in my opinion, as well as I knew him, he never would have struck any other human being in anger, least of all Taylor. Steve may have had a lot of personal demons chasing after him—he never was as successful as I know he wanted to be. But he was a good man."

After a moment, Annie asked Keith if he could think of anyone else who might be able to tell her about Steve's state of mind in the months before his death.

"Lemme think ... I know he was all upset about Taylor throwing him out—spitting mad, to tell you the truth."

"Was he opposed to the divorce?"

"Oh, yeah. He knew they were having their troubles, but he wanted to work it out. He felt that if they just separated, and didn't divorce, that they might eventually get back together."

Annie thought for a moment. "Was money an issue?"

"Not really, for Steve. He said he'd talked to a divorce lawyer, who told him he wouldn't get much. Something about the way he owned his part of the business, that she wouldn't be forced to buy him out, or something. We didn't talk about it that much. His main concern was Taylor. He was crazy about that woman."

"Do you remember the name of his lawyer, by any chance?"

Keith thought hard. "Let me see. . . . The day he told me that . . . he came by the church and we shot some hoops. He was in Spokane that day because he'd just been to see the lawyer." Keith started to shake his head. "He told me, but I can't seem to . . . wait, wait I do remember, because the name was the same as one of my Sunday Schoolers. Phillip Greene. That's the kid's name—Phil Green—only the lawyer's name is spelled with an 'e,' because I asked if there was any relation. He practices here in Spokane. Funny the things you remember, isn't it?"

Annie agreed, and hoped that this little tidbit might provide yet another missing piece of the puzzle.

Chapter 24

BY THE TIME noon rolled around, Jed Delacourt was looking at three strikes in a row. His search of county police and court records revealed that neither Steve nor Taylor had ever filed a complaint against the other, and there was no indication that Steve had ever been arrested. Civil records showed no lawsuits, no prior marriages, no ownership of property.

Jed's next search had been a telephone call to Steve's former employer, Nu-chem, a chemical supply company headquartered in Seattle. Steve's former boss was more than willing to talk, but had little to say. Steve had been a commissioned salesman with the company for about a year and a half. His territory included central and eastern Washington, and the western part of Idaho. Each salesman was responsible for storing their own samples. Some worked out of their homes, but the boss said that Steve had rented an office in the Larson Building in downtown Yakima to use as his base of operations, and gave Jed the address.

"He might still have some stuff there. I know he had some office furniture, filing cabinets and whatnot. He told me he was subletting the space from a friend who worked in the same building, so his rent was dirt cheap."

"Did he say who he was subletting from?" Jed asked.

"It was that guy that owns the chain of mini-marts, I think."

Jed asked why Steve had lost his job.

"Hey, what can I say? I liked Steve, but sales is a tough job. The guys have monthly quotas they've got to meet. They're allowed to slide for a month or two here and there, but oh, maybe six months ago, Steve's figures really went down the toilet. We knew he was having some problems at home, which must have had something to do with it, but there's only so much leeway we can give somebody. But whatever was going on, his sales figures were in the basement. When he couldn't get his numbers back up, he was told to move on."

That was it, Jed learned. No personality disputes. No controversy. And certainly no indication that Steve had a problem with fighting or violence. Except for one minor incident.

"There was one time," the employer had said, chuckling. "Hell, I thought it was pretty funny. Steve had a big sale fall through. He was over here at the main office when he got the call. Boy, he was spittin' mad. He held his cool on the phone to the customer pretty well, even though I could see he was getting hot under the collar. But when he hung up, he was so steamed that he hauled off and kicked the desk he was standing next to. It was a cheap, plywood thing. Put his foot right through it."

"What happened after that?" Jed asked.

"Nothing, really. He offered to pay for the desk, but I told him it was a piece of junk to begin with. The guy had a short fuse, I won't deny that. But hey, that's not that unusual for somebody working in sales. It's a tough business, not like other jobs where you get paid just for showing up. If you're not successful, you don't eat. But he calmed right down, apologized. I really didn't pay it much mind. Like I told that reporter, it wasn't that big a deal."

"What reporter?"

"Oh, some guy from the Yakima paper. He called me first thing on Wednesday, the morning after Steve was killed. Helluva way to find out somebody you know is dead, let me tell you. Here the guy was murdered, and this bozo was trying to dig up dirt, like somehow Steve did something to get himself killed. Really pissed me off. I mean, Steve wasn't my best salesman, but he was a decent guy. Those reporters, they salivate at the sight of blood."

"Do you remember his name?"

"Yeah, 'cause I told my gal not to put through any more of his calls. Lopez. Tim Lopez."

Jed thanked him for the information, left his number in case he thought of anything else that might be significant about Steven Vick, then drove to a fast-food restaurant for a bite to eat. Munching on a quarter-pounder with cheese, Jed thought about what he'd been able to discover—or not discover. All that he'd learned so far was that Taylor's husband was a somewhat less-than-adequate salesman who occasionally got angry when things didn't go his way. Jed took his cellular phone—his favorite new toy—out of his pocket and dialed information for the number of the Yakima newspaper. When he called there, he found there was a reporter named Lopez, but he was out on assignment, and due back about four. Jed made an appointment to come by and see him.

When he had finished eating, Jed couldn't think of much else to do but drive by the office building where Steve Vick had rented space. If his supplies were still there, they might provide some clue to the murder victim's personality.

The Larson Building reminded Jed of the kind of place Philip Marlowe or Sam Spade might have had an office. The reader board in the lobby listed Steven Vick and Associates on the fourth floor. An ancient elevator creaked and groaned its way up, then opened onto a hallway tiled with squares of brown and tan linoleum that looked as old as the building. The individual office doors even had the names painted in fading gold leaf on frosted glass.

Suite 411 was at the end of the hall, around a corner, with STEVEN VICK AND ASSOCIATES painted in small print. The lights behind the frosted glass door were off. Jed turned the handle on the door and it opened.

It looked like someone had cleaned out the office in a hurry. A scarred wooden desk stood in one corner, all the

drawers half-open and empty. There were multiple uniden-
tifiable stains on the fading brown carpet. A calendar on the
wall was turned to the correct month, and a pile of newspapers on the floor bore that week's dates. The only conclusion Jed could draw was that the office had been emptied
after Steve's death. He left, closing the door behind him.

Further down the hall was an office with the lights on,
and the sound of a television emanating from the open
door. Jed walked toward it to see if whoever was there
could tell him anything about when Steve's office had been
evacuated.

There was no name on the door. Jed stepped inside. Despite the presence of half a dozen cigarette butts in the
ashtray with a lingering smell of smoke, a small black and
white television turned on to a soap opera, and an empty
child's playpen, the office appeared to be empty.

Jed glanced around. The single room looked like it had
been decorated in the late sixties and never updated. The
carpet was a dense, industrial-grade pile in a garish floral
pattern of pink, orange, and lime green. The walls were
paneled in chocolate brown veneer, which someone had
tried to lighten up with large prints of lions and tigers in
gold-painted frames. Jed had seen such things in discount
stores, but never knew who bought them.

Three filing cabinets stood against one wall, and half a
dozen unlabeled cardboard boxes with frayed corners and
water stains were piled in the corner. A battered wooden
desk that looked like the companion to the one in Vick's office stood near the door. A typing table near the desk held
a clunky old electric typewriter, something Jed hadn't seen
in an office for several years. The only clue to the office's
possible occupants was a jumble of keys on the desk on a
large lucite key chain that read DARLENE.

Jed heard a flushing toilet across the hall, and moments
later a young woman carrying a chubby, fruit juice–stained
toddler shuffled into the office. She wore black shorts, a
thin cotton tank top, and plastic thongs. Her stringy,
shoulder-length hair was frosted blond, with the dark roots

starting to show. She lifted the toddler into the playpen, then moved behind the desk and put her hand on the phone. She narrowed her eyes at him. "What are you doing, snooping around here?"

Jed grinned. "I'm not snooping."

" 'Cause if you are, I gotta call Martin. He can be down here in five minutes if I call him."

"That's pretty fast."

The woman had an idea. "You're not Martin's boss, are you, checking up on him? I'm just filling in for a couple days, really. He's right upstairs if you need him."

"No, I'm not anybody's boss."

"Then what are you doing here?"

The woman was so nervous and defensive, Jed figured that direct questions would get him nowhere. He had to think fast. Giving her what he hoped was his most winning boyish smile, Jed improvised. "I got the time wrong for a job interview with a guy down the hall, and I'm about an hour early. I saw this TV on, and well"—he tried to look sheepish—"I hate to admit it, but I'm a soap fan myself. I thought maybe I could sit and watch with you while I wait for my appointment."

Hearing the words, Jed wanted to kick himself. It was positively the lamest excuse he'd ever heard. Amazingly, she bought it.

"Hey, no problem. Pull up a chair."

There was a folding metal chair in the corner. Jed brought it over and set it up where he could see the TV. He'd actually never watched a soap opera in his life, and hoped the woman wouldn't press him with questions.

She cooed to the toddler in the playpen, then sat down behind the reception desk. After rummaging through her purse for a cigarette, she pulled the last one out of a pack and stuck it between her lips. "Want one?" she asked. "I've got more." She held up a fresh pack of Eves.

"No thanks."

"Gum?"

"Sure." He took a stick of Juicy Fruit, then watched the

soap opera for a few minutes. A blonde was accusing a brunette of sleeping with another woman's husband. It wasn't easy to follow. When a commercial for breakfast cereal came on, Darlene hit the mute button on the remote control, and smiled broadly at Jed, revealing crooked, nicotine-stained teeth. "My name's Darlene." She jangled the lucite key chain and giggled. "But I bet you knew that already."

He didn't see a wedding ring. The whole scenario was starting to remind him of the nightmare of personal ad dating. "Hi, Darlene. I'm Ted."

"Hi, Ted."

"Hi."

"I'm sorry I was so jumpy there. I was kinda weirded out when I saw somebody in here. Till now, I've never seen anybody come by here, 'cept Martin. And he told me to keep an eye out for anybody snoopin' around."

"And Martin is . . . ?"

"Martin Grubenmacher. He's the bigwig that owns all them mini-marts. You know, Short Stops. Like out on the highway? He's probably the richest guy I've ever met."

"Does he work here, too?"

Darlene snorted, blowing cigarette smoke through her nose. She kept one eye on the playpen and the other on the muted commercials. "Nobody 'works' here, unless you count me, and this is hardly work. I just got this job through the temp agency. All I have to do is sit here, make sure nobody takes anything. I brought the TV myself—nobody said I couldn't—'cause I got bored as hell just sitting here the first day. I wasn't going to bring Jessie. She usually stays with my mom, but Mom wasn't feeling well this morning, and I thought, what's the big deal? I sure as hell can't pay a sitter on the minimum wage they give me here."

"That's for sure. Is Martin the person you work for?"

"I guess so. He came down my first day and helped me get set up. He said he was supposed to sit and watch this stuff himself, but he was too busy. Couldn't get his other work done."

"His other work is running the mini-marts?"

"Better than that. He's the guy that gets to design all the window displays. Doesn't that sound cool? But he said he can't be creative if his office doesn't have a window. Upstairs, his office is on the top floor in the corner. It's got a great view. He said he just couldn't work down here. But that's why I asked if you were Martin's boss. 'Cause he said if anybody came by asking for him, to say he was in the bathroom. Then call him real quick, 'cause he's supposed to be down here himself."

The soap opera came back on, and Jed pretended to watch. On the next commercial break, he asked, "You know anything about this Steven Vick guy that has the office down the hall?"

"Only what I read in the papers."

"He's been in the paper?" Jed feigned amazement. Deep down, he had always wanted to be an actor. He knew he was at least as good as the clowns on the soap they were watching.

"Oh, yeah. It was a big deal. My aunt lives in Harmony, she called and told my mom about it. This Steven Vick, he got killed at a party out there at one of the wineries, some big posh shindig."

"Wow." He tried to sound interested, but didn't want to lay it on too thick. "Was it, like, a drug deal or something?"

"Oh, no. Nothing like that. The papers said that his old lady bonked him over the head—nobody saw it, but she was found standing over the body waving this wine bottle at him."

"Why did she do it?"

"The newspaper story kind of hinted around that he beat her up. Man, that takes guts, let me tell you. And I should know. I've had the stuff kicked out of me a few times. It's hard to fight back."

"Did you ever meet him?"

"Meet him? Nah, I only started here on Wednesday. I had to help Martin move his stuff out of there, over to this office. It seemed tacky to do it before the funeral and everything, but Martin said sometimes the police confiscate stuff, and he was worried about the things he'd loaned to Vick. That's why he had to move it over here." She turned the television sound back on. It was a party scene, and Darlene was saying something about how the other actress who had played Jeanette was so much prettier, and how could they possibly expect them to believe that she'd gone in for plastic surgery, and come out shorter and uglier? Jed mumbled affirmatively, as if he'd been thinking the exact same thing.

"So this is all Martin's stuff?" Jed asked while pretending to be thoroughly engrossed in the soap opera.

"That's what he told me." They watched in silence until the next commercial.

"So," he said, when Darlene hit the mute button again, "have you looked in the files?"

"Have I looked? Are you kidding? Of course I've looked. Somebody hires me to come down here and sit on my fanny all day with nothing to do, of course I'm gonna look. Who wouldn't?"

Jed leaned forward, and whispered conspiratorially. "So was it good stuff?"

Darlene stubbed out her cigarette. She picked up the pack, as if considering having another, then changed her mind. "Nah, it's all stupid. Xeroxes of articles, and scientific magazines. None of it makes any sense to me."

"Like what?"

"Well, there was a bunch of stuff on apples. From a while back, you know, when nobody would eat apples because they sprayed that Ajax stuff on 'em?"

"You mean Alar? The pesticide?"

"Is that what it's called? There were all these studies and reports about how nobody was buying apples, and what a disaster it was."

"Anything else?"

"Other stuff like that. Nobody's buying apples. Nobody's buying Tylenol. Nobody's buying fast-food hamburgers 'cause some little kids died from germs. It was just all old stuff."

"Sounds pretty boring."

"It was. I read through some of it, 'cause the first day I didn't bring nothing to read. How was I supposed to know there wasn't going to be anything for me to do? I thought this was supposed to be some sort of job. But then I took a lunch break and bought a *National Enquirer*."

Jed shook his head. "Seems pretty dumb, have you sit here and guard a bunch of articles."

"Tell me about it. I mean, there was some other stuff, too. Maps and stuff about water canals and wells and stuff."

"Any particular places?"

"Mostly out in the valley. The Roza Canal, near Harmony, that area."

"And what's in the boxes?"

She shrugged. "I dunno. I didn't look."

His eyes got big. "You didn't? Then that must be where the important stuff is."

"You think?"

"Maybe." Jed was worried. The credits began to roll on the soap opera. He was going to lose his excuse for being there in a few minutes. He held his breath.

"I'm gonna look," Darlene said.

Jed exhaled. "Are you sure you should?"

"Ah, who's gonna know?"

"I won't tell."

She giggled and went over to the boxes in the corner. "Come on, help me look." He joined her and they opened the first box.

"Oh, yuck. It's just chemicals. Gross."

"They look like really old bottles," Jed said, pulling one out. It was dark brown glass with a faded Nu-chem label. He took it to the window to get a better look, while Darlene opened another box. "This one's the same stuff," she said. "Can you tell what it is?"

He read the label. "This stuff's been banned for twenty years."

"What is it?"

"It's DDT."

Chapter 25

ANNIE LOCATED two attorneys named Phillip Greene in the Spokane telephone book, but only one spelled his name with an "e" and specialized in domestic relations. Since her appointment with Dr. Montgomery wasn't until four, Annie decided to try an informal drop-in, to see if Greene would see her without an appointment. But first, she needed to place a quick call to Val O'Hara.

About a hundred times a day, Annie thanked Val for coming back out of retirement. It might have been possible to run a law practice without her, but it certainly wouldn't have been easy. Within minutes, Val was able to pull up a prior brief on her computer, and read Annie the case citations she needed before she talked to Greene. She'd run by the county law library to make photocopies on her way to Greene's office.

Val also passed along a couple of messages. Dr. Butterick, at St. Elizabeth's, needed to talk to her about Taylor. He would be assisting in surgery until five, but she could have him paged at the hospital after that.

The second message was from Jed. He told Val to tell Annie, if she called in, that the court records and police reports were all negative for any incidents of reported violence between Steve and Taylor, but that he was "hot on the trail" of another lead.

"Did he say what it was?" Annie asked.

"No," said Val. "Only that there was some link to a guy

named Martin ... I didn't quite catch the last name. . . . Gerbermeister, maybe?"

"Grubenmacher?"

"That was it. He didn't tell me what he was working on, only that you shouldn't worry if he wasn't back at the motel when you got there tonight."

The Gable Building, with its chrome escalators and off-white walls could have been any nondescript office building in any medium-sized city. Greene's office, which Annie found on the twelfth floor, was as nondescript as the building—white walls, beige industrial-strength carpet, budget furniture. There were no clients waiting in the reception area, and a bespectacled, thirty-ish man in a white shirt and loosened tie sat behind the reception desk talking on the telephone. He looked up, smiled, and held up one finger for her to wait.

After he hung up, he turned to Annie. "Hi," he said with more enthusiasm than the typical front office person. "Can I help you?"

"Yes, I'd like to speak with Mr. Greene, if that's possible. I don't have an appointment."

"That's do-able," he said, without looking at an appointment book. "My next client isn't due until three o'clock. As long as you don't mind my catching the telephone if it rings."

"Oh," she said in surprise, "you're . . ."

He held out his hand. "Phil Greene. Pleased to meet you. And no, I don't usually run a one-person office from the reception desk. My staff's throwing a baby shower for my paralegal, and they decided that my gift would be answering the phones for a couple hours so they could all go to lunch together. So, were you referred by someone?"

"It's a little more complicated than that." She gave him her card, and explained, as briefly as possible, her relationship to Taylor, Steve's murder, and the information she was after.

Phil Greene stood up and came around to the front of the

desk and sat in the chair next to Annie. He was a small man, very boyish in appearance. Annie noticed for the first time he was wearing jeans and Reeboks. He tapped her business card against his teeth while he thought. "Let me think about this for a second. You say the wife is suspected of killing Steve?"

"At this point she seems to be the only suspect, although no arrest has been made."

"And you think the prosecutor will try to prove a financial motive, that she wanted to kill him to avoid a division of property?"

"If I were prosecuting the case, that's what I'd do."

The lawyer shifted in his chair. "Then my file is certainly relevant. Steve was my client, so there's confidentiality to think about. I've never had a situation come up where I've been asked to reveal information after a client's death."

Annie nodded. "I knew you'd be concerned about that. But this is something that does occasionally come up in murder investigations." She handed him the photocopied statutes and case law she'd obtained at the library.

"Boy, you come prepared, don't you?" He read through them, and seemed satisfied that he could discuss Steve's file. "Hold on just a second." He locked the door, and hung a sign saying that the office was closed for lunch. "Let's go back to my office, and I'll pull Steve's file. Coffee? Take anything in it?"

"Please. Black is fine."

Greene's office was little more than a cubbyhole big enough for a desk, chair, and computer. Files lay in stacks on practically every inch of floor space. He squeezed around behind his desk and offered Annie a chair, also filled with files. "You can just throw those anywhere." She moved them to the floor and sat down. Greene swiveled in his chair, gazed at the teetering stacks for a moment, and then reached for a file about two-thirds of the way down the first pile. Miraculously, he had put his hands right on Steven Vick's file. He shrugged and grinned. "It's kind of a talent I have. Like that old game, Concentration. Comes in handy."

Annie agreed. It was a talent she needed, but didn't have. She waited while Greene flipped through his papers, refreshing his recollection of Vick.

"It sparked my interest, when you were describing what the prosecutors would try to do. Because the way I see it, there wouldn't have been much of a financial motive for the wife in this case. I really felt sorry for the guy when he came to see me for just that reason. If his wife really wanted to go through with the divorce, I told Steve that he was basically going to get screwed."

Annie was interested. "How so?"

"He first came to see me, let's see, I've got the date here. It would have been six months ago, right after his wife asked him to move out. 'Asked' is a euphemism in this case. From what I understand, she moved all of his stuff into storage and changed the locks." Greene stirred his coffee with the end of a Bic pen. "Steve was really distraught. He hadn't seen it coming. He knew there had been problems, but nothing that he thought was that serious. The way he described it, they'd always had a volatile relationship—lots of screaming matches and tantrums—but they usually made up within a few days. This time seemed different, she wouldn't take him back. He'd recently lost his job at a chemical supply house, and that wasn't helping his state of mind, either."

Annie scribbled notes on a yellow legal pad. "What about community property? Wouldn't there have been a division?"

"That's where things got complicated. They had been living together, as man and wife, for many years, and had one daughter together. But for whatever reason, they hadn't actually gotten married until three years ago." It was the same story that Annie had just learned from Keith Curran. "There are no significant assets other than the house and farm. And Taylor North inherited those, equally with her brother, *before* she and Vick were legally married. Now, you said you do some domestic relations work, so you know there's no such thing as common-law marriage in the state of Washington, although there is a recent precedent for the kind of lawsuits that have been termed 'palimony.' "

"But it's not clearly defined."

"Exactly. That's what I told Vick. I said that his *legal* claim to her share of the property was pretty thin, although there would be ways to fight it. It could be an expensive lawsuit, without any guarantees. I told him that I personally wouldn't take on the case without a thirty-five hundred dollar retainer, and that I wouldn't promise I could get results for him. He said he'd think about it."

Checking back through her earlier notes, Annie said, "When I talked to Taylor's brother, Gerald, about the property, he got very defensive. I didn't get the impression he owned any interest in Taylor's business."

"Okay, here again, it gets a little messy. This family apparently didn't have a very high regard for lawyers, because they drew up their own business transactions without any help. If they'd gotten a little bit of legal advice, a lot of headaches could have been avoided." Greene flipped back in the file until he found what he was looking for. "The father died a little more than twelve years ago, without a will, so Taylor and her brother inherited the property equally. The brother, Gerald, is some kind of artist. He had no great love for the farm, but wanted cash. Something about going to study painting in New York. Steve had about fifteen thousand dollars set aside—remember, this is *before* they're married—and he agreed to buy Gerald's half. Gerald was so desperate, that he didn't even bother to get a valuation on the property, he just took the money Steve was offering. At that time, the farm hadn't been worked in a couple of years, the buildings were run-down. Gerald went on 'intuition' and didn't think the land was worth very much. He spent his money living and studying in New York for a year, and came back penniless. Taylor and Steve, on the other hand, were well on the way to building a decent business. According to Steve, Gerald was convinced he had been conned."

"Had he?"

"I don't think so. It was a sloppy deal, but neither party was guilty of any wrongdoing."

"But if Steve owned half the property, wouldn't Taylor have had a financial motive to kill him, rather than go through a divorce?"

"I don't think so," said Greene. "Because of one other fact. Steve's interest wasn't recorded properly. The title was still in Gerald's name. When they did this transaction, they went to the stationery store and got some forms. Drew up a bill of sale and a quitclaim deed. Basically handled it as if they were selling personal property, like a car or piece of furniture. When I looked at the documentation, I just cringed. The purchase agreement wasn't notarized and the signatures weren't even dated. I told Steve that a sharp lawyer would make mincemeat out of the deal. At best, he might prove that he'd invested fifteen thousand in the business, but he'd be lucky if he could even prove that."

"So if Taylor divorced Steve . . ."

"My guess was that with a savvy lawyer, Taylor could have walked away with everything. With him dead, basically what she saved herself was some protracted litigation. You tell me. Is she the type of person who'd off her husband just to save herself the hassle of a lawsuit? There wasn't even any life insurance. I remember asking Steve that. He said the only insurance he had had was through his job, and that ended when he was terminated. Now, her best position from a financial standpoint was to do exactly what she was doing—nothing. Stay separated from Steve, but not divorce him. He wasn't pressuring her for a divorce, and she could use her cash flow to build the business, not pay lawyers to litigate a property settlement."

"But Taylor was ready to start divorce proceedings. At least she said she was. That was the reason she invited me here."

Greene sipped his coffee and closed the file. "I guess

that's what makes domestic relations work so interesting to me—we give advice regarding what the best *business* or *financial* decision would be—then our clients go and do just the opposite. It's important that we lawyers don't forget that these cases aren't *business* transactions. They involve love, marriage, parenthood, companionship. If Taylor was willing to divorce Steve, even though staying married was a better deal for her, then the chances are she had some reason other than money for not wanting to be married to him anymore. He was out of the house, willing to give her some space . . . What do you think?"

"She wanted to marry someone else?"

Greene shrugged and smiled. "That sounds like a good guess to me. Love makes us all do crazy things sometimes."

Chapter 26

THE OFFICES of the *Yakima Herald-Republic* were on North Fourth Street downtown, near the mall. A receptionist directed Jed to Tim Lopez's desk near the back, where a young man was cradling a telephone receiver on his shoulder as he typed copy into a computer.

"Right . . . uh huh . . . what time will the ceremony take place today? . . . And the mayor will be talking about kids' issues, right?" He gestured for Jed to take a seat. "Okay, that's about all I need for now. Can I call you back later if I have some more questions? Great. Thanks a lot." He hung up and looked at Jed. "Kind of a slow news day. Our lead story will be about a speech the mayor is giving at a ground-breaking ceremony for the new children's hospital. Life in the big city, huh? What can I help you with?"

Jed sat down across from Lopez's desk, and introduced himself. The reporter frowned when Jed mentioned Steven Vick's name.

"Lemme get this straight. You're one of the defense attorneys for the wife?"

"That's right."

"Did Shibilsky give you my name?"

"Shibilsky? Who's that?"

"I guess he didn't." Lopez shook his head in disgust. "He's the homicide detective who's supposed to be working the case. I called him as soon as I heard about the story. I tried to tell him what I knew, but the guy just wasn't interested. So how did you get my name?"

Jed told him about Steve's employer. Lopez said, "Yeah, I could tell the guy was p.o.'d. I tried to call him back and apologize for hitting him with the news like that, but I couldn't get his secretary to put the call through."

"You said you called the homicide detective to tell him what *you* knew?"

"Yeah, not that it did much good. You try to be a good citizen and come forward with this stuff. Soon as I saw Steve's picture, I mean, I knew it was something that should be followed up on. Hold on a second. Let me save my document here." He punched a few keys, and his computer screen went blank. "Steve Vick came to talk to me about, uh, let's see, it was a week ago, Monday. I didn't know who he was until later, when I saw the picture we got to run in the paper. He never gave me his name."

"What did he want?"

"He wanted money for some information he had. The talk shows are making it really tough to be a reporter these days, you know? Everybody hears how they can get big money selling their story, nobody wants to talk for free anymore. Problem is, newspapers don't have that kind of money to throw around. Half the time, I give a ten dollar bill to an informant, it comes out of my own pocket."

"What kind of information did he have?"

"He wouldn't give me many details, because as I said, he wanted to be paid. But when I told him I wasn't authorized to buy stories, unless I had some idea what I was buying, he told me a little, but it was pretty vague. He said that he had uncovered evidence of a major scheme that would harm the public. Man, I thought he was a paranoid nut, to tell you the truth. We get people come in here all the time, think they know somebody who's got the atomic bomb. But anyways, he thought it would be a huge story if we could blow this thing wide open, and publicize it before the harm reached the public. Then he and I would be hailed as heroes. I could tell he really got off on the hero angle. Well,

I told him I didn't think the public would get quite that excited about a story that hadn't happened yet, especially if he wouldn't tell me what it was about. Now after somebody gets hurt, that's a different story."

Jed looked perplexed. "So you told him *not* to go public with the story until somebody got hurt?"

Lopez laughed. "Hell, no. I wouldn't do that. No, I just told him I'd have to check with my supervisor about the cash, and get back to him. But I wasn't very encouraging about him getting much money for the story. I also told him he might have a better chance coming forward with the story for free, if what he wanted was the public recognition. Then maybe a talk show would pick it up. I definitely told him he should reveal what he knew, especially if there was going to be harm to the public. And I warned him that if he didn't come forward, that he could be considered an accessory to the crime. He didn't like that, but then he thought about it and laughed. He said, "I can hardly be charged as an accessory if nobody knows who I am.' "

"Then what did he do?"

"We chatted a little longer. He asked if it would help if he brought me the documents that proved what he was talking about." Lopez shrugged. "That was one of the things that made me doubt the guy, to tell you the truth. Of course, it would help to have documents. Did this guy just fall off the turnip truck or something? If he had documents, why didn't he bring them in the first place? At this point, I was starting to think the guy was a flake, but I told him, yeah, go get me hard copies. There was something weird about the way he said it, though. Just a second, I kept a few notes on the conversation." Lopez swiveled in his chair and brought up a document on his computer, then scrolled down the screen. "Here it is. . . . Yeah, when he brought up a reference to the military, that's when I figured he was a genuine nut case. . . . Okay, Vick said he'd seen the production notes and the distribution schedule in the colonel's desk drawer, but it shouldn't be a problem to get, because he—Steve—was good friends with 'the old softie'—meaning the colonel, I guess. Then he kind of chuckled at his own joke, know what I mean?"

"Did you talk about anything else?"

"I chatted him up some more. Don't get me wrong, if there was a real story there, I wanted to be the one to get it. I just didn't want to pay for it. I was trying to kind of cajole him into telling me something. I pretended to go talk to my editor about the money."

"Pretended?"

"Yeah, the kind of money he wanted—I think he floated twenty-five thousand as a figure—the paper could never have paid. We pay five hundred to a source, we think it's the big time. I was just stringing him along to see if he'd give me anything else. But he didn't. I showed him out, and he said he'd call when he got the stuff, but I didn't think any more about it. When he did call back, it took me a minute to remember who he was."

"When did he call back?"

Lopez checked his computer screen. "Tuesday morning. That would have been the day he was killed. He told me he had the documents in his possession, and he wanted to meet. We made an appointment for Wednesday at one. He wanted to come in right away, but I was working on some other things, and frankly, thought this guy was just going to waste my time. In retrospect, I probably should have put a little more effort into getting the story out of him."

"You mean because of the murder?"

"Hell, yeah. A guy comes in to see a reporter, says he's got a hot story, and the next day somebody smashes a bottle over his head? That would tend to make me believe he knew something that somebody didn't want revealed."

"When did you hear about Steve's death?"

"Our guy who monitors the police beat had the news Wednesday morning. When I saw the photo the paper was going to run, I knew Steven Vick wasn't going to be keeping his one o'clock appointment with me."

"So what did you do?"

"As soon as I saw the guy's picture, I called up the detective and told him everything I knew."

"This was Detective Shibilsky?"

"Yeah. And to tell you the truth, he didn't give a damn. He said it was a domestic quarrel, and no further information was necessary to wrap up the investigation. Now, if he was doing his job, he would have been required to keep notes of our conversations, and turn them over to whoever is defending the wife, meaning you."

Jed smiled. "I was a public defender for a while. Believe me, those guys are very good at not doing their job. It's hard to turn over what's not written down. I bet he has a faulty memory about the conversation, too."

"I hear you."

A beep sounded on Lopez's watch. He reached in his pocket and pulled out a packet of gum with a prescription slip attached. "Nicotine gum. I can only have one every hour. You ever try to quit smoking? It's murder. Sorry, no pun intended."

"After Steve was killed, you could have printed the story. That would have embarrassed the detective."

He shrugged. "Yeah, but I'm not out to gore anybody's ox. We get a lot of stuff from the sheriff's office. No sense in mucking up that avenue of communication. And who knows, maybe the detective had already checked it out, found out it was nothing." Lopez sat back, looking like he was deriving great satisfaction from his nicotine gum. "Now, if something happens *tomorrow* that looks suspicious, you better believe we'll print this story in a second."

"Tomorrow?"

"Yeah, that was the one hard fact Vick would give me. Whatever it was that was going down, it was going to be set in motion tonight. According to the documents he'd gotten his hands on, the stuff was going to be moved into place Friday night. He said folks might start getting hurt as early as Saturday the fifteenth. I don't know about you, man, but the next few days, I'm going to watch my step."

Chapter 27

ANNIE STILL HAD half an hour before her appointment to see Dr. Claire Montgomery, so she decided to take a walk down by the river. The day was chilly and overcast, and the trees in Riverside Park were turning various shades of red and gold. She walked past the angular bronze sculptures of runners and onto the pedestrian bridge that crossed the river at Spokane Falls. Because it was October, the water level was low, but the river was still beautiful. She stared into the water and listened to the rushing sound, trying to organize her thoughts.

Talking to Keith Curran and Phillip Greene, it was clear that Annie would not be able to establish that Taylor North was a battered spouse striking back at her husband out of fear and desperation. Such cases were, unfortunately, all too common—but this wasn't one of them.

Why then was she still searching for answers? The physical evidence pointed to Taylor as the killer. Steve was struck in the back of the head, with sufficient force to kill him. Taylor was found near the body holding the weapon, and she attempted suicide shortly thereafter. And, at least for now, Taylor's loss of memory prevented her from testifying that she didn't kill Steve. What could be a more perfect case for the State?

Annie had been a prosecutor long enough to know when a case was strong. The only thing she could conclude was that she didn't *believe* Taylor had killed Steve in cold blood. It just didn't fit.

Dr. Montgomery's office was in town in the downtown commercial district one block from the river. Annie found the waiting room elegant but cold, with a dark burgundy carpet contrasting starkly with white leather furniture and bare white walls. The only adornment was a single flower arrangement, a glass vase holding half a dozen red anthuriums, on a square black lacquer table. No magazines, no brochures, not even a box of Kleenex for distraught patients. And like most psychologists' offices, no receptionist.

Annie took a seat on the white leather loveseat a few minutes before the hour. Precisely at two, the inner door was opened by an extremely thin, dark-haired woman wearing a black silk jumpsuit. She wore red lipstick and fingernail polish in a shade which perfectly matched the red anthuriums, an effect which Annie was sure was intentional. She wore no jewelry, no makeup except for the red lipstick, and no shoes. Her toenails were painted, of course, a matching shade of red.

"You must be Annie MacPherson. Please come in." Inside the inner office, Dr. Montgomery indicated one of two armchairs facing each other. "You may sit there, by the window." Like the reception area, the inner office had stark white walls and modern furniture. There was very little about the room that would have made Annie feel like opening up her inner self. The psychologist handed Annie a clipboard with a new-patient questionnaire on it, and a copy of a fee schedule. "Might as well get the unpleasant details taken care of first. Do you have insurance?"

Annie stopped her. "I really have to explain. I'm not here for myself. I'm here to talk to you about a client." The thin woman stiffened. "You're an attorney." It was a statement, not a question.

"Yes. But I have a letter of representation and a signed release. I'm sure you'll find it in order."

The doctor responded in a peeved tone, "I wish you'd

made that clear. I limit my legal consultations to two a week, and those slots have already been filled."

That was precisely why she hadn't mentioned the purpose of her visit, Annie thought.

The woman sighed dramatically. "Well, I guess the time is booked, and you're here. My fee for legal consultations is three hundred an hour, which I expect up-front." Annie reached for her checkbook, while the doctor took thin wire-framed reading glasses from some invisible pocket. "Who is it you need to know about?"

Annie handed the doctor a copy of the medical release. "Taylor North. Perhaps you saw the news about what happened to her husband on Tuesday night?"

Dr. Montgomery stiffened. "Yes, yes I did hear. But I'm afraid someone's given you the wrong information."

"About what?"

"Taylor isn't a patient of mine. Never has been. She's an old friend. I've known her for years."

The doctor removed her glasses and shook her head. She glanced at Annie's checkbook. "No, please. Put that away. You say you're representing Taylor? The news has been very scant. All I really know is that Steven Vick was killed."

"The sheriff's department is still investigating, but I expect them to charge Taylor. She was found standing over the body, holding a wine bottle which they believe was the murder weapon. The detectives are not investigating any other suspects."

"My Lord, that it would come to this." She shook her head sadly. "I knew Taylor was troubled, but that she would actually . . . Can I get you something, a cup of tea?"

"No, thank you, Doctor. But please go ahead."

"Yes, if you'll excuse me for just a moment."

She returned in a few minutes with a porcelain teacup filled with something smelling faintly of oranges. "Taylor and I were students together in Pullman. I was getting my graduate degree at Washington State University, Taylor was involved in theater classes. Steve and Taylor had an apartment across the hall from me." She took a deep breath. "Taylor's friendship has meant a lot to me, and until fairly recently, we've seen each other quite often. I have a house on Lake Coeur d'Alene, about thirty miles from here. Taylor would come over and stay the weekend five or six times a year. Now why is it that you assumed I was her therapist?"

"Taylor asked me to come to Harmony to discuss a divorce. When we first started talking about Steve, she implied that the relationship was an abusive one, but that she'd been seeing a woman therapist in Spokane to deal with her feelings about it. When I found your business card in her address book, I assumed that you were she."

"Well, I can see how you would have thought that. Taylor . . . how can I put this . . . has a tendency to exaggerate or embellish the facts when it suits her purpose. It was one of the reasons why I would never have taken her on as a patient. It would have been very frustrating trying to ferret out the truth. Actually, such exaggeration is not inconsistent with her particular personality disorder."

"I thought you said she wasn't a patient. You sound like you diagnosed her."

Dr. Montgomery looked up. "Well, actually, I did. It's an occupational hazard. After enough years of this, it becomes difficult *not* to diagnose one's friends and acquaintances. Basically, Taylor is a thrill-seeker. It's one of the qualities that makes her so attractive. She's bold, adventurous. If one is not quite so bold, like myself, perhaps like you, one is attracted to her energy."

Annie could see the pattern. In high school, she had certainly hoped that some of Taylor's recklessness would rub off. The doctor continued. "But Taylor carries her boldness to an extreme. That's why I mentioned a personality disorder. I came to believe that she has what is known as a borderline personality, with histrionic features. That sounds complicated, but what it really means is that she displays a pattern of instability of self-image, uncertainty about goals, career choices, friends, lovers. One of the typical features of this personality type is an endless sense of emptiness and boredom—the bold behavior is a means of trying to fill that emptiness. She needs to be the center of attention—and will achieve that by playing various roles—victim, seducer, loyal friend—whatever will achieve the desired result."

Annie said, "So this would explain her mercurial relationship with Steven Vick?"

"Absolutely. There would be times when Taylor would undervalue herself so much that she would stay with a man who was angry frequently, whom she fought with, out of a lack of her own self-worth. Other times, she would be disgusted by him, not want anything to do with him, tell him to get out of her life. Days later, she might be madly in love with him again—do anything to get him back. Steven Vick was as unpredictable as Taylor in many ways. It was one of the reasons she didn't grow tired of him and kept coming back for more."

Annie told Dr. Montgomery about Taylor's behavior following the Wine Gala, taking the pills, being rushed to the hospital.

"That sounds very consistent, actually. Borderline personalities often make shallow suicide attempts that are really cries for attention, or a response to boredom. In this case, I doubt that Taylor really wanted to die. It's more likely that confronted with Steven's death, she wanted to thrust herself into the role of victim, rather than aggressor. From the way everyone around her responded, it sounds like it worked."

"But I've spoken to her doctor. She was in terrible shape after the overdose—that wasn't an act."

"She probably misjudged the effect of the pills she was taking. Maybe she thought that she wouldn't suffer any great damage if her overdose was discovered quickly. It sounds like she guessed wrong."

"So you wouldn't see the suicide attempt as an indication of guilt?"

"No, I don't think you could draw that conclusion. Sorrow, despair, neediness—almost anything could have triggered that type of behavior for Taylor."

"You mentioned something about histrionic traits?"

The doctor continued, "Yes, personality disorders rarely fall into neat little boxes. Taylor's personality, in my mind, was primarily dominated by the borderline traits, but she also displayed traits associated with the histrionic personality disorder—in other words, the flamboyance, the flirtatiousness, the attention-seeking behavior. This type of person is often very engaging, very seductive—and very aware of their own attractiveness."

"I see." The description of Taylor North sounded like a perfect fit.

"Let me ask you something. Taylor hinted to me, and to her neighbors in Harmony as well, that Steve was beating her. Her friends said they saw the bruises."

"Taylor? A battered spouse? I would find that very hard to believe. Remember, I've known both Steve and Taylor a very long time. I've never seen any evidence to support that, and it simply wouldn't fit either of their personality profiles. Oh, they fought frequently. You wouldn't believe the terrible shouting I heard from across the hall back in those early days. But as often as not, Taylor was the aggressor. Steve was more of a blusterer, full of sound and fury as they say. Steve would bully and yell, but Taylor was the one more apt to get violent. I'd seen them fighting where Taylor was taking wild swings, and Steve was doing his best to push her away."

Annie remembered Harry Braithwaite's description of the night Steve was killed—Taylor pounding on Steve's chest, him repeatedly shoving her back until she fell in the gravel. At the time, she had thought Harry was making the whole thing up, but the scenario was identical to what Dr. Montgomery was describing.

"But the bruises? Several people in Harmony told me they saw them."

"Hard to say. She craved danger and might have gotten herself into rough situations. But if she was angry at Steve,

I'd say it was more likely that she was trying to make him out to be a monster. Push the blame for their breakup onto his behavior, making him look bad to their mutual friends. In other words, it might have all been an act."

"An act?" There was a pause, and Annie remembered something both Dr. Montgomery and Keith Curran had said about Taylor's time at WSU. "You said Taylor was involved with theater at school?"

"Yes. It was practically all she did. She flunked out of her other courses, but she loved every aspect of putting on productions. Acting, directing, costumes, sets . . ."

"Makeup?"

Dr. Montgomery looked at Annie and instantly understood. "Yes, theatrical makeup was one of her interests."

"The only injuries anyone saw were black eyes, partially concealed by dark glasses."

Dr. Montgomery nodded. "That wouldn't have been difficult for Taylor. She was very, very good with stage makeup."

Annie stopped, and tried to comprehend what she was hearing. The thought of Taylor faking injuries was chilling. But if what Dr. Montgomery said was true, it was consistent with Taylor's personality. "Doctor, throughout this entire episode, I've been unable to believe that Taylor could kill Steve. Have I been deluding myself?"

The psychologist paused, thinking. Finally she said, "No, I don't think so. Steven Vick played far too important a role in Taylor's life. Even in her moments of hatred, she needed him. She fed on his anger. She often desired him most when they were apart. Virtually everything she did was either to please Steven or to infuriate him. No, I would agree with you, I cannot imagine her destroying the central focus of her life."

Annie stood up and walked to the window overlooking the city of Spokane. There were gray clouds to the south that looked like a storm was coming. "You said that until recently, you'd seen Taylor often. What did you mean by that?"

"She hasn't visited me in five or six months, although we have talked a bit on the telephone. This most recent separation from Steve has been a very intense time for her. From what I understand, she's become very involved with a business associate, although they've made an effort to keep their relationship a secret. Again, I think that the intensity of her love for this new man in her life is in direct proportion to her need to manipulate Steve and make him jealous."

"A business associate?" Annie asked, her pulse quickening. "But I understood that *ended* about the time Taylor threw Steve out?"

"Oh, quite the contrary. The last few months, it's been increasingly passionate, according to Taylor. In fact, the last time I talked to her—it must have been about a week before the Wine Gala—she told me that he'd asked her to marry him."

"Really?"

"She told me she said yes, just as soon as she was free from Steven Vick."

Chapter 28

JED SAT in his car in the newspaper's parking lot and looked at his watch. It was twenty minutes to five, which meant that Darlene with all of her toddler paraphernalia would be leaving the Larson Building office very soon. He took the cellular telephone out of his pocket and dialed the number for the Cherry Court Motel. Finding that Annie wasn't back from Spokane yet, he left a message for her to call him as soon as she got in.

He made it back to the Larson Building at a few minutes before five, and prayed that Darlene was conscientious enough not to leave early. He sat for a moment and took a few deep breaths. His plan to get back into the office wouldn't work if he seemed harried or nervous. He got off the elevator and sauntered up to the door just as she was folding the playpen and loading little Jessie into her traveling car seat. "Hi," he said.

She turned around. "Oh, it's you again. How did your job interview go?"

Jed smiled broadly. "Really well, I think. I was only expecting it to last half an hour or so, but they kept me there all afternoon, meeting this vice president and that marketing director. I think that's a good sign."

Darlene's eyes were wide. "All that time for an interview? I think I would've wet my pants or something. I've never had one that lasted more'n ten minutes or so."

Jed was hardly surprised. "You've got a lot of stuff there, haven't you?"

"Yeah, it's always this way when I take Jess someplace." She stopped and eyed the mound of baby stuff. "I guess I'll have to make two trips."

"Oh, no. I can help you. Is your car nearby?"

"Yeah, it's at a meter on the street, right down there." She pointed out the window.

"No problem."

She looked so relieved, Jed wished he didn't have to deceive her. She would undoubtedly get in trouble when it was discovered that someone had gotten into the office after hours, and it might be a long time before the temporary agency sent her out on another job. "You take the baby and go ring for the elevator," he said, taking firm control of the situation. "I'll be right behind you with the playpen."

"Okay. The door locks automatically. Just pull it shut behind you."

"Right. You have your keys?"

"Right here." She jangled the lucite key chain.

"Great. I'll shut the door." On his earlier visit, he'd noticed the office door had a standard lock. All he had to do was switch the push buttons, and the door would stay unlocked until he came back up. He pulled it shut loudly and made a show of twisting the knob. "It's locked."

Down at the curb, he helped Darlene load the gear, Jessie's car seat, and the baby into a lemon-yellow Chevy Vega. From the sound of the engine, Jed suspected the car was suffering from terminal old age, and probably wouldn't last out the year. Darlene reminded Jed of a lot of the clients he had represented as a public defender. He knew he ought to feel compassion for them, but mostly, all he felt was bewilderment. Their lives were so different from his, he couldn't figure out how they found the strength to make it through the day. As was his custom, he tried not to think about it too hard. He stood on the curb until she was out of sight.

Back upstairs, Jed checked the other offices on the floor.

All looked closed for the evening, and there was no sign of a night watchman. He slipped back into the office and locked the door behind him.

He looked around. Now that he was back in, there was plenty of time to do a thorough search, and no reason to think he'd be interrupted. The intense silence made him nervous, so he turned Darlene's little television on, keeping the volume low. Jed then went to the filing cabinet, and starting with the top drawer, pulled every manila folder, methodically searching for a distribution schedule, references to a colonel, or anything that hinted at a scheme that would harm the public.

Chapter 29

Martin Grubenmacher crept slowly up the stairs to the Widow's Perch, avoiding the third and the fifth steps from the bottom. They were the ones that squeaked. Perhaps if he'd been allowed to take wood shop in high school, he would know now how to fix them. But his mother had been adamant that no son of hers would ever work with his hands. Instead, he'd had to spend hours every afternoon going to Junior Achievement and Future Businessmen of America meetings, working on a marketing plan to sell light bulbs door-to-door, when what he'd really wanted to do was learn how to work on cars or build toolboxes like other boys his age.

It was four stories up in a tight spiral. When he'd first started coming up here, the climb had winded him. But now that he'd come up every day for a very long time, it was no trouble at all. He rather enjoyed the exercise.

He finally reached the opening in the floor to the little room. In a while, he would use the special binoculars he'd bought himself for his birthday. They were so powerful that Taylor's bedroom seemed like a few feet, not a mile, away. She didn't even realize that she could be seen, and never bothered with the drapes. Martin stood in front of the window and gazed out toward North Faire with a happy sigh.

Once inside his little fortress, Martin could surround himself with his photographs and his magazines and enjoy himself in peace. He'd learned years ago that anything left in his bedroom, no matter how well hidden, would be instantly located by his mother's X-ray vision and destroyed. The sun was setting, so he lit a tiny candle. He didn't think Mother could see such an insignificant glow from downstairs, and besides, he liked the way the candlelight flickered on the wall.

Lately, Martin had taken to secreting a few bottles of red wine in his sanctuary. A lightweight Styrofoam cooler under a blanket kept them protected from the heat, and a glass or two added to his mellow mood of relaxation. His mother didn't approve, of course, but that was neither here nor there. There wasn't much she did approve of, when it came right down to it. He always made sure that a bottle lasted several days, and that the smell of alcohol could never be detected on his breath. He patted his pocket, checking that he had a full tin of Altoids to freshen his breath afterwards.

Martin retrieved the half-full bottle of pinot noir from its hiding place, poured himself a little nip, and plopped down onto his beanbag chair. His private sanctuary was more comfortable to him than any room in the big mansion. He took a sip of wine and closed his eyes, relishing this most perfect part of the day. Soon, things would be even better. He'd be paid for the work he did the night of the Wine Gala, and then, maybe he'd buy a night vision scope for his binoculars, or even take a trip away from Mother. The possibilities were endless. Martin had never had any spending money of his own to speak of.

And after that, maybe he'd get up the courage to talk to Taylor. He'd heard she was doing better and would be out of the hospital soon. Steven Vick was an evil man; Taylor deserved to be free of him. When she learned what Martin had done, she'd be so grateful, she might . . . she might . . . Martin could barely contain himself thinking about it.

"Oh, is it cocktail hour already, Martin? You won't mind a little company, will you?"

The deep voice made the tiny man jump, spilling half his

glass of wine on the front of his white shirt. He started to get up out of his beanbag chair.

"No, don't get up." The man climbed the rest of the way into the room. Even though he wasn't overly tall, his hat brushed the ceiling. He removed it and held it in his gloved hand.

"How did you know I would be here?" Martin asked nervously.

"I've watched you, Martin. You come up here every evening at the same time. Kind of a creature of habit, aren't you?"

Martin's eyes flicked from side to side. He felt like a caged animal with nowhere to run. "Why . . . why are you here?" He tried to sound like he was making small talk, but his visitor just chuckled. "Can't I stop by to have a drink of wine with an old friend?" The guest lowered himself until he was seated cross-legged on the floor. "Dixie cups, Martin? Not exactly the best for wine testing, are they?"

"I . . . I didn't want Mother to miss any of her good glasses. She gets suspicious, you know."

"I see." The guest poured himself what was left in the bottle. "An '89 Oregon pinot noir. That's a good choice, Martin. I'm glad to see that at least I've managed to teach you a thing or two about wine." He sniffed, then sipped. "Not bad. I probably would've given it another year or two, but it's pretty drinkable as it is. So, first things first. The bottles from the Wine Gala. I take it they're finished and ready to go?"

Martin bit his lip and nodded, eager to please. "They're in the basement, in boxes."

"Good. I'll transport them to North Faire tonight and mix them in with the others. We have to make sure that the entire winemaking region is well-represented, don't we?"

Martin nodded. "Do you want me to help?"

A thin smile. "No, Martin. I don't think that would be a good idea. Frankly, I'm having a hard time understanding why I should trust you to do anything else on this project."

"But . . . but . . . why? I've done a good job, haven't I?"

"What do you think?"

"I did everything you said. I got Steve out to the rose garden. That, in itself, wasn't easy. He didn't know why we had to go out there, and he didn't want to. He wanted to talk to Taylor, and I told him that Taylor would be out there in a few minutes."

"Mmmm."

"And I took the wine bottle out with me, and was very careful about the prints. I left it like you said, on the third stone bench. Steve really wanted to leave but I was able to stall him until she arrived. I'm telling you, it wasn't easy."

"But you ran away, Martin. You were supposed to stay so you would be our witness. I'm very disappointed in you. When Taylor finds out, she probably will be, too."

Martin's eyes widened. "But . . . but I thought Taylor would be happy. . . ."

"She would have been, Martin, if you had completed your assignment. You were supposed to be the witness, and tell the detective that you saw Taylor swing the bottle in self-defense. You've let Taylor down, Martin."

Martin hung his head like a school boy being disciplined in front of the class. His hands were shaking so badly he had to set his Dixie cup on the floor.

"I could lie. I could go to the detective now and say I saw it all."

The man shook his head. "But you didn't, Martin. After this much time, they'd know you were lying. They were supposed to interview you at the scene, right after the incident, so there would be no question. If there had been an eyewitness, this would have been an open-and-shut case. No investigation. They wouldn't believe you now."

The guest hoisted himself up off the floor. "I don't like it when the people I hire disappoint me, Martin. You've made me very unhappy. Taylor might go to jail because you weren't able to do your part. Or worse yet, they might suspect that she didn't swing the bottle, hmm? And then this afternoon, I find out that you've let me down yet again."

"What?" Martin's lip was quivering.

"Don't play the fool with me, Martin. Your job was to destroy the remainder of the supplies. *Destroy*, Martin. You never should have let Steve acquire the chemicals in the first place—it made him suspicious, and that's when he started to look around. But we dealt with that, Martin, by getting Steve out of the picture. All you had to do was eliminate the evidence so that no one else would cause problems for us. I went by the office this afternoon, and you know what I found? I found that you had directly disobeyed me."

"I took precautions. I moved everything to a completely different office. And I hired someone to keep an eye on it. It's all perfectly safe."

The visitor was growing impatient. "I had no idea when I hired you that anyone could be so stupid, Martin. Not only do I have to go back there and get rid of the stuff myself, but now I have to do something about the girl. What if she looked in the boxes?"

"Darlene? She wouldn't have looked. . . . Darlene just needed a job for a few days. No, please, you won't . . . she has a baby. . . ." Ignoring him, the guest looked at his watch. "I can take care of the girl at her home, swing by the office, then be back here by . . . hmmm, it's going to be a busy night."

A sound halfway between a whimper and a cry emanated from Martin's lips. "Martin, are you crying? My, but aren't you the sentimental one."

"I'll . . . I'll be all right." He wiped his wet eyes on his sleeve. "As soon as you pay me my share, I'll never say another word. I promise. You'll never hear another peep out of me."

The guest laughed. "You believed me, didn't you? That I'd actually pay you?"

Martin was frightened now. He pushed himself deeper into his beanbag.

"No, Martin, I don't have any cash on me right now. But that doesn't matter. Because I never intended to pay you. It seems that you're going to have to have a little accident."

"Accident?" Beads of sweat were popping out of Martin's forehead.

"It's too bad about your alcohol problem, Martin. Drinking as much as you do makes you quite unstable on your feet."

"But I don't have a—"

"Shh. Let me finish. We're going to sit here and have a few more glasses of wine, you and I. You'll have most of it, of course. It'll look like you went out on the balcony, Martin, and stumbled. That old wooden railing simply couldn't hold your weight."

Martin opened his mouth, to protest, or argue, or even scream. But he couldn't. He couldn't think what to do.

The guest was calm. He pulled another bottle of wine out of Martin's Styrofoam cooler and opened it with one pull. Without even pouring it into a glass, he handed it to Martin. "Drink, Martin. It's a lovely cabernet. You'll enjoy it."

Martin took the bottle, and brought it to his lips. He was too frightened to try to resist.

"That's it, keep drinking."

Martin finished half the bottle, then stopped to take a breath. The room was spinning. He tried to stand, but the visitor moved quickly. Using a maneuver he'd learned many years before, he grabbed Martin in a headlock and twisted, snapping the small man's neck like a twig.

The guest snuffed out the tiny candle and opened the balcony door. Holding onto the doorframe for support, he broke the flimsy wooden rail with one swift kick. Martin's body hardly made a sound as it landed facedown in the soft mud below.

Chapter 30

IT WAS DARK by the time Annie got back from Spokane. At the Cherry Court Motel, she glanced down the exterior hallway toward Jed's room, but saw no lights on. She entered her room and without even turning on the light, slipped off her shoes and lay down on the bed. Riding in small planes had never been one of her favorite pastimes, and the turbulence they'd encountered on the way back as the storm moved in had brought her close to the edge of queasiness several times. She needed five or ten minutes to reassure her stomach that she was back on solid ground.

When she was ready to return to the land of the living, Annie got up, washed her hands and face in cold water, and only then noticed the blinking message light on the telephone. She called down to the clerk, who was clearly perturbed at a guest who had the unmitigated gall to receive so many messages—three from Dr. Butterick at the hospital, one from Gerald North, and one from Jed, instructing her to call him on his portable phone. Galen Rockwell, the one person Annie would have liked to have heard from, hadn't called.

She tried the hospital first, but Dr. Butterick did not respond to his page. The switchboard operator couldn't tell if he was tied up in surgery, or whether he'd left the hospital, but took down Annie's name anyway. Next she tried Gerald North both at home and at his campus office, but here again, got no response. She wasn't terribly surprised. Friday evening was usually not an easy time to get hold of people.

Finally, she responded to Jed's message.

Jed Delacourt nearly jumped a foot when he heard the ringing telephone. He glanced around quickly, then realized the ringing was coming from his own pocket. He took out the portable phone and answered it.

"I hate to admit it," Annie said, "but it is convenient to be able to reach you on this blasted contraption."

"I'm telling you, everyone should have one." Jed took out his handkerchief and wiped his forehead. He hadn't noticed how nervous he was, searching through a strange office at night. Talking rapidly, he told Annie everything he'd learned, from the boxes of DDT to the story Steve wanted to sell to the Yakima newspaper. "I'm trying to follow up on the military angle now, looking through Steve's files for anything that might lead us to the officer who had the documents."

"What was that again? You were going so fast. What military angle?"

"That's where Steve told the reporter that he had seen the documents—in some colonel's desk, apparently a good friend of Steve's. But I'm not having much luck. I tried the V.A., but Steve wasn't a veteran, and . . ."

"Hold it, Jed. There's no military connection."

"But I just told you. . . ."

Annie chuckled. "There's no way you could have known. Steve's 'colonel' is not exactly a high-ranking officer in the U.S. armed services. His name is Bob, he's furry, weighs about twenty pounds, and has a penchant for fresh mice."

"You're kidding me, right? The colonel is a cat?"

"It's kind of an in-joke. Everyone at the winery refers to Colonel Bob as the chief of security. And his favorite napping spot is on top of Taylor's rolltop desk in the winery. That's got to be where Steve found the documents."

"From the winery? Wait, I saw some papers that had to

do with wine distribution, but I couldn't make anything of it. Hold on."

Jed pulled out a folder he'd passed by earlier.

"I saw this, but it hardly looked like the key to a scandal."

"Tell me what it says. Maybe I'll recognize something."

"Okay, there's one piece of paper with a bunch of names listed. Fifteen in all." Jed read the list.

"Those are all of the Yakima Valley wineries that were at the Wine Gala. They're all within a fifteen- or twenty-mile radius of North Faire."

"Okay, next to the names of the wineries are some numbers and letters. Two B-T-S, six B-T-S."

"What does it say for North Faire?"

"Eighteen C-s. All the others say B-T-S."

"Cases and bottles?"

"You think this is just a wine list for the party, then?"

"No," Annie replied. "Why would there be eighteen *cases* of wine from North Faire, and only a few *bottles* from all the others? What else did you find?"

"Okay, there's another sheet with dates and items listed. One oak barrel, two boxes labels, two hundred fifty corks . . ."

"Those could be the thefts that Taylor and Galen were talking about. Taylor thought Steve was behind it, but her brother was accusing Galen Rockwell."

Jed shifted the telephone to his other hand. "Well, this looks like an inventory all right. With check marks and handwritten dates down the list."

"So the thefts weren't random acts of vandalism, after all. That never did sound right."

"Someone was bottling wine on the side?"

"With those quantities, a few bottles here and there, what would be the point?"

"Not money, certainly. And if they wanted it to drink, why not just steal the wine?" Jed laughed and said, "I know. They were going to put cheap rotgut red in the bottles, pass them off as the real thing, and make North Faire look bad."

"Wait a second, you might be on to something."

"I wasn't serious. . . . who would go to all that trouble. . . ."

Annie could feel her heart beginning to race. If her hunch was correct, many innocent people could be at risk.

"You said something about distribution. Was there anything about that?"

"No. I haven't found anything that might say when or where the wine would be going. All I know is that Steve told the reporter that the plan was going to be set in motion late tonight, the fourteenth."

"What do you think we should—wait . . . the first and the fifteenth. That's when Galen said the distributor comes to pick up the North Faire Wine. Tomorrow's the fifteenth. There will be a truck coming by at dawn tomorrow to pick up whatever's on the North Faire loading dock." She looked at the clock on the bedside table. "It's still early. I'm going out there."

"What? Annie, are you crazy? Steven Vick might have been killed because of what he knew. You don't even know who you're dealing with. You can't stop them by yourself."

"I won't try and stop anyone. I'm pretty sure I do know who's behind this, but I have to be sure. All I'm going to do is watch the loading dock and see who meddles with the shipment."

"Wait, and I'll meet you there."

"No. Two of us probably would be seen. You finish looking through the files. I'll call you if I find anything."

"Okay. But be careful."

The low buzz of the television was doing little to calm Jed's nerves. It was clear now that the filing cabinet had been from Steve's office. Most of the files contained his sales records, income tax receipts, nothing having to do with whatever story he was trying to sell to the newspaper.

At nine, the local television station broke in with a news

update. Jed flinched when he heard that continued random violence would lead the headlines at eleven, but barely paid attention to the words. "No more than twenty minutes ago, a young single mother was the victim of a drive-by shooting," the reporter said in a grim tone. "Multiple shots were fired into the woman's one-bedroom bungalow, injuring her in the shoulder, but miraculously leaving her toddler daughter unharmed. Police have no suspects, but are assuming gang-related activity is involved." Jed glanced up as a picture of the woman's home flashed on the screen. In front of the broken front window was parked a lemon-yellow Chevrolet Vega.

Chapter 31

ANNIE DROVE UP the gravel road toward North Faire, and stopped at the cottages. Both were dark. She parked her car behind Celia's cottage out of view from the road, and walked up over the rise until she could see Taylor's house. Like the cottages, it was completely dark. A tiny sliver of new moon shining through the clouds cast light on the house and the barn, giving their white exteriors an eerie glow.

It was a long shot, hoping to see someone meddling with North Faire's wine shipment, but she couldn't think what else to do. Unless Jed could find some clue in the documents, there would be no way of proving who was behind the plot that Steven Vick had discovered. Going back over the pieces of the puzzle, Annie was virtually positive that she knew who was responsible, and why, but a hunch wouldn't stand up in court.

For a brief moment, Annie saw a flicker of light inside the winery, near the front of the barn in the vicinity of the rolltop desk. There were no vehicles parked anywhere near the building.

She walked slowly, toes first to keep the gravel from crunching. Keeping to the shadows, she was able to get closer to the barn, thinking that if she could get to the far side, she could look in the window to see who was inside. It looked like the double doors at the front of the barn were slightly ajar. She rounded the corner into almost total darkness, the thin light of the moon blocked by the barn.

In dismay she looked up at the window, its edge half a foot above the top of her head. There were few moments when Annie wished she were tall, but this was one of them. She had remembered the windows were at eye level inside, but had forgotten that the barn's floor had been raised.

She inched along the side of the building, feeling with her foot in the dark, hoping to find a box or a used part to stand on. Her foot landed only on dry dirt and weeds.

Annie heard the sound of a file drawer slamming. She glanced up. The light was moving, with the sound of footsteps going toward the loading dock at the back of the barn. Annie held her breath to listen, but the footsteps had stopped.

If the building had had only one exit, her choice would have been simple. She could simply wait in the shadows in the dark until whoever was in the building came out. But she remembered there was a side door as well, opening only twenty feet from where she was standing. If she waited where she was, she ran the risk not only of missing the person when they came out, but of being seen if they exited through the side door. There was no single vantage point where she could see both exits, but not be seen herself.

Unless, of course, she went inside the building. She pictured the interior of the winery. If she stayed in the shadows just inside the front door, she should be able to have a clear view of both exits.

Annie listened from the top step before opening the door. She heard no sounds from inside the barn. She crouched low and peeked in. A vague shimmer of light—it couldn't be more than a penlight—was visible from behind some crates in the back. Moving slowly, Annie was able to open the door enough to squeeze in, then close it behind her without making a noise. She could still see the glow of the penlight near the loading dock, moving slowly. She couldn't risk going any closer.

Annie moved to her left and bumped into a table that had not been there before. Feeling blindly ahead of her, she felt a metal contraption on the table, with a V-shaped basin and tubes running out of it. To her right was the wine bar and behind it, the rolltop desk.

She slid under the plank that formed the wine bar and crouched low until she was hidden in the shadows. By craning her neck, she should be able to see both the loading dock and the side door, once her eyes adjusted to the dark.

Suddenly there was a loud thump on the floor next to her. Annie jerked but didn't make a sound. Colonel Bob had awakened from his bed on top of the desk and jumped to the floor. He sensed her presence and turned to investigate. Annie held her breath.

She doubted the cat would make a fuss, but couldn't be sure. He sauntered over to where she crouched, extended his nose for the briefest of sniffs, then flicked his chewed-off tail and ambled off in the other direction. On the other side of the room, she could hear the cat crunching on a midnight snack of dry food. Annie slowly let out her breath.

Time passed, fifteen, maybe twenty minutes. The person with the penlight was still moving slowly around the cases of wine ready for shipping. Afraid she might be visible, Annie lowered herself into the space under the desk, while trying to keep the glow from the penlight within view.

Suddenly there were heavy footsteps coming from the back of the barn. It sounded like boots, but she couldn't tell if the footfall was made by a man or a woman. She leaned sideways to see which exit the person would use, then ducked back under the desk when she saw the light moving toward her. She pushed herself farther back into the shadows to wait as the figure passed. The footsteps came closer, paused in the middle of the room, then started walking back toward the side door.

It was too dark. Annie had waited for her eyes to adjust, but there simply wasn't enough light. Clouds must have blocked what meager light was coming from the moon. Annie couldn't distinguish a face.

The penlight flashed on at the side door. She heard what sounded like a key in the lock, turning a deadbolt. Then she heard fiddling with the windows.

The footsteps drew nearer again, slowly. Annie forced herself to open her eyes. The penlight was off. She couldn't tell if the person was looking around. It was still too dark from her vantage point on the floor to discern any features. The feet came parallel to the wine bar, and she could finally make out some detail. That was when she saw the boots.

Annie stared in disbelief. Gray eelskin cowboy boots. Galen Rockwell's gray eelskin cowboy boots.

The boots weren't moving. Annie prayed that there wasn't anything else in the filing cabinets Galen wanted to look for. Why was he standing so still?

Finally, after minutes that seemed like hours, Galen moved toward the front door. Annie could barely see the silhouette of his broad-brimmed felt hat as he took a last look around. Then quietly, he went out the front door and shut it behind him. She again heard a key in the lock. No problem, Annie had noticed that the lock on the front door could be opened from the inside. But the next sound was more ominous. It was the sound of a chain being looped through the exterior door handles and fastened with a padlock. Annie was locked inside.

Chapter 32

ANNIE STRETCHED HER LEGS and tried not to panic. She reviewed the situation step by step, not wanting to jump to conclusions. The gray eelskin cowboy boots were too distinctive to belong to anyone but Galen Rockwell. They were the same ones she'd seen him wearing at the Wine Gala. Nevertheless, she couldn't believe that Galen, himself, was responsible for the scheme that Steven Vick had uncovered.

She had to find a way out of the barn. Her eyes were a little more accustomed to the dark, but it was still hard to see. She couldn't risk turning on the lights—Galen would surely see them and come back to investigate. She started with the front door, knowing it was probably futile. Sure enough, when she unlatched the deadbolt and tried to open the double doors, they wouldn't budge more than an inch. A thick chain doubly wrapped around the handles held the two doors firmly together.

Feeling blind and vulnerable, Annie felt her way to the side door near the back of the barn. Again, she found it bolted and padlocked, this time from the inside. Annie thought about the private detectives she read about in novels who always happened to carry a set of lock-picking tools that a "friend" had given them. She'd never thought that was terribly realistic. Annie knew no one who owned such tools, nor anyone except a professional locksmith who would have any idea how to use them. Perhaps it was time to branch out and make new friends.

She started on the windows. As in many old barns, the large square-paned windows were tightly spaced along the length of the building to let in natural light. They were large enough to climb through, and not too far off the ground to jump. But again, she didn't hold out much hope. She'd heard Galen fiddling with a window. He was probably making sure they were all secure. Systematically, she started at the back of the barn and tried each window in succession, feeling for loose or missing panes. The double hung windows had opened at one time, but now she found they were sealed tight with what seemed like several layers of dirt and paint. She pushed hard on each one, but none would budge so much as a millimeter.

It took about fifteen minutes to check one side of the barn. When she got to the end, Annie stopped to think. This wasn't working. All of the windows were well-caulked and securely locked. Her hopes of finding an easy way out of the barn were dwindling fast. There was the trap door off the second-story loft, but that idea didn't sound too encouraging. First, it was probably padlocked like the doors. And even if she could get it open, it was at least a thirty-foot drop to the ground. If it came to a choice between breaking a window and breaking her neck, Annie thought a broken window sounded a lot less risky.

She started checking the windows on the other side of the building. If she could get out on that side, she would be inside the fenced yard where the winemaking equipment was kept. The chain-link fence was about eight feet high, but she was pretty sure there was no barbed wire on top of it. It wouldn't be fun to climb, but certainly not impossible.

Annie was so tired, and so resigned to having to break a window, that she almost didn't test the latch on the fourth window from the end. She'd gotten into a rhythm—running her hands along the panes to look for cracks, then sliding her fingers over the caulking, then pushing on the frame from below to see if she could crack the paint. As she proceeded along the wall, her effort on each window diminished.

That's why she almost missed it, that slight movement on the fourth to the last window, the one next to the table set up for gluing labels. She stopped and pushed again. The window was stiff, but it went up. Yes!

Annie suddenly remembered Celia telling her how all of the labels were glued on by hand. Of course they would sit by an open window when working with glue. Annie chided herself for not thinking of it sooner.

She shoved hard, and the window slid up and stayed. She gladly breathed in a gulp of the cold night air, not realizing quite how claustrophobic she had started to become trapped inside the winery. She stuck her head out the window and saw that the drop into the fenced yard was only about seven feet.

Feeling exhilarated by her freedom, Annie climbed through the window, bracing one foot against the outside of the barn until she was sitting on the window frame, then pushed herself out, landing with a thud on both feet. She brushed the dirt from the windowsill off the seat of her pants and stood up to catch her breath.

In the shadows, she could barely see the barrel of Galen Rockwell's shotgun pointed at her stomach.

Chapter 33

THERE WAS SCARCELY ENOUGH moonlight in the yard to make out the silhouette of Galen's hat. "Aren't you going to tell me what this is all about, Annie?"

She stared at the gun. "Galen, I really wish you'd put that down. It makes me very nervous."

"That's what guns are supposed to do to trespassers."

"Galen, why are you—"

He didn't let her speak. "You know, I read the papers every day, and it seems like politicians and lawyers and such are always acting like their degree or title or office puts 'em right up there above the law. And every once in a while they get caught, and sent to one of them low-security, country-club prisons where they get to practice their tennis serves and golf swings. Is that how it works, Annie? When you graduated from law school, did they hand you the diploma in one hand, and your exemption from the law in the other?"

"Galen, you don't—"

"No," he replied. "I'm talking here. And I'm ready to get to the bottom of whatever the hell's been going on. For the last few months, supplies have been disappearing. Bottles, corks, labels, foils, storage boxes. Little bits at a time, as if I don't keep careful enough records to notice. Then, for the last two or three nights, coincidentally right about the time you arrive," he said bitterly, "somebody has been getting into the winery late at night. *Somebody with a key.* I haven't seen it happen, but in the morning, I could tell that someone had been in here. And while I was waiting tonight to see what would happen, if anybody would break in, I checked the stock that's ready to be picked up by the distributor in the morning. And what do I find? Along with the regular shipment, there's twenty cases of wine that I didn't put there, plus bottles from a whole slew of other wineries. And the invoice for the distributor has been re-typed. Now, I may be a little slow at figuring out criminal activity, but this here's gotta be some kind of bootleg operation or something. I don't know what. Or maybe you're helping Taylor and that Marchand character set me up, send me to jail for stealing from North Faire. All I know is, this stuff's been happening the same time every night, and I figured that tonight I'd wait and see who showed up. I gotta say it surprised the hell out of me that it was you, Annie. At first, I thought it was Taylor. Then I smelled your perfume and knew it was you." He laughed bitterly. "I always did like that perfume you wear."

Annie felt confused and relieved at the same time. Her theory was correct. Galen had been doing exactly what she had—watching for whoever was meddling with the wine shipment. She wanted to explain, but first she asked, "What did you mean, you thought it was Taylor? Last night at the hospital, her doctor said she wouldn't be released for days."

"You mean you haven't heard? Her doctor and Gerald have been calling everyone they can think of. She left the hospital this afternoon against medical advice. No one knows where she is."

Annie remembered all of the messages Dr. Butterick and Gerald had left for her. "Galen, I can explain everything. I was doing the same thing as you. We found evidence today of a scheme involving North Faire and other local wineries. Steven Vick was killed because he found out about it."

He lowered the barrel of his gun. "A scheme? What kind of scheme?"

As Annie was about to tell him, there was a sound on the other side of the chain-link fence. Dr. Charles Marchand unlocked the padlocked gate and entered the yard. "Yes, Ms. MacPherson. Why don't you tell us all about this little scheme? I'm very interested in what you have to say."

Chapter 34

"PRODUCT TAMPERING," Annie replied, trying to remain calm. Galen stood by silently. "It's the only thing that makes sense, considering the methodical thefts of bottling supplies, and the additional cases of wine added to North Faire's distribution. I assume you've laced the wine with the DDT we found along with the documents Steven Vick got hold of. How did that work? Did Martin Grubenmacher con Steve into acquiring the pesticide from the Nu-chem warehouse? Did Steve think he was providing it for some other purpose?"

Annie could see that Dr. Marchand was smiling, but there was no humor in his smile. "Why are you asking me?"

"Because you're the one who planned it."

He laughed loudly. "And why would I want to tamper with wine? What a ridiculous idea. Are you suggesting I'm trying to bump someone off by sending twenty cases of bad wine into the marketplace? My least favorite wine critic, perhaps?"

Annie took a deep breath. She could feel her heart racing. It was hard to talk and also plan what to do. "There have been cases of product tampering that were intended to kill a specific victim, while making the harm appear random, like the cyanide-laced painkillers in Seattle a few years back. But I didn't see that happening here. With so many cases of tampered wine being shipped, there might be tens, even hundreds of innocent victims. A lot of death for a single intentional murder, don't you think? And I would have my doubts that a lethal dose of pesticide could go undetected in wine."

"Hmmm," was all he said.

"But if the wine tasted bad, and was found to contain even slight amounts of DDT, what result would that have on the local wine industry? Stock would be pulled. Rumors would run rampant. With representative bottles from all of the local wineries, the regional industry would be devastated."

"But I was thinking of investing here. Why would I want to destroy a business I'm thinking of buying?"

"You had no real interest in investing here. You have significant money already invested in small wineries in California. Those wineries are suffering badly from the phylloxera infestation. My guess is that you wanted to buy time, Dr. Marchand. Prevent Northwest wines, which have not been affected by the root louse, from gaining market share while your holdings go bankrupt, and while it takes you five or more years to replant your vineyards. You had to arrange for Steven Vick to be killed, because you found out he was planning to go to the media and expose your scheme before the tainted wine could hit the market. Close enough?"

"Quite perceptive, Ms. MacPherson. I should have hired you as my assistant, rather than that dolt, Grubenmacher."

"So it is true," said Galen.

"I'm afraid so." He removed a small, snub-nosed handgun from his pocket. "And you were right. The amount of DDT in each bottle was minute, but it would have shown up when the wine was tested. Now, if you'll both come with me now, my car's right outside. I'm not sure where we're going, but I can't afford any more deaths tied to North Faire. It starts to look suspicious after a while, you know. Oh, and don't bother to bring the shotgun. Taylor told me you fill it with blanks to scare the birds."

Galen stood his ground, and Annie could see he was seething with anger. "How did you get keys to the winery?"

The doctor jangled the key ring in his hand. "There are lots of things one acquires in the middle of the night. You, of all people, should know what a heavy sleeper Taylor is. Out like a light. Snores, too. All too easy to lift her keys and have a copy made. She never even knew I'd taken them. And you. You were so gracious when she broke off your affair six months ago. She said you never even asked her if there was someone else. She really thinks you're a gentleman. Dull as dirt, but a gentleman. She and I have been having quite a time. Oh, don't think that Taylor was in on any of this. She didn't have a clue. I believe she actually thought I was spending so much time with her because I loved her."

"Why DDT, doctor?" Annie had to keep Marchand talking. She didn't know what else to do.

"I'm surprised you don't know. You seem to have deduced the other parts of the plan. I think I was being quite clever with that. There have been Federal studies lately showing a high level of residual DDT in the groundwater near the Yakima River."

"And North Faire has the deepest well in the region," Galen said. "That's why you centered your plan at North Faire."

"Very good. You two make a good team."

Without warning, Galen Rockwell lunged forward, swinging the shotgun with full force. The blow struck Marchand's hand, sending the pistol flying to the ground.

Annie bolted. She remembered the stairs up to the crusher-stemmer. The catwalk platform was near the top of the fence. If she could make it to the top she might get over the fence, and the equipment would shield her as she dropped to the ground. Annie tripped once as she grabbed the handrail and started up the metal stairs, but quickly regained her footing and kept going. Four or five steps up she thought she was going to make it. Then a hand grabbed her ankle and pulled her down.

She landed on her right hip, and slid down the metal stairs, kicking as hard as she could with her free foot. She aimed for arms, a groin, anything she could make contact with. She landed a kick in Marchand's stomach, and as the wind was knocked out of him, she got her leg free and scrambled to get up.

She stumbled on something as she darted for the other side of the yard, then realized it was the gun. She picked it up and tried the trigger but nothing happened. There must be a safety, or something she didn't understand about firing the gun. She flung it high, hoping to send it over the fence. She looked around, but couldn't see Galen.

"Annie, over here." The winemaker was standing near the side door to the winery, which he'd managed to unlock. Marchand was still on the ground, but he was blocking her way. Annie found herself near the barrels of recently crushed grapes. As Marchand started to get up, she grabbed the first she came to. It was hard to tip over, incredibly heavy, but once some of the lees had poured over the edge, the barrel fell, sending a cascade of sticky pulp toward Marchand. It slowed him down long enough for her to get past him and into the winery. Galen slammed the door behind them as they escaped into the barn.

Inside, it was pitch-black. Annie couldn't tell which direction Galen had gone. She crawled behind and underneath one of the steel tanks and tried not to move.

She heard Marchand enter through the side door. Somehow, he must have retrieved the gun, because a shot rang out in the darkened building. Annie crouched lower behind the tank.

Someone moved on the catwalk that ran above the tanks, but all Annie could see was a flash of white. There was the sound of footsteps running up the ladder onto the catwalk. Suddenly, Annie was dazed as all of the lights in the winery went on at once. Galen was in the back of the building near the electrical panel and standing on the catwalk near an open vat of red wine was Taylor North, holding a gun on Charles Marchand.

"I heard everything," she said, her eyes wild. "You never meant to invest in North Faire. You never meant to marry me. You were using me."

"Taylor, no." Marchand, his hands empty, tried to back away, but there was nowhere for him to go. He was trapped on the catwalk, with Taylor blocking the stairs.

"Last night, in the hospital, after Annie left, I started remembering. I remembered fighting with Steve, but I always knew I didn't kill him. There was someone else . . . someone else. I could never have killed Steve."

"Of course not, Taylor. Now put the gun down. We can talk."

Annie began to hear the faraway sound of a siren, out on the highway.

"You killed Steve," Taylor was mumbling, over and over. "My Steve. You murdered my husband. . . ."

Marchand, all routes blocked, abruptly turned and dove into the open vat of wine, the crusty cap collapsing under his weight. A minute later he came to the surface, gasping for air, arms flailing. As the siren drew closer down the gravel road to the winery, Taylor aimed the gun at Marchand's head and fired five shots.

Chapter 35

THE WINE COUNTRY looked very different on the day before Thanksgiving. The apple trees and vines were bare, and the ground was tinged with frost. There was a stark beauty to the landscape that was unlike the richness of the harvest season.

"Well, what's the verdict? What do my very first paying guests think of the Vineyard View Bed & Breakfast? Are your rooms to your satisfaction?"

Harry Braithwaite couldn't wait until they came down, but was yelling at them from the kitchen. He was still working on his first culinary masterpiece, a German chocolate cake made from scratch, and was afraid that if he left the kitchen while it was still in the oven, disaster would surely strike.

Annie came down the stairs of what had formerly been the Grubenmacher Mansion, with Jed Delacourt, Ellen O'Neill, and Joel Feinstein right behind her. She was still getting used to the idea of Jed and Ellen as a couple. Joel, on the other hand, was delighted, thinking that a little stability could only be good for Jed's billing practices. "My room is delightful, Harry." He had put her in the room at the top of the stairs, the room that had once been Florence Grubenmacher's *private* sitting room. "I'm so glad you got rid of all that beige. The new decor is fabulous. It makes me think of a country house in Provence."

"It is wonderful, isn't it? Gerald North has really been a

lot less moody since he gave up teaching, and went into interior decorating full time. I think he did a marvelous job with the whole place. He told me that before Florence decided to sell it and move to Scottsdale, every time he set foot in it he thought about how to redecorate it. Having it as his first major contract really gave his new business the boost that it needed." Harry looked at Joel. "Where's the baby? You didn't leave her somewhere, did you?"

"No, Val is upstairs helping Maria change a diaper, as if a mother of three needs help. They're fine."

"Good, good. Annie, I've set out a plate of cookies. Will you do the honors and make the coffee?"

"Of course." Her housewarming present to the B&B was a large-capacity European coffeemaker, a grinder, and five pounds of Starbucks beans. No bed-and-breakfast could ever have survived on Harry's percolated coffee. As she made the first pot, she walked him through the process.

"I'm so glad you decided to have your first firm retreat here. It gives me a chance for a shakedown cruise of sorts, and frankly"—he looked at Jed and Annie—"you two need the rest and relaxation after what you went through." Harry's timer dinged, and he gingerly opened the oven door. "What do I do now?" he asked in a whisper. Ellen showed him how to test the cake with a toothpick to see if it was done. After he'd removed the pans and set them out to cool, everyone moved into the living room, where Harry had intermingled his own antiques with those sold to him by Florence Grubenmacher.

"Do you miss your old house?" Annie asked.

"Oh, no. The place just wasn't the same without Eleanor. Here, without all of those old memories haunting me, I'm feeling much more enthusiastic about things. I was actually able to clear out the clutter."

Ellen said, "Annie told me how you tried to send yourself to prison."

Harry grinned and shrugged. "I don't know. It seemed like a good idea at the time. But this is much more fun. I've got a number of guests booked for the winter, and everyone tells me the real crowds come in the spring and autumn. The cooking lessons are going well, and I get my daily exercise by hiking up to the Widow's Perch. What more could a man want?"

The coffee was ready, and Harry did the honors. His doctor had given him a clean bill of health, and told him all he really needed was a little more exercise and fresh air. With the activity of getting the B&B up and running, his health was improving on a daily basis.

Maria and Val came down the stairs, the latter happily cuddling the baby. "How are the other children doing?" Harry asked.

"They're upstairs, happily watching a video," Maria replied. "That's a great playroom you made up there."

"I wanted to encourage families with children. I think it will be fun having the little monsters around."

"Have you heard from Taylor, Harry?" Joel asked.

"Yes, we talk almost every day. She's miserable, as I knew she would be. I still think I would have rather enjoyed the people I would have met in prison, but she sees it only as a loss of freedom. I keep reminding her that her lawyer predicted she'd be out in twelve or thirteen years, if she behaves herself. That's not such a long time. She's pleased to have Galen Rockwell running the winery. And he's happy, because Edna Hinkel is loaning him the money to buy out Gerald's half-interest in North Faire. For a reasonable sum, this time."

"I'm surprised Taylor didn't try to use the insanity defense," said Maria. "From what that psychologist told you, she certainly didn't sound normal."

"She may not have been healthy, but Taylor was sane, all right. She clearly knew right from wrong, and that's what counts in criminal cases," Annie said. "When she shot Marchand, she knew exactly what she was doing. This time, when Detective Shibilsky rushed in, she really was holding a smoking gun."

"How did Shibilsky . . ."

Annie looked at Jed, who said, "When I heard on the

news that the woman I'd met in Steve's office had nearly been killed, I got out of there in a hurry and called nine-one-one on my handy-dandy portable telephone. Annie, if you had one of these, it might have saved you a lot of grief."

"You can be insufferable, you know that?"

"Uh-huh." Jed smirked.

"I still can't believe that Taylor was just playing a role, pretending that her husband was abusing her," Ellen said, incredulous. "That's so . . . sick."

"The state's psychiatrist who examined Taylor confirmed what Dr. Montgomery believed. Being a 'victim' was just one of the roles she needed to play to get attention and affirmation. Her entire life was structured around Steven Vick. She had affairs to make him angry. She tried to get attention by making people believe he abused her. And then when he was utterly furious with her, she'd become seductive to win him back."

Annie got up to refill her coffee. Harry beamed at her. "This really is good. Why didn't I get a coffeepot like this before?"

Joel was still trying to comprehend the strange sequence of events. "So it was Charles Marchand who planned Steve's death?"

"Right," said Annie, "because Steve discovered and was going to expose his plan. Steve suspected Taylor of trying to hide assets from him, so he broke into the winery one day to search for hidden accounts. He knew, like everyone else, that Taylor hated using the rolltop desk for her regular business. He pictured the locked drawer as a good hiding place. Apparently, so did Dr. Marchand.

"Charles Marchand cared about only one thing. Money. He was basically a high-stakes gambler who gambled by investing in small businesses. Over time, he had sunk a fortune into small California wineries, and was feeling helpless as he watched one after another of them succumbing to financial difficulties, due primarily to the phylloxera infestation. And as the small California wineries suffered, the

Northwest wine-growing region continued to prosper. He saw Washington wines winning acclaim in Europe and on the East Coast, at a time when his businesses needed to replant and take a few years to develop mature vines. Rather than see all of his investments go down the drain, he decided to do something about it. He figured a product-tampering scheme could work provided he distanced himself from the key activities—such as acquiring the DDT. He used Martin Grubenmacher as his toady, intending all along that when he had served his purpose, Martin would 'have an accident.' "

"Martin sounded like such a strange little man," said Jed. "How did he and the doctor get together?"

"When Marchand met Martin, as the Wine Gala was being planned, he pegged him as someone who would be easy to manipulate. Although the family was rich, Florence kept little Martin on a pretty tight leash, so that he was constantly in need of cash. Taylor also told Marchand about Martin's crush on her—it had been going on since they were in grade school together—and Marchand actually led Martin to believe that Taylor would be pleased by Martin's actions, and reward him in some way. That, plus some spending money, was all the incentive Martin needed."

"So Taylor knew nothing about Marchand's plan?"

"No. She never would have gone along with any scheme that would have destroyed her winery. She loved it too much. And when she found out that Marchand had arranged Steve's death, she flew into a rage. He was the only thing she truly couldn't live without. Her entire affair with Marchand had just been a way to torture Steve."

"How did Marchand find out that Steve knew?"

"Taylor called Marchand after Steve came to her house on Monday. She was playing her victim role again, telling Marchand how scared she was of Steve's threats. Marchand put it together that Steve knew about the plan, and decided to kill him."

"So there's still one big question. Who swung the wine

bottle?" Jed asked. "It couldn't have been Marchand. Annie saw him inside talking to Celia Vick at the time the murder occurred."

"Well, it had to be Taylor, didn't it?" said Ellen. "Her fingerprints were on the bottle."

Annie shrugged. "I don't think so. When I finally saw the lab report, I noticed something that Detective Shibilsky hadn't bothered to tell me. Taylor's fingerprints were on the bottle, all right, but they were right side up. In other words, the way they would be if someone picked up a bottle by its neck to carry or pour it. If Taylor had used the bottle as a weapon, the thumb print should have been upside down. For whatever reason, the fingerprints of whoever used the bottle to kill Steve aren't on it. I guess it's something we may never know."

Jed looked troubled. "I know it doesn't make any real difference, since Marchand and Martin Grubenmacher are dead. But still, it would be terrible not to know, after everything we've been through."

Annie noticed Harry nervously nibbling a cookie, looking distressed. "What is it, Harry? What's wrong?"

"No, no, it's nothing." He picked up his coffee, spilling some on the front of his shirt without noticing.

"No, what is it?"

He set down his cup. "I know after my little scene at the sheriff's department that I have not earned a great reputation for veracity."

"But we understand why you did what you did, Harry. You loved Taylor. You wanted to protect her."

He brushed crumbs off his wool pants, hemming and hawing a bit. "Well, you know the second tale I told you? About the mysterious figure in black?"

"Yes."

"Well, I fully understand why you chose not to believe me, but every word that I said was true. It *was* someone besides Taylor who wielded that bottle."

Jed wrinkled his brow. "But even if we believe you, that

doesn't answer the question. Who was the figure in black? It was too dark that night for you to see a face."

Harry fidgeted. "That's true." He rubbed his chin. "Since we all know that Marchand was the mastermind behind this episode . . . and that he's dead . . . and if I assure you that appropriate steps have been taken . . . is there any reason for what I'm about to say to leave this room?"

The others exchanged glances. Annie, for one, had no desire to share information with Detective Shibilsky. "I guess not," she replied.

"What I said was the truth; I could not see the person's face. But what I didn't say was this: I didn't have to. I could still tell who it was."

"How?"

"By her walk. The figure in black was my granddaughter, Mimi. My suspicions were confirmed when she showed up the next day with all that cash and told me she was leaving on the next Greyhound for L.A. to be with her boyfriend. I knew there was a good chance she'd use the money for drugs, so I alerted the authorities and had her picked up when the bus reached Portland. It turned out that she'd been paid substantially more than the one thousand dollars she showed me and had spent almost all of it on drugs to take to her boyfriend in California."

"What's going to happen to her?" Annie asked quietly.

"Because she was transporting the drugs across state lines, she could be charged with a Federal crime. I met with her and explained what I had seen, and convinced her to plead guilty. She'll be sent to a boot camp in California for youthful violent offenders—if that kind of discipline can't straighten her out, then nothing will." He looked around the room. "But promise me you'll say nothing. If no one in Harmony knows about this, then perhaps someday she can come back here and stay with me."

Everyone in the room was silent for a moment. Finally Harry said, "I believed Taylor because I wanted to, you see? My family has been such a disappointment to me over the years, I wanted a perfect daughter. She had so much vitality, so much life. She was family to me. Maybe ... I don't know. Maybe I still have a chance to have that with Mimi."

Chapter 36

THE NEXT MORNING, Annie rose early and walked from the mansion over to North Faire. She spotted Galen's truck on the hill overlooking the vineyards. He smiled when he saw her approach.

"It's mighty different in wintertime, don't you think?" he asked as she got closer.

"But it's still beautiful, all these bare vines stretching for miles."

"We try to use this time to get caught up. Do a little paperwork, mend some fences."

"I hear you and Taylor are business partners now."

He nodded. "Yep, with Edna's help, by the time Taylor gets out of prison, I'll have bought out Gerald's share. Oh, I know what you're thinking. You think I'm still in love with her, don't you? That that's why I won't leave here?"

"The thought had crossed my mind."

He ambled over to where she was standing and put a strong arm around her shoulder. "There may be a kernel of truth in that." He gestured out at the vineyards. "But this is why I'm staying, Annie. With this climate and these slopes, what we're standing on is a little piece of heaven." He chuckled to himself. "And, who knows, maybe by the time Taylor gets out, I'll be a happily married man with a minivan full of kids."

She looked up at him and circled her arm around his waist. "I hope so, Galen. You deserve that."

"So, I guess that means you're not interested in applying for the job?"

She shook her head. "I don't think I'd ever get over the feeling that Taylor was there in the room with us, always on your mind."

He looked down at his boots. "I couldn't make you any promises."

After a pause, he said, "I'm sorry I doubted you, that night when I found you in the winery. I guess, after what I've been through with Taylor, I have trouble trusting anybody."

Annie shrugged. "We both got caught up in trying to protect her, didn't we? When I heard from her that day, for the first time in so long, I thought it would give me the chance to recapture my friendship with her. Those high school years were exciting because of her. It nearly crushed me to discover that Taylor's loyalty was just part of her act."

"I'll let you in on a little secret for dealing with Taylor, Annie. Don't try to forget her, because it probably won't work. Just remember the good times, and leave it at that."

Galen walked Annie back to her car, and gave her a hug. "Harry's agreed to let us use the mansion for a wine-tasting party in April. It won't be as grand as the Wine Gala, but nobody wanted to repeat that particular event. You should think about coming."

"I will," said Annie, returning Galen's embrace. They looked over at the mansion and saw a puff of smoke coming from the chimney.

"It looks like folks over there are getting up now," Galen said. "You should be getting back."

"You sure you don't want to come to Thanksgiving dinner? We're serving North Faire wine. I hear the gewürztraminer is excellent with turkey."

Galen smiled and shook his head. "No, thanks. I . . . I'd rather be alone."

"We'll drink a toast for you."

"Yeah, I'd like that. A toast to old friends."